COILED PHANTOMS

KAIROS

GWYDION ROYCE

ORACLE OF LOST PATHS BOOKS

Cover Design by Damonza.com

1st edition 2024

Oracle of Lost Paths Books

author@gwydionroyce.com

979-8-9916145-6-6 (eBook)

979-8-9916145-7-3 (Paperback)

Chapter One

"Time to get up, lass. You've got a visitor."

Derfael's voice roused me from sleep, and my eyes cracked open. I raised my head, brought up short by the book stuck to my face.

I'd fallen asleep at the table in Derfael's library, poring over some ancient texts. There was no way I was taking his word for it that we couldn't locate Adrian.

"A visitor? Who?"

"That mousy girl, Frige's second."

"Oh." I rubbed my cheek and yawned. "I'll be down in a minute."

I trudged to the bathroom and ran some cold water over my face, staring at my reflection in the old, cracked mirror of mercury glass. With the dark circles under my eyes, I looked as terrible as I felt. An unexpected visit didn't bode well. I sighed and plodded down the stairs to meet her.

The smile on her face evaporated into concern. "Are you all right?" she asked.

I deflected the question. "What happened now?"

Morgan looked at me, surprised. "Wow. Who hurt you?"

My brain took a moment to reboot. "Why else would you be here except to deliver bad news from the Council? They like to switch it up and send different people so I don't get too suspicious."

"Well, I just wanted to check on you. I haven't heard from you in a few days." Her eyes searched mine for answers. "Nobody has. You kind of fell off the grid after the attack at the press conference."

I was having a hard time wrapping my head around this. She was just being nice?

"Oh, um. That's all fine—I'm fine, I mean." Lies. All of it lies. "A human militia isn't much of a match for us. I guess the Council won't be firing me just yet," I said, forcing a smile.

Morgan looked at me shrewdly. "What aren't you telling me?"

I swallowed, the lump in my throat working its way down. "I can't find Adrian."

"Tensions are high, I'm sure he's just off decompressing somewhere, yeah?"

"I mean, I *can't find* him. He's gone." Calm slipped away and I filled my lungs. "Missing. Completely off my radar."

Morgan's face paled, the blue-purple veins standing out even more starkly. "The sisters?"

"Yeah."

"Oh, no." She gripped the chain around her neck, zipping the pendant across the links. "You haven't found a body?"

"No. Which just makes it worse. What are they holding him for? I didn't give them what they wanted, so they killed my team. Now they took my familiar. And as of right now, I'm helpless to do anything about it." I sat heavily at the table. "We'd just reforged our bond. The two of us were getting along great, like old times but... better. Without all the backstabbing and bullshit stunts that we pulled on each other."

Morgan sat across from me and reached forward, clasping my hands. I tensed and she released them. "Sorry." She laughed nervously.

"It's not your fault. I'm just not used to people being friendly."

She gave me a "bless your heart" look. "That's kind of what friends do."

"We hang out in far different circles," I said, laughing. "The last time I visited Ishani, she started a fight just to show off her new metal prosthetics."

Morgan nodded, mouth quirking. "You're right, that is very different. What avenues have you tried so far? To find him?" she asked.

"I've been sifting through every one of Derfael's books, starting with the most archaic stuff and working my way to the modern day."

She nodded thoughtfully. "And I'm assuming you tried tracking spells?"

"Of course. We got an image of the twins before it burst into flame."

She grimaced. "But they have to know that if they kill him, you have no reason to help them? They should just be using him as more of an incentive."

"Or they're evil and waiting for me to break, just because."

Morgan put a hand on my shoulder, and this time I didn't flinch away. "It'll be all right. Let me look into a few things. You know I have my ways."

"That didn't go so well last time. Slightly different circumstances, but it's a huge risk to take."

She nodded. "It's worth taking. We need to find him. Trust me, all of my defenses are much better than they were last time. Frige made sure of it."

"Do you really think there's a chance that they're just going to hold them hostage?" I asked. I wanted to believe that.

Morgan suppressed a flash of doubt before nodding. "If they haven't been able to take that power from you by force, then they have to convince you." Morgan reached over and put a bookmark in my place before closing the text in front of me. "If anyone can find an answer, it's me. Now why don't we go over and have a seat in some comfortable chairs?"

I let her steer me toward the living room, where Derfael was just setting down the tea tray full of snacks. "How'd you do it? I've been trying to get her to take a break for days."

He handed me a cup and I added a few mini scones, obsessively arranging them around the teacup saucer.

Morgan took a few bites of an oatmeal square and her eyes widened, crumbs stuck to her lips. "Mmm. This is delicious. Did you make these?" she asked Derfael.

"Aye. It's an old recipe—"

"A really old recipe," I mumbled.

"—but I think it's a lot better now with sugar instead of honey. One of those marvels I can't get enough of."

"Oh, I know. I make a butter cake that is so sweet, it'll take the enamel off your teeth."

The druid chuckled. "I'd be more than happy to sample that if you need some more input."

"I'll make sure to bring some the next time I come over," she said, finishing the oatmeal square and dusting her hands off. As she took a sip of her tea, I could sense an air of hesitancy.

"What else?"

"I know that it's not a great time to ask, but have you heard from Tristan?"

Hearing his name brought me less pain these days, but losing Adrian had turned all the sadness over Tristan into anger. Adrian stood by me and he's suffering for it, while Tristan is doing the gods know what and living the high life. With *my* dog in tow. "No."

At the mention of his name, Derfael mumbled angry words under his breath. I couldn't hear them clearly, but I got the gist. He shook his head. "Of all the ways I imagined that relationship going badly, this wasn't one of them."

"I can't tell if I should be insulted by that?" I refilled my teacup and grabbed a cookie, biting into the lemon shortbread while delivering side-eye.

He laughed derisively. "Probably."

I looked at Morgan, wiping some crumbs off the table. "Why do you ask?"

"The nobles are being more... standoffish than usual. The Council hasn't had any contact with Tristan either, and there are rumblings—"

"Let me stop you right there. You don't need to worry about any kind of treason from them."

She hesitated. "Are you positive? There's no chance that he's changed since he..."

I considered it. "I mean of course there's a chance. But to do something like that would be against everything that Tristan has ever stood for. Even with *Sophia* whispering in his ear, I don't think that would be enough to change his mind toward striking out at the council."

I thought back to that curious conversation I overheard, the night I missed our anniversary dinner. "Has anyone been discussing some kind of summit?" I asked.

"A summit of nobles?" Morgan shook her head. "No. At least not that I heard. Sebastian has been their go-between for most of the talks with the Council."

"Sebastian is still around?" I asked, eyebrows in my hairline. "Did you pull him out of storage and dust him off first?"

Morgan laughed. "He's more of a sad concierge these days, but he's been hanging around. Now that new talks are in the works with the remaining nobles, Sebastian has been working his way back to having a seat on the Council."

I whistled. "I never thought I'd see the day when the Council made a positive change."

Morgan rolled her eyes. "Miracles do happen. We don't have much of a choice but to change. If we don't, we get left behind. And if we get left behind—"

"So does all of the Strangefells," I finished.

"I will make sure to ask Sebastian about it, but he hasn't seemed cagier than normal. Where did you hear about this?"

I briefly explained the situation, sitting back on the sofa and crossing my arms. "They were trying to bring the heads of two of the most reclusive remaining noble families out of hiding. Highgate and Azure. So whatever this is, it's big. At least in Sophia's mind."

"Tristan didn't seem like an unwilling participant in that conversation from the way you've described it, Talulla," said Derfael. Tristan's leaving had hurt more than just me. Derfael had placed a lot of trust in him, and we were both realizing how little we really knew him.

"Why the sudden interest?" I asked her.

"Faced with current tensions, the Council wants to wrap up any loose ends."

I nodded, looking back at the library and the pile of books waiting for me to leave an imprint of my face on them. "Let me know what you find out, on both fronts."

Morgan caught my eye before she spoke. "It's going to be okay."

She seemed so confident. If only I could feel the same. My phone chirped, and I pulled it out of my pocket. "And that's a wrap, folks," I said.

Derfael and Morgan looked at me quizzically as I held up my phone. "Detective Ryan. He's calling off the task force. Tensions are getting a bit high and it's not safe to keep holding meetings to try and smooth things over between Strangers and humans." I tossed my phone on the table.

Morgan sighed. "I was truly hoping this would be just another hothead, losing their temper and riling people up. But things haven't been simmering down. It truly looks like war is on the horizon."

After Morgan left, I went back to the books for all of an hour before I gave up. I couldn't stop thinking about Tristan. What was *Sophia* whispering in his ear right at this minute?

"Don't waste any more energy on him," said Derfael, closing the book he was reading and rubbing bloodshot eyes.

"How'd you know?"

He couldn't fight a yawn, and I had to wait for his answer. "Melancholy. You're terrified for Adrian, but you still miss Tristan terribly." He gave me a sad smile that I suddenly wanted to slap off his face for being so on point. "Are you hanging onto hope for the two of you?"

I couldn't stop fidgeting under the scrutiny. I huffed out a breath. "Why are you asking me this now?" A stray hair tickled my face and I searched for it, finally swiping my hands through my messy mane and tying it into a loose ponytail. "I have more important things to focus on."

Derfael pursed his lips and nodded. "You're right." He stood and patted my shoulder on his way to bed.

I angrily returned to my studies. I wasn't holding a torch for that asshole. He left me high and dry, after all that bull about this "not being the end." He didn't even try. Not *one single word* from him.

The burning behind my eyes only made me angrier, and I dug knuckles into them. Damn allergies acting up again. I slammed the book shut, pausing to apologize when it chittered at me, and trudged off to take a shower.

I stood under the stream of water, slamming the knob to cold and staying there until my teeth chattered. Then I went in search of a warm-up, taking my usual place on the couch and wrapping myself in a blanket.

"Are you sure that's a good idea, Talulla?" Derfael asked, shuffling out of his room.

"What?" I held up the bottle of bourbon in my hand. "This?"

"I don't need to tell you—"

"You're right. You don't need to tell me. I'm fine." I hunkered down and took a swig of whisky just to prove my point.

"I think that's debatable," he said, looking at me sternly over his glasses.

"Night, Derfael," I said, pulling the blanket tighter and dialing the volume down on the TV.

I heard him sigh and walk back to his room. When his door closed, I drained the bottle of bourbon and grabbed another. Every time my fears crept up on me, I took a swig. It was almost gone in ten minutes.

None of the books had proved helpful so far. There was still plenty more to go through, but I was putting my money on Morgan finding the answers. So in the meantime...

Everything good I tried to do fell apart. Like it always did. Neither side trusted me, either because of past interactions or my desire to work with both sides. It didn't matter that my heart was in the right place. All they saw was trouble and a potential traitor. I had no idea if the Council would keep me involved going forward or if they would use the escalating tension as an excuse. Can't have a loose cannon wandering around at the edge of war.

My exhaustion caught up to me, and my head fell heavily onto the pillow. I thought about getting up and going to bed, but figured it would be too much trouble.

For the first time since Adrian disappeared, I slept.

I'd had constant nightmares of the event that sent me into hiding fourteen years ago. They stopped after the battle with the Ancients and not much had replaced them. Not since the sisters began to pay me visits.

My booze-addled brain wasn't helping anything. It would make it easier for them to infiltrate, but I hoped there would be a trade-off. I could talk to them, try to find some answers. Maybe, if I was lucky, I would dream of him.

It was incredible how fast I'd fallen apart. I'd spent most of my years in hiding alone until I got Jake shortly before returning to the city. But I never really *felt* alone. Now, even with Morgan and Derfael providing support—despite my best efforts to shrug them off—I felt isolated.

Vision swirled to life and I found myself caught in a classic Lewis Carroll acid trip. A blazing fury of images danced around too fast to grab any single one and focus on it, turning to fire, death, destruction. Bodies lying everywhere as the city burned. And I was standing at the center, wreathed in blue-black flame.

Then it switched. My parents dead, our home destroyed, and my siblings missing, never to be seen again.

That too tore away, back into the deep hole that I kept those memories locked in. Then one single image caught my attention. It wasn't a memory. Before it could rush away, I used all my willpower to grab it and hold on.

My heart leaped. Adrian, strapped tightly to a stone chair, his head lolling forward onto his chest. He wasn't moving, but I thought I saw the slightest rise and fall of his breathing. The room was dark, just a hint of firelight in the distance. Controlled. Like torches. I couldn't discern much other detail besides flagstone floors strewn with sand with wavy patterns drawn into it, evidence of something slithering. The chair itself was covered in strange markings, a mix of cuneiform and Linear B.

Adrian stirred. His eyes flickered open, then looked right at me. There was hope and recognition, and then a shadow loomed over him. His flesh tore and he bit back a scream. Then a blinding pain shot through my body and my head felt like it would explode.

Fighting through the pain, I desperately attempted to hang on to the vision, the visitation, whatever it was, but I couldn't. With one last stab of agony I was thrown out, tumbling off the couch with a shout. Breathing was difficult as I tried to ignore the searing burn splitting my skull in two. My face pressed into the carpet as my breaths came in gasps and ragged exhalations, covering the intermittent sobs that punctuated in between. I would have curled into myself if I'd had the strength to move.

I don't know how long I lay there, but when the pain finally subsided I got shakily to my feet. It had felt so real. That brief instant had realized all my fears. Adrian was alive, but his suffering had only just begun.

"Describe those runes again," said Morgan. We'd been attempting to sketch them out, but dragging them from a dream was just as hard as you'd think.

"A little more squared on that side, I think," I said, pointing to the right side of the chair. "Yeah, that's more like it."

"But you don't remember anything about the room itself?" she asked.

"No. That part is still a blur."

Morgan grabbed another piece of charcoal and continued to sketch. The table was littered with previous attempts, but they were all impressive.

"You're really good at this."

She smudged a line she'd just drawn with her fingers. "Thank you." She wiped her nose and left a smear across her face, but she didn't even notice. "I studied art for a long time. Being Frige's second was my backup plan. My initial career choice was ancient art recovery."

"That sounds fun."

"It would've been." Regret flashed across her face before she put a few finishing touches on the sketch, including the wavy lines in the sand on the floor. "How's this?" She blew off the excess charcoal and turned the page to me.

"That's it. Just missing Adrian, sitting in the chair." The sight of his terrified face, fighting back a scream of pain, was the only detail that was crystal clear.

"I've already got a few leads," said Morgan, giving me a kind smile. "We'll figure out how to find him."

I nodded, wiping sleep crust out of my eyes.

"When's the last time you had a full night's sleep?"

I snorted. "About a year ago."

"You look like shit."

"I know." What was the point in arguing?

"Why don't we go out somewhere tonight? We can go dancing? Or see a movie or something."

"Maybe. I don't know. There are a few other books in the library that I wanted to look through. There were some promising leads in an old Alexandrian text."

"Evyn, you can't just spend every waking moment scouring every book in existence, hoping it'll lead you to answers."

"I can't just do nothing either," I snapped. I shook my head and calmed myself. "You didn't see what I saw, Morgan. My familiar is being subjected to whatever torture those monsters can dream up, right now, as we speak. Do you have any idea how much damage mercs like us can take?"

"I can't imagine what stress you're under. I've asked the Council to look into some of it and I've got my ghosts on the hunt. There are a lot of avenues being explored." She rolled up the sketch and put it in her bag. "Think of it this way. If you're too brain-dead to focus, you might miss what's right in front of your face. You need to do something to rest your mind."

I looked at her through bleary eyes.

"It's not your job to save the world."

I stifled a yawn. "Since I largely contributed to the world being in this situation in the first place, I kind of owe it to... everyone... to try."

"Why are you still trying to take that responsibility onto yourself? If Moreno hadn't picked you, she would've picked someone else. This was going to happen. But she underestimated you. We are all lucky that she held a grudge, otherwise things might've turned out different."

"Exactly. I just delayed the inevitable. Now instead of being over quick, it's just extended suffering."

Morgan gave me a pitying look that still held a hint of annoyance. "No matter how bad things get, there's still hope. The world isn't going to end. Of that, I am confident."

"Then you are far more optimistic than I am."

"I have enough optimism for both of us. So whenever you need some—like right now—just ask." I nodded my head and gave her a conciliatory smile but she kept staring at me, deadpan. "Seriously. Take some."

"Alright."

Morgan grinned.

"But would you be okay if we just ordered in and watched crappy TV?"

She grabbed her phone. "Sure. One question. How do you feel about pineapple on pizza?"

Thirty minutes later, on the dot, the delivery driver pulled up. It was one of the family pizza joints in town. Great sourdough crust, stretched thin, wood fired. I handed Morgan her Hawaiian pie—it was the first time I truly questioned our friendship—and took the triple mushroom with goat cheese and roasted garlic for myself.

"So what are you in the mood for?" I asked, crashing onto the sofa. "Housewives, ex-cons, cults, true crime?"

"Let's start with cults and see where the evening takes us."

"I like where your head's at." My streaming account was primed and ready with suggestions, and we were halfway through our first episode when Morgan's phone rang.

Her brow furrowed. "It's the Council."

I paused the show.

"Hello?"

"Okay. I'll be right there. Do you want me to bring Evyn?" she asked, glancing at me. "Got it."

She hung up.

"What happened?" I asked.

She shook her head. "No time." She grabbed her pizza and slung her jacket over her arm. "Let's talk while we drive."

I nodded and grabbed my jacket off the back of a chair. It drove Derfael nuts when I eschewed the coat hooks. Just like Tristan and the damn key rack.

Derfael was just coming up the stairs as we were leaving. "Trouble?"

"I'll pull the car around," said Morgan, continuing on.

"Seems like," I said. "The Council called and they want her to bring me with her."

"Shite," said Derfael. "I'll keep the news channels on. Good luck."

I sucked in a breath and nodded. "I'll give you updates when I can."

Morgan beeped her horn, and I hurried out the door, jumping in the passenger seat. I barely had the door closed and she was pulling away from the curb. White knuckles gripped the steering wheel, and her eyes were tight with worry. "Here we go."

Chapter Two

We arrived at the Council building in record time. The parking lot was full and as soon as we stepped inside, it was a hive of activity. I couldn't remember the last time I'd seen any Council gathering this intense.

Morgan pushed through the crowds of people, mostly support workers and staff that rarely ever appeared in the main Council hall. At one point, she took my hand because the crush of people was so tight. We were heading for a private antechamber that was sealed with privacy wards and she knocked once before entering.

A sea of grim faces met us as the door sealed shut. Morgan had explained what little she could, but she didn't know much. The entire Council was present, along with their lieutenants, and Morgan went to join Frige. I made a beeline for George. He and Ishani were whispering about something as all the other Council heads talked among themselves.

"Evyn, I'm glad you could be here," said George, giving me a quick hug.

"This interrupted pizza and true crime night. Better be good," I said, trying to keep things lighthearted.

The two of them just exchanged rueful grins, the usual reaction to my gallows humor.

"We're waiting on a speech?" I asked.

Ishani nodded. "We are expecting the president to be on the air any minute." She motioned at the projector playing a major news network on the pull-down screen. "Whatever he says, we need to have a quick strategy meeting and then George needs to give the reply."

"But we're anticipating it's for sure a declaration?"

They both nodded. George's jaw set in a tight line. "I can't believe these fools have actually gone through with it. How did things escalate so fast?"

Before either of us replied he waved us off. "You know what I mean. Those damn sisters..."

A look must've passed across my face because he blanched. "I'm sorry. Morgan mentioned what happened to Adrian. I meant to reach out but—" he looked at me helplessly. "Half the time, I can't tell if I'm coming or going these days."

I gripped his shoulder. "I understand."

"Obviously we will do whatever we can to help," said Ishani. "As far as is in our power, anyway. I'm honestly not sure what kind of resources we'll have available after tonight."

"Are you sure he's alive?" asked George. "I don't mean to be insensitive, but do you really believe that?"

"Long story short, yes. I'm positive he's alive. And I am almost certain he'll stay that way until they get what they want."

"Why go to the trouble?" asked Ishani. "Why bother inciting war? If you claim that your primary goal is to exact vengeance on a very specific group of people, why bring the entire world into it? If you have no intention of turning your sites on this realm? It just seems reckless. Needless."

"They wanted to keep us busy so we couldn't focus our forces on them?" I ventured.

"Hell of a way to do that," she said, folding her arms. Her real nails tapped a staccato of anxiety on her metal arm.

"It's on, turn it up!" someone shouted.

Senator Yards was standing next to the president of the United States, flanked on both sides by leadership from the Known. He had a smug smile on his face, the look of a man who just got everything he wanted. The evil gleam in his eye made me sick.

President Nolan stood with an air of solemn sincerity, and all of us pressed closer to the screen. "Ladies and gentlemen, I have called you here today to make a grim announcement. This is the kind of moment every leader dreads. Something we hope to avoid at all costs. But we find ourselves at an impasse." He gripped the podium and bowed his head in a fake show of regret. "After extensive attempts at peace talks and resolutions, the Stranger High Council of the United States territories has refused any further discussion."

"That's bullshit," I snarled, several others in the room echoing my outburst.

"We have no choice now. We can no longer wait and hope for the best. They have forced our hand." He motioned at the top brass standing with him on the stage and I recognized General Hicks—one of my overseers at the DIWR—and that sniveling brown-noser that did his dirty work, Brentwood. I was very glad I'd never have to deal with them personally again.

President Nolan continued. "I have mobilized domestic military units to be dispatched to major cities. A large part of our forces will head to Michigan. We will seek the High Council's surrender, but if they refuse, we will have no choice but to declare martial law."

The gathering of congressmen and women behind him was no longer split in their reactions like at Yards's rally that Adrian, Percy, and I had spied on a week ago. Back then, it was clear that at least half of them were not in support of this. But now they all had the same resolute stares of determination. They wanted this.

President Nolan cast his eyes skyward. "I pray it doesn't come to that. But we are fully prepared to take this as far as it needs to go. I know these words are frightening, and never in a million years would I have imagined that this would be the defining moment of my time in office. I promise you, none of these actions are taken lightly. Right now, all I ask of you is to be strong. Hold your families close. What we do now is for the betterment of all humanity. Together, we will stand and fight against this supernatural scourge. We will show them who is truly meant to inherit this earth! And we will not back down until our enemy is defeated!"

His entourage clapped and Yards shook hands with the president before turning aside to his buddies from the Known, exchanging quiet words on the edge of the screen.

A deadly silence filled the room.

"I don't suppose there's any magical reset button we can press?" I asked George. "Maybe something super-secret that you've been sitting on?"

His ruddy face was pale. "Unfortunately, no."

I was honestly at a loss. I've fought many battles, even some as part of a larger war, but it's never been on my doorstep. And never an "Us versus Them" scenario.

"Okay," said George to the room at large. "We need to decide on which response we're giving them."

The newscast switched back to the anchor; he looked shellshocked. "As you've heard here tonight, well..." He blinked rapidly. "The president has just declared war. Against Strangers. Uh... we will obviously keep you apprised as more details are released, and plans made clear. But as it looks right now, our worst fears have happened."

Somebody pressed the mute button.

"What were the options?" I couldn't see the speaker, but I'd know that wheezing voice anywhere. Thatch, head of the Magi Guild.

"We offer restraint, or we go full aggression," said Ishani.

"We don't offer them a damn thing," said the Matron.

I turned, gaping at her. "You don't want to make any kind of contrition?" I asked.

She raised her chin and stared down her nose at me. "You are here as support staff. Not for input."

I bristled. "Excuse me?"

"Theresa," sighed George, and I did a double take. What was going on? He never referred to her as anything other than the Matron around other Council members. And her attitude was completely unwarranted. This time.

George motioned to me. "I'm willing to hear anybody. Including Evyn."

My aunt gave me a menacing look, warning me to keep my mouth shut, regardless.

Fuck that.

"If we go at them guns blazing, they'll panic. Do we have any idea what they're planning? How their troops are moving?"

All I received in reply were blank stares. "Nothing?" I asked. "What happened to the people I trained to replace me?"

"They got themselves killed or fired," said Thatch. "You didn't train them very well."

"Or you pushed them too hard, too fast. Training can't make up for experience," I snapped.

"It doesn't help that our primary spy burned her bridges with the DIWR," said Theresa. "That might've been helpful."

I gritted my teeth and turned to her slowly.

"Okay, that's enough," said George. "I want to hear what she has to say," he said firmly, glaring at my aunt.

Her nostrils flared, but she didn't say anything else.

"If they've got full military units set to move in right now, we need to tip-toe. Unless you want the entire city to come down on us tonight. Mass panic won't accomplish anything. Assure the humans we'll look to resolutions but make sure our people know to stand up for themselves."

"No, tell them to fight!" said Thatch.

"The Unseelie will not support that," said Finvarra, his pointed face etched with his usual sneer. "I won't send my people into the fray."

"We need to hit the humans hard!" Thatch tried again. "Get them now, before they have time to organize!"

"They've already organized!" I said, stepping between Thatch and Finvarra and putting myself in a precarious danger zone. "Haven't we been preparing for this?" I asked. I looked around at each of the Council heads. Regret, anger, defensiveness, or denial were the pervading body languages. I shook my head. "Fine." I turned to George. "Tell our people to get out."

"What?" asked Ishani.

"Tell them to go back to the Strangefells. If at all possible. Get out and stay safe while our teams deal with shit here. It'll keep causalities down." I frowned. "And if worse comes to worst, we can hit them with everything we've got and not have to worry about our own getting caught in the cross-fire."

Thatch waggled his finger at me. "Now that idea, I can get behind."

"I'm thrilled," I said, rolling my eyes.

George chewed the inside of his cheek while he thought. With a slow nod, he said, "I'm good with that. Any objections?"

Nobody spoke up. George turned to Rami. "Let them know we're going live with our response in ten."

Remi had his phone to his ear, already dialed, in an instant.

George placed his hands lightly on me and Ishani's shoulders. "You two come with me." He looked like he might be sick. "Moral support."

We followed to his office where a camera was already set up. He took a seat behind his desk and Rami came in, giving us both a curt nod. He stood behind the camera and waited on the phone for the go-ahead from the network.

George took a few deep breaths, and his demeanor changed into the picture of steady leadership, not looking the least bit frazzled—even though he was about to make a speech that was about to change the way of life of the people he'd been bound to lead.

"Good evening. It brings me no great joy to have to make this announcement tonight. I know for many of the humans listening, you will not believe me when I say that your people are lying to you. They have made no attempts at working out a peaceable agreement. We have made a more concerted effort than they have, in that regard. Our missives have gone unheeded. Our liaisons have been shut out. We want conflict even less than you do. But clearly, it is unavoidable now."

He folded his hands in front of him on his desk. "To my Strangefells community, I beg you to take caution. These next few days will more than likely be violent and chaotic. Keep your heads down. Be very careful who you trust, especially human neighbors and acquaintances. I urge you not to utilize violence or magick unless you have no other choice. Defend yourselves, but if conflict can be avoided, do so. Lines will be drawn in these next few days, and for the life of me, I don't know what will happen. I wish I could give you a confident answer. This is the last thing you want to hear from me, but if we know nothing else, it's that humans are predictable in their unpredictability. They do crass, stupid things when they're afraid. Don't give them a reason."

I winced. A bit harsh, but alright.

"Council forces are being deployed, and we are working closely with the global Council organization. You will not be lacking in support, you will not be alone. We must take shelter in each other. Escape to the Strangefells if at all possible. For many of you, I know that's a lot to ask. You've built your entire lives here. Many of you have never even been to the Strangefells. But seek out your elders. Ask them for guidance. It's a terrifying concept to give up everything you've ever known, but it is the safest option. This war cannot follow you there. Give us time to work things out in this realm while you stay safe and out of the line of fire. It will be far easier for us to function if there are as few citizens to worry about as possible.

"But let me make this abundantly clear. We are not ceding. We will not surrender, run, or hide. We will not give the humans an inch. We have made our homes here for millennia. We... are not... leaving."

George looked at Rami and nodded. The djinn cut the live feed and clicked the small TV on. The news anchor was having the worst night of his life. His skin was several shades paler than it had been before George's address and sweat beaded on his forehead.

The anchor's lip trembled as he spoke. "Well there you have it. I'm afraid I-I don't even know what to say. We are in uncharted territory. Stick with us for further updates."

Without even waiting for a cut to commercial, the man got out of his seat and walked off camera. There was a moment of confusion in the background before it cut away to some B-roll story about the recent changes to electric vehicles.

"He seemed fine," said Ishani.

I leaned against the wall. "You did great, George." And I meant it. "But can someone please explain to me what you assholes have been up to?"

A week later, and I still hadn't heard from Morgan. Time flies when armies are mobilizing. Life was continuing on relatively normally, for now. Several mobile guard units had set up stations all around the city, concentrating heavily at the High Council's headquarters, which I was avoiding until they got their heads out of their asses. So maybe forever.

A slow filter of people trickled from the city heading toward more rural areas, but the presence of Strangers still seemed consistent.

There had been multiple minor incidents with militia groups and vigilantes, but most of the people that were hurt were also human. Strangers had been heeding George's warning and staying out of sight.

It was the breath before the plunge. Everybody waiting to see who would fire the first shot, and what would happen when they did.

All this also meant that any help I may have been getting from the Council, or Morgan, was tied up with other matters, and I had run out of books in Derfael's library. I was at my wits' end.

"Call your aunt," said Derfael, on my twentieth circuit of the room. My restlessness was torture. Every time I went outside, someone recognized me. It was only a matter of time before I was mobbed by the angry villagers.

"Did you not hear my breakdown of our last chat?"

"They clearly need you back."

"They've let everything fall apart!" I shouted. Derfael nearly dumped his tea down his front at my sudden outburst. This had been weighing on me all week, building up into a maelstrom. He'd just said the words to let it loose.

"I gave them the keys to setting themselves up for success. But they got lazy. They watched the ship sink and did nothing to correct it!"

Derfael's voice was infuriatingly calm. "A gradual decline is easy to miss."

"How many times should I have to warn them? It's like all our strategy meetings over the last year went in one ear and out the other." I paced faster, wringing my hands together as they itched to do damage to something. "It seemed like we were on the same page. When I started training Bex and advising Council security, I made it clear that they needed to give them oversight. I couldn't be everywhere, nor could I anticipate their shortcoming if I wasn't there to supervise. They *assured* me they'd stay on it!"

"You're too good at your job, Talulla," said Derfael with a wry smile. "You made it look easy, so they didn't think it was necessary."

"That's a piss-poor excuse. And now we've got a war on our hands, and they aren't prepared!"

"So help them prepare!" Derfael said, standing. "Dammit, lass! Why are being so bloody difficult?"

I stopped my pacing and stared at him.

"Being angry about the situation doesn't help," he said, sweeping his robes behind him as he crossed the room and grabbed my phone, tossing it at me. "How many missed calls do you have?"

My lip curled, and I shoved the phone in my pocket. "I'm tired of it. They use me for my skills and knowledge, turn me into a punching bag, let me become a demon to Strangers and humans alike, beg me to help again after they fuck up, and then the cycle repeats."

I stared at Derfael, daring him to contradict me. He didn't. "The only reason I've never done anything about it before is because the perks were too good. Now all it's doing is causing a distraction from what I should really be focusing on."

"Until Morgan or the council come up with a solution, we are at an impasse. The only thing you can do for Adrian right now is worry. And that is clearly not helping you. Or him."

"No. I can't stop looking for answers. The Council library should be accessible again tomorrow. I've already checked the alignments twice. There have to be answers there."

"Fine," he sighed. "But in the meantime..." He motioned outside. "It'll be dark soon. Why don't you take a walk? It'll help."

"Help you or me?"

Derfael chuffed, but didn't answer.

I grabbed my coat, shaking my head in frustration. "Fine. I'll get out of your hair."

"That's not what I meant."

"I know what you meant," I said, adding my keys to the ensemble. "I'll see you later."

"Be careful," he called after me.

"Always," I called back, taking the back door out of the shop to avoid being seen.

The shadows were already lying thick. I zipped up my coat, the frosty night settling in as each breath puffed in the air. I didn't have a destination in mind, just let my feet set the path.

It was maybe twenty minutes before the familiar thumping of music got my attention. Right down the street was Exodus.

"What are you doing? You damn well know you shouldn't go in there," I said to myself. The last time Morgan and I had visited the exclusive Stranger club in the bar's basement, I wanted to give my brain a bath. The club owner was a sleaze.

But... it sounded a hell of a lot more appealing than going back home and repeating my usual ritual of downing two or three bottles of bourbon before I fell asleep on the couch. And then the inevitable nightmares that followed.

I closed my eyes against the horror. Every night, Adrian would be even worse. More injuries, screaming, pain, fear. Sometimes I would get a glimpse of the monsters and then they would throw me out, and I'd be unable to stop them. Unable to save him.

But he would always make eye contact with me. And lately, the pleas had started. He begged for help, asked me to put him out of his misery. Staring into my eyes the whole time.

After the lancing pain from being forcibly removed from that place subsided, I would find myself in a heap on the floor of the living room, bawling my eyes out. I didn't know how much more of this I could take. I added another bottle of bourbon to the count every night, just so I could hope for a blackout instead of dreaming. How long would it be before I saw a body? Torn to pieces and barely recognizable?

After the first incident, I stopped telling Derfael about them. He was a heavy sleeper, so he never heard me fall on the floor, crying, in the middle of the night.

I was so tired. All the time. People kept telling me it's not my job to save the world and then they would come to me looking for help. The circumstances are always dire. Maybe it was time I left them to drag themselves out of the holes they dug.

The icy wind battered my jacket as I stood across the street from the club. It was packed, but nobody was lingering outside. Life must go on, even in a city under the watchful glare of emboldened zealots and a military ready to invade.

The debate raged within me, and I stepped off the curb, my desire to lose myself just for a little while pulling me toward Exodus. But I stopped. Not tonight.

I turned back to Wolfe's, oblivious to the Stranger watching me from the shadows.

Chapter Three

"Are you going to answer that?"

I glanced at my phone. "Nope." I clicked it to silent and went back to studying the book laid out in front of me.

Derfael harrumphed. "Council again?"

"Mm-hmm."

"You can't keep ignoring them," he said, continuing our argument from last night. "They want you back in full capacity and you're going radio silent?"

"I don't have the patience or bandwidth to do anything but search for a way to get Adrian back. They'll have to figure it out."

"Right," said Derfael, moving aside a stack of books. "Because they have so many replacements to choose from."

"That's their own fault," I said.

"Do you really want Malcolm taking over?" A plate with a deli sandwich and some chips appeared in front of me. I pushed it aside to where all the other food Derfael had brought me went to languish.

I shook my head, still not looking away from the grimoire in front of me. "If that's what they need to do."

"Evangeline Louise Urquhart."

I froze and blinked, processing the hit. I flicked my eyes to Derfael. To describe my glare as *annoyed* would be an understatement.

"First of all, eat that," he said, pointing angrily at the sandwich. "Or I will force feed it to you. It's been days since you've had anything."

"I—"

"Second, no matter how angry you are with the Council, are you going to let everybody suffer because of it?"

"I thought you said it wasn't my fight, alone? That I shouldn't take the burden onto myself?"

"Evange—"

"Don't you dare," I snapped.

"Then stop acting like a child," he fired back. "Sequestering yourself among the books until you find answers won't get you anywhere. Think about it from a rational perspective. You still have contacts that could help you. Being on the inside of the Council is sure to get you further than if you were just looking at a bunch of books. And what about that agent at the DIWR? She seemed to be pretty friendly. No chance that she'd be interested in helping you still?"

"I haven't thought about that," I begrudgingly admitted. "I doubt I could even get in to see her. And for all I know Agent Greene's been shitcanned like everyone else."

"There's only one way to find out, and you can't do that from here. And are you really implying that you can't break into DIWR headquarters?"

"Of course not."

He grabbed a chip off the plate and popped it into his mouth. "You aren't any use to Adrian if you just hide away here."

"I'm not hiding." I took a bite of the sandwich. Derfael was right. I wasn't going to make any progress if I didn't take care of myself. "I'm just trying to find... hope," I finished lamely. "Is that so wrong?"

"Of course it's not," said Derfael. "But you have a lousy way of dealing with heartbreak. Don't slip outside yourself. You're no good to him otherwise."

I chewed, swallowed, took another bite, and unabashedly spoke with my mouth full. "Do you actually believe this is possible?" I asked.

He sighed heavily. "I can't say for sure. I'm not going to get your hopes up. It's hard enough to find someone that doesn't want to be found. But when we're talking about inter-dimensional hide-and-seek? It's going to be all but impossible. That's just a fact."

"What if I can't find him?" My voice was quiet.

My phone buzzed and Derfael seemed relieved to not have to answer. He grabbed my phone before I could silence it and punched the answer button. "Evyn's phone." His eyes held an evil gleam. "Why, yes, Percy, she's right here."

He handed me the phone.

"Hello," I said, more of a groan than a greeting.

"Evyn, what the fuck? Why have you been ducking my calls for a fucking week?"

"Hi Percy. How are you?"

"Don't even start with that shit. We need your help, we're sorry, yada yada. Get your ass down to headquarters."

"Sorry, can't. I'm in the middle of something," I said, staring at Derfael defiantly.

Percy made a strangled noise. "Gods, Evyn, are you going to make me beg?"

"It wouldn't hurt."

"Evangeline—" said Derfael.

"Evyn—" said Percy.

"Alright, fine," I snapped.

"That was fast," said Percy, meeting me at the front door.

She led the way inside and I followed, spinning my car keys on my finger. "Everything is fast if you don't pay attention to traffic lights."

Percy led the way through a part of the building I hadn't seen before. It was far from the luxe excess of the main chamber. This looked more like your standard office building. Signs labeled every door we passed. Each Council member's office had a name tag and there was even an employee lounge.

"Do you want to talk about it?" she asked.

"You idiots, or Adrian?" I replied, raising one eyebrow.

"Either?" she offered, casting me a sidelong look.

"No."

Percy rolled her eyes, and we turned a corner. One side of the hallway was lined with windows and looked like a waiting room in a hospital.

"This seems out of place," I said.

Percy snorted. "It's Thatch's. He wanted a meeting room made specially for the magi. This is his idea of comfort."

"You know," I considered. "That's not at all surprising. Does everybody get their own special room?"

"Of course not. We just didn't want to listen to him wheeze."

When we reached a nondescript door at the end of the hall, Percy opened it to reveal George waiting for us.

My face relaxed into a smile. "Hey."

I thought he'd looked exhausted before, but now—guilt crept up on me.

"Don't," he said.

"Huh?"

"Feel bad about ignoring us."

Percy made a sound of disagreement, a kind of spluttering snort.

A bemused frown twisted my mouth. "Am I that predictable?"

George shrugged. "You had 'guilt' face. It's like constipation face, but... sadder." He motioned for me to take a chair.

"Noted." I sat and looked around. This wasn't the same office we'd been in before. "I thought you had an office," I said.

"This is the spare one he hides in when he wants to avoid people," said Percy.

"Checks out," I said, crossing my legs. "I forgot to ask before. Did you fire Bex?"

George waffled a bit before answering. "Fired is a bit overstating it. We've allowed them to continue training. If Bex wants to stick around and work their way back up, that's up to them." The wolf leaned back in his chair, placing his palms flat on the desk and stretching.

"So what's the latest news?" I asked.

He groaned. "Yards has been making the rounds. Gathering more support. And he's getting it. Him and that smarmy dick from the Known." More to himself, he said, "I am so sick of seeing their faces."

"Common sense is failing fast," said Percy.

George slapped his hand on the desk. "Which brings us to the point. We clearly need you back. I'm not proud of how we failed to maintain what you'd worked so hard to set up. You've already sacrificed a lot, and when you needed our support, you didn't have it. For that, I am sorry. Are you willing to give us another chance?"

Percy reached over and grabbed my chin, pushing my mouth closed. "I know it's shocking," she said with a grin. "It's not every day you get an apology from the Council."

"No matter what may have happened in the past, you were our best. And, especially right now, we need you back on our team," said George.

"Are we talking full reinstatement? Team leader?" I asked.

George nodded, smiling. "Yes."

There was no point in thinking it over. It was my best option and we all knew it. "Okay," I said, holding out my hand. "As long as I can still have full access to resources to keep looking for Adrian, we have a deal."

"Excellent," said George, taking my hand and sealing said deal. "Let's make some introductions."

The war rooms were a little used and much maligned chamber, hidden away in the Strangefells away from the prying eyes of humans and Strangers alike. We traveled there with a quick portal, conveniently located in one of the back offices of the Council headquarters.

"It's been a long time since I've been back to this place," I said.

"It hasn't changed much," said George, winding his way ahead of me through the narrow hallway that served as a chokepoint in the event of an outside attack. Percy had opted to stay behind.

A heavy iron door at the end had a small crack of light spilling through the edges and I could hear brief snippets of conversation. "I had the full team assemble," said George. "They, uh, don't know you're coming."

I rolled my eyes over to him, already annoyed. "Why do you do these things to me?"

He gave me a sheepish smile. "It wasn't going to take the sting out of it anyway. And maybe you can avoid some walkouts."

"You have a lot of confidence in my charm."

We walked through the door and into a cave with a high, vaulted ceiling.

There was already a large group of people waiting for us. Some I recognized, but most were unfamiliar faces.

"Hey, Evyn. I knew you couldn't stay away for long." The smarmy voice alone made me want to punch the owner of it and when I saw his face, that desire only doubled. Malcolm Finny. Because of course it was.

"Of all the mistakes the Council made, you're the worst." I said it with a wide smile on my face and a pleasant tone that didn't hide the animosity in my eyes.

"One of these days, I'll win you over," said Malcolm, waggling his eyebrows and flicking out his tongue. I rolled my eyes and continued after George.

Now that I looked closer, these rooms had seen *some* updating. Most of the tech they'd had the last time I was here consisted of devices developed long ago that worked purely with magick. Vessels, focuses, a magickal switchboard that acted as our communications hub. But now some modern equipment had joined the lot.

"Did some mages rob a Radio Shack?" I asked.

George laughed. "Radio Shack? You can't come up with a better reference than that?"

I shrugged. "It was the first thing that popped in my head. Call me old fashioned." I winked.

"We have had some magi take interest in combining tech and magick. We've been thinking of developing it into its own branch." He winced. "Now it seems too little too late."

"Hindsight. Nothing ever seems like enough when you're looking back on it down the barrel of a gun." I took a moment to peruse the interesting set up. Consoles with strange, blinking lights that made little sense, antenna with energy crackling around them, spires reaching to the ceiling that hummed with power. None of it seemed to have rhyme or reason. I almost felt like I was walking into a Cold War bunker long hidden in some canyon somewhere with a collection of random experiments that had been abandoned.

George clapped his hands together and turned to the room at large, where everyone had been watching us with a keen interest. "As I'm sure you've gathered, there's a new team member in your midst." He waffled his head before correcting himself. "Although, I guess I should say she's not joining, as much as taking over leadership of this team."

My stomach sank as I watched the expressions on everyone's faces sour.

"You suck at this, you know that, right?" I asked him.

Most of these people hadn't worked with me before, but had undoubtedly heard of my reputation. Half of them probably didn't trust me, because of my working with both sides. And now George was coming in and telling them all that they were my subordinates whether they liked it or not? That was a great way to make a first impression.

The angry rumbling had already begun. I stepped in front of George and raised my hands placatingly. "I'm sure what George meant to say—if he knew what tact was—is that I'm going to be advising in a supervisory capacity. I don't want to step on anyone's toes—"

"Too late for that," said a woman at the back of the group. There were murmurs of agreement.

"It is, and the abruptness of it isn't fair. But you are sadly in need of new leadership." I stared down anyone who looked like they were about to defy me. I liked to be open and honest with people, but if they thought this was a democracy, there were going to be problems.

"This team has been working together for months." Malcolm stepped forward. As much as I hated the man, he *was* the best substitute that they could put in charge of this group. And the people here seemed to default to him easily enough. "We would love to have you on the team, but I think you can see why we're hesitant."

George was about to interject, but I waved him off. I took a few steps toward Malcolm and the smug smile on his face faltered just a bit. "Normally, I would agree with you. I would never seek to usurp anybody after months of being a team leader."

The expression on Malcolm's face changed to one of suspicion. Rightly so.

"But I hate to break it to you. You've been doing a shit job." I crossed my arms in front of my chest and invited the subsequent backlash, which was quick. Angry outbursts and curses came flying in my direction. Not actual curses, of course. They wouldn't risk George getting caught in the crossfire.

I stood there and weathered the onslaught, and when it died down, I continued. "I don't want to point fingers or direct blame at any one person," I said, aiming a direct glance at Malcolm. "As a team we're a single unit that succeeds or fails together. You have no idea how disappointed I was to find out that you have had so long to get a handle on things, but when we entered a whole-ass war, we were so grossly underprepared it was shameful. There is plenty of blame to go around, not the least of which lies with me. I wrongfully assumed that I could set everyone up for success and leave you to continue in that trajectory. Clearly, I was mistaken."

Some of the angry looks were fading into acceptance, if not outright resignation.

But there was a strong holdout. "That's not fair," said Malcolm.

"It's plenty fair," I said. "You guys have dropped the ball in pretty much every way possible. There were no tactical plans, you didn't have reinforcements set to deploy, as far as I can tell there is no intel coming in from anywhere, even though there were several available sources to draw from stationed within human organizations. Contacts that I painstakingly set up for you."

Malcolm's tone turned defiant. "If you were so confident that all this would be foolproof, clearly you were mistaken. I've been doing the best I could with what I have."

I didn't even bother stifling my laugh. "Did you just outright call yourself a fool?"

A few titters of laughter from the group behind him had Malcolm's face turning red. "That's not what I meant," he grumbled.

"What's done is done. My primary goal is to get us back to where we should be, and prepare to meet our enemy." The temperature in the room had changed somewhat. I wasn't getting a sense that there would be outright mutiny, anyway.

George, satisfied with what he was witnessing, gave me a sharp nod of approval. "How many auxiliary teams do you have?" I asked.

Malcolm looked uneasy at that. "This is pretty much it. We have some reserves, but—"

That took me by surprise. "Nothing? How are these the only people you have?"

I turned to George for that answer, who looked at me apologetically. "Unfortunately, we've had some trouble with retention. And a whole lot of deaths on the job."

"Do you not have anybody else coming up in training?" I asked. When I had been in the merc "academy," there had always been at least a hundred people training at any given time. It was the only reason the Council was truly feared; there was never a shortage of folks like me ready to do its bidding.

"This life doesn't appear as illustrious to Strangers as it used to," said George with a small shrug of his shoulders. "Recruitment's been down."

I blew out a breath. "Okay." I looked around at my new team, hands on hips, already wondering if I made a bad choice accepting the job. "We'll figure it out."

Chapter Four

After thirty-six hours straight of hashing and rehashing every protocol and procedure of the Council teams, we'd finally made some progress. I'd reestablished the lines of communication with my contacts, not that it was worth a whole lot now. Maybe we'd still get advanced warning from them before an attack was launched, but that was the most I was hoping for.

Luckily, their actual battle training was fine. I still didn't relish the idea of taking such a small force into a head-to-head fight with a human military unit three or four times our size, but as long as our tactics held up, I was keeping my fingers crossed that everything else would too.

I was floating along on autopilot when I realized I was close to Exodus again. The music wasn't as loud, and there were even fewer people scurrying back and forth. Before I even registered what I was doing, I'd parked my car and was heading back toward the club.

A shape caught my eye, a man standing on the corner, leaning against the building. I couldn't see his eyes, but I felt him staring at me and when I stopped to stare back, he pushed away from the wall and walked out of sight. My hand gripped the cold metal door to Exodus and I stepped inside, immediately letting myself get lost in the swell of noise.

The same bartender was working that I'd met when I came here with Morgan, so I flagged him down. In no time, I was being escorted down to the club. It was a different bouncer this time. Sure, it was the same gruff personality, similarly built, same haircut, but this one didn't have nearly the same helpfulness. This guy seemed detached, much less invested in the well-being of the customers.

The vibe, too, was different.

It felt dingier, a little more sleazy. I didn't necessarily feel unsafe, but I wouldn't be letting my guard down. And I would most definitely be shielding myself better from whatever magick Ranzick had buzzing in this place.

A woman in a slim black cocktail dress bearing a silver tray stopped in front of me, offering me the drink sitting on it.

"Old-fashioned?" she asked.

"I really need to stop being so predictable," I said, taking the drink. She smiled, her blood-red lips a perfect Cupid's bow.

"There's nothing wrong with knowing what you like," she said with a wink, and walked away.

The halls were empty, and Geoff didn't appear to give me another tour. I tried to remember the color-coding that he'd mentioned last time. Purple was pay-to-play, green was groups, and orange was low-key casual, right? I poked my head into several rooms with various levels of intrigue ranging from salacious to "back away slowly," but none of them really spoke to me.

Not until I reached the blue room.

I sought in my memory for any mention Geoff may have made of what the blue rooms were. This was the only one I'd seen. I thought I'd been in this hallway before, but I would've remembered something so out of place. Wouldn't I?

I shrugged, deciding to check it out, anyway. There wasn't much that I could walk into that would really shock me, so I wasn't worried about that. But what I found when I opened the door wasn't what I was expecting.

The room was largely empty. Art hung on the walls, but it was nothing earth-shatteringly interesting, and a small bar with a single bartender standing at it sat to the right of the door. A living wall planted with moss and other greenery flourished amid the Edison bulb lighting along the back, and there were a few plush pieces of furniture.

But the real point of attention was the one man sitting on a couch in the middle of the room, looking at me with an interested expression as I stood in the open door. I would've walked back out immediately, thinking I'd interrupted a private party, but he smiled and gestured me forward.

"I've been waiting for you, Evyn. Come on in."

I almost did the classic "check over my shoulder to see if there's someone behind me named Evyn," because no way was he speaking to me, but I resisted.

The man chuckled. "Yes, you. Please." He motioned again, his smile wider.

I took a few steps inside the door and let it close behind me. There was nothing amiss here. The bartender was minding his own business, wiping at the spotless bar top with a pristine white rag. That same binaural drone that was ever present hummed away in the background. But there was no music in this room. Just the droning beat.

"Do I know you?" I asked, not taking a seat.

"We haven't yet become acquainted, but I've seen you around. I'm hoping to get to know you better."

I frowned. "In a good way or a bad way?"

"Only good." He crossed his middle and index fingers, holding them up to me. "Promise."

I narrowed my eyes at this man, unsure of his game. I pegged him for some kind of fae, but I couldn't tell exactly what type. Then the dots connected. "I saw you outside. You were watching me."

He nodded. "Guilty."

There was a love seat positioned directly across from the sofa he was sitting on, and I perched myself on the edge. The next sip of my drink put my glass almost on empty, and I noticed the bartender spring into action, mixing another one.

"Do you often hang around in rooms by yourself at a club like this?" I asked him. "Are you an owner?"

"A silent partner," he said, with a smile that suggested there was a joke to go along with it, that I wasn't in on.

"This is quite an establishment you have here," I said. "I wasn't sure I was going to come back, but..."

He nodded deeply in acknowledgment. "We do try to give people memorable experiences."

The bartender brought over the fresh drink and swapped it out for my empty glass. I toasted the mystery man and took another sip.

"Mmm," I said. "Give this guy the award for mixing up the best old-fashioned."

"Ned is excellent at his job. We tend to hire the best people away from their current establishments when we find them. Doesn't make us too popular with the other bars in town, but we don't hesitate to acquire talent. Or anything of interest."

His gaze became hungry, but not in the way you typically see in a joint like this.

"Why do I feel you're about to give me some kind of proposition?" I asked.

"Nothing untoward, you have my word."

I raised the glass to my lips. "Except for finishing this delicious drink, I'm not interested in anything else you have to offer. If you'll excuse me." My heels clicked on the mirror-shined concrete floor as I headed for the exit.

"Okay, you win. No propositions, but won't you stay and chat? It does get rather lonely, and Ned isn't much of a conversationalist."

I shot a glance at the bartender, who gave a one-shoulder shrug.

"And what would you like to talk about?" I didn't move back into the room.

The man splayed his hands. "So many things. Anything you'd like. I'd just like some company, and you seem like an excellent choice."

I rolled my eyes. "Cut the bull. Tell me what you're aiming at, or I walk out right now."

"Do I seem that untrustworthy?" he asked.

My eyebrow hiked up. "If you know so much about me, you should also know what my relationship with the fae is like."

He tilted his head back and laughed. "That's no concern to me. I'm not part of the queen's court anyway."

"You're one of Finvarra's?" I couldn't hide my sneer of disgust. Moreno's family had been part of the Unseelie king's court before he turned on them and encouraged their kin to do the same. He was partly responsible for creating the monster that she was. And he personally tortured one of the few fae I actually counted as a friend.

The man saw a look on my face, and the corners of his mouth turned down. "Perhaps I shouldn't have said anything."

"I don't have a direct outward animosity with your king, but I'm no friend of his either."

"Not many people are," he said, waving his hand dismissively.

I took a few steps closer. Warning bells weren't clanging, and I had to admit that this man intrigued me. "If we're going to have a conversation, can I at least get a name?"

"Any old name?" he asked, a mischievous smirk on his face.

"Whatever one you're willing to give me." I shrugged. "Unless you'd like me to call you 'asshole in the black suit' for the entirety of our time together."

His smile this time revealed the pointed incisors common to dark fae that he no longer bothered to glamour. "That doesn't really roll off the tongue. Let's go with Ivan."

"Ivan?" I took a seat, leaning back and crossing my legs. "Odd choice, but alright."

He cocked his head. "Hell of a thing, isn't it?"

I waited for him to furnish a subject, but he didn't. "Can you be a little more specific? I can think of a lot of things I'd describe like that."

"The war, of course. I've been racking my brain to remember the last time a war of this scale broke out between us and the mortals."

"A long fucking time ago, that's when." I raised an eyebrow. "Is this really what you wanna talk about? Not exactly light conversation."

"Who said I was looking for light? I thought it might be interesting to hear from someone on the front line."

I snorted and shook my head. "I hear the weather is a nice thing people talk about when they're getting to know each other."

Ivan gave me a sideways smile, showing off one of his sharpened incisors again. "Very well. A change of subject then." He seemed to search around for a new topic of conversation and what he came back with almost made me drop my drink.

"Amazing what the nobles are attempting to pull off, isn't it?"

I stared at him, trying to keep my face neutral. Nothing of Tristan's work should've been known to anyone outside the Council and the noble families themselves, and even the Council wasn't up to date anymore.

Ivan continued. "You know I thought for sure you'd be at the shindig this weekend. Isn't your lover one of the Iraklidis clan?"

I couldn't resist; I took the bait. "There's a party going on? Now?"

The fae man hummed and pulled out his phone, typing in a few things and scrolling the pages until he found what he wanted. "Oh, I stand corrected," he said, feigning surprise. "Apparently someone else is hanging off his arm for the event."

He flipped the phone over to me and my blood boiled. Sophia Brennan. That bitch. At the sight of Tristan's smiling face, posing for the camera in his tailored suit, his dimples standing out perfectly, my heart gave an uncomfortable thud. That discomfort turned to a painful twist as I saw Sophia, dressed to the nines and looking every bit the royal consort.

So he'd replaced me then.

I didn't know whether to be heartbroken or angry, or both. The least he could've done was call—hell, I'd have settled for a messenger pigeon—to tell me it was over. So I didn't have to find out like this. Sitting in a room in a shady club with a perfect stranger.

It didn't take long for the anger to take over the heartache. My house wasn't safe to return to. My trusty canine companion couldn't be with me because Tristan practically kidnapped him. And worst of all, my familiar who I'd gotten a second chance to start a life with had been taken, and if the nightmares I was having were anything close to the truth, he was being tortured by the vile creatures that took him.

But at least his highness could get dressed up and smile pretty for the cameras.

Ivan reached over and snatched his phone back out of my hand when my tight grip threatened to break the device.

He checked his phone over for damage while giving me a pompous grin. "Apologies. Apparently you didn't know."

"We've been separated for a while. This just confirms he's not coming back. Thanks for that I guess."

I downed the rest of my drink, and Ned brought over a fresh one before I'd swallowed. I spent the rest of the night venting all my frustrations to Ivan. Perhaps a little reckless, but who was I hurting? I left the Council out of it, and by the looks of things, I didn't know Tristan as well as I thought, anyway.

By the time Ivan walked me to street level and saw me out the door with a smile and a warm handshake, I felt like a weight had been lifted off my shoulders.

"I'm here most nights, if you'd like to continue the conversation," he offered.

"I just might take you up on that."

There was a pep in my step on the walk home, and I actually made it into my bed before I fell asleep that night.

I didn't dream.

CHAPTER FIVE

I woke feeling more refreshed and ready for the day than I had in months. There was none of that lasting gloom hanging over my head, just ready and waiting for the next disaster to happen. Missing Adrian was a dull ache in the center of my chest, but instead of feeling panicked, now I only felt prepared and ready to tackle the problem. I don't know what kind of magick Ivan worked on me last night. Maybe it wasn't him at all, I just needed to vent to someone. Either way, it worked.

Derfael must've already gone down to the shop, so I made a pot of coffee and planned my day. The team would be fine unless we got called out; that much was the same no matter whose side I was working for. So it was an easy call to devote the day to searching.

Since I'd already burned through the druid's entire library, I needed to up my game. The Council didn't like to advertise it, but their library was one of the greatest resources they never talked about. Plenty of rare gems could be found, if you knew where to look.

Now, what did I do with that key?

I filled up a thermos and headed downstairs to find Wolfe's was unsurprisingly busy. There had been a constant stream of Strangers coming in for defensive items since the declarations. Derfael had a hard time keeping things in stock.

The atmosphere was glum as I wove through the nervous customers. Most turned their eyes away upon seeing me and busied themselves with their purchases or took a sudden interest in an item on the shelves.

Derfael gladly took a break from answering questions when I tapped him on the shoulder. "Heading out?"

"The Council library might have some answers. But I have to stop at the house first."

His face darkened. "Are you sure that's a good idea?"

"I have to get the key. Unless I want to try to bypass the wards the hard way."

He wasn't happy about it, but he settled for a sharp nod. "Be careful. Call me if you need anything."

"Promise," I said, before working my way to the front door.

My car rumbled to life, and I headed for my old neighborhood. I hadn't been back since I'd moved, and that ache of homesickness tugged at me.

The drive was quiet, traffic low as people continued to evacuate the city. That was the only good thing about impending war. When I pulled onto my street, it was obvious that something was wrong and a second later, it became clear.

"Oh, no."

There had been no shortage of shenanigans on my street after my departure. I pulled into my driveway. The usual barriers to entry didn't slide across the car like they usually did, but I would've known they weren't there just from looking at my house.

And the neighbors'.

My house and the two on either side had been attacked with fire, force, and foul graffiti. I got out of my car, stomach sinking as I surveyed the damage. The first things I noticed were the shriveled bodies of the servitors that had guarded my home so well. Their vessels had been destroyed and all their power evaporated with them. That alone told me a Stranger had a hand in this.

They must've started by throwing incendiary devices at my house, probably a molotov cocktail or two and when they bounced off my shields, they hit the neighbor's house instead. Scorch marks marred the side of the house on our left, the siding melted and dripping onto the ground. The windows of the house on our right looked like shattered, broken teeth grinning through the pain. Police tape surrounded both houses, but there was none around mine.

That seemed to be the worst of the damage, for my neighbors anyway. When they broke through my wards, it had become a free-for-all against my home. I circled around the outside, looking for evidence they'd broken in, but those protections had held. The vandals had instead settled on scrawling hateful messages and graffiti everywhere. They smashed the porch in several places, broken bits of the railings used as battering rams and batons as they tried to force their way in.

They'd even dug up the landscaping and... my heart twisted. They'd demolished the arbor and torn up all the plants that Tristan and I had put so much effort into building together.

How hadn't I sensed the attack? The minute those barriers came under attack, it should've notified me. Clearly, whatever Stranger was helping them wasn't strong enough to get into my home, but blocking the wards from sending out an SOS would've taken a lot of power and knowledge in itself. It didn't make sense.

"Evyn."

I turned to find the Jacobsons in my driveway. They owned the house to the right of us.

"When did this happen? Is everyone okay?" I asked.

They nodded and Mrs. Jacobson put a hand on her husband's shoulder as his face reddened. "The only damage is what you see. They were here for you. About a week ago."

Shortly after war was declared, then.

"Bastards," said Mr. Jacobson. Neither Tristan nor I bothered to keep secrets from our neighbors. They knew who I was and what we did. The Jacobsons and the Millers, who were in the house on the left, hadn't batted an eye. They even invited us to cookouts and other neighborly things. Our schedules always prevented us from being able to attend, but it was nice to be invited and welcomed to the neighborhood. I had volunteered to ward their homes as well, out of common courtesy of living next to a high-value target, but they turned me down.

"And the Millers?" I asked.

"Fine," said Mr. Jacobson. "They weren't home."

A sigh of relief hissed between my lips. "I'm so sorry. I should've given you a heads-up."

Mrs. Jacobson's mouth pressed into a thin line, and I thought she was about to blow up at me. But it wasn't me she was angry with. "Those idiots were of a mind to destroy whatever got in their way. They just appeared out of nowhere, raging, and shouting. They hurled anything that could get their hands on at your house and fire-bombed the Millers once your—" she circled her hand as she tried to think of the word.

"Wards," I supplied.

"Yes, thank you. When they saw everything just bouncing off it, it only made them angrier. Somebody started shooting at it. And then someone showed up who was definitely not human." She shook her head. "I'm not sure what kind of Stranger she was, she just raised her hands and clapped once. There was this cascade of light as the barriers fell, and then the crowd surged."

She motioned at the destruction they'd wrought. "Once they made it onto your property, they left ours alone. By then the cops were already on their way." Her brow furrowed as she thought. "It was so strange... odd, I mean. That woman just watched, smiling while they tore at your house. Satisfied with what she was seeing. But I got the feeling that if she wanted to, she could've destroyed the whole thing by herself. I don't know why she didn't let them in your house. But she could've."

Mr. Jacobson looked at his wife. "How do you know?"

She shrugged. "It was just a feeling. When you can tell someone is dangerous just from one glance. She exuded"—she made a motion with her arms, drawing herself up—"confidence. Power."

"What did she look like?" I asked, decently sure I already knew the answer.

"Long black hair, darker complexion. Very tall. Extremely thin. Even from my vantage point peeking out our window, I could see her eyes, just dark pits. I almost had a heart attack when she looked at me."

Mr. Jacobson shot her a look. "You didn't tell me that."

"I didn't want to upset you. You already told me to stay away from the windows," she said, a sad grin on her face.

"But the rest of them, you got the sense that they were all human?" I asked.

They both nodded. "Half of them were wearing Known t-shirts."

Mrs. Jacobson's phone rang, and she glanced at the screen. "It's our daughter. We're staying with them until—" she motioned at their house. "She has a little one, so we didn't want her coming with us to collect a few things, just in case. But we should check in."

"Of course," I said. She stepped away to take the call, but Mr. Jacobson didn't follow.

"Do you think it'll be safe to come back? Will all this die down before it boils over?"

Spreading fear isn't high on my list of things to do anymore, but I couldn't lie to him, either. I owed him that much. "If you have someplace to stay, away from the city, you should go there. Take everything with you that can't be replaced."

He nodded and extended his hand. "Thank you."

"Be safe," I said, clasping his offered hand. "And if you need anything, don't hesitate to ask. You and the Millers were both wonderful neighbors."

"We hope to see you again, Evyn," he said, giving me a strained smile and heading off after his wife. I watched them hurry into their house before turning back to mine.

After stepping over the pile of actual shit somebody left on my doorstep, I walked into my empty home that wasn't a home anymore. It was just a soulless four walls holding up a roof. It had only been a few months since I'd left, but I hadn't put any kind of maintenance framework in place. There was a layer of dust over everything, it smelled musty, and I might've heard the scurrying of a few mice in the walls.

I kept several hiding places around the house. I'd cleaned most of them out when I moved to my apartment, but some were so well hidden and secured, it has been easier to leave them here.

We found lots of hidden things as we renovated that hinted at some... extracurricular activities of a criminal nature, by some of the home's former owners. A couple of the cubby holes hadn't been found by previous residents, and still contained old bottles of liquor, newspapers, personal photos, and a couple of wads of cash from the early 1900s. Bank robberies weren't uncommon around here, especially with Dillinger running around.

I headed straight for the guest room, not wanting to spend any more time here than necessary. We'd taken out the back staircase and found a secret cutout in the bottom of the newel post. Behind it was a compartment cut into the wall that hid a switch to the real secret compartment down the hall. It was so ingenious and still worked beautifully, so we preserved it. The switch compartment was behind a vent now. After I deactivated the jinxes surrounding the switch, I reached in and triggered it. A fast rolling sound echoed down the hall as the wooden panel concealing the compartment dropped down.

There were further hexes on the items within the compartment, and I pulled them all out for good measure. Who knows if next time they'll actually get in or just burn the place down?

My key for the library was hidden here, along with a couple of cursed relics I'd taken from Moreno's museum—the Council confiscated the rest—my personal grimoire, Solomon's ring, and a few knickknacks from Tristan's childhood that he'd been sure to hang onto. A small toy hand carved from wood in the shape of a war horse, a journal of his mother's, and a necklace that belonged to the first queen of his family line.

Why would he have left these here if he hadn't intended to return?

I hesitated, hand hovering over the toy horse. On the one hand, these were Tristan's, and I didn't want to remove them, but on the other, if something happened to the house, they'd be destroyed.

Eventually, I swept everything into the satchel at my side before going around and clearing out all the others. There were only a few odds and ends left. I'd taken most of the furniture and household items in the move to my new apartment, and nothing else was all that special to me.

I slung the bag over my shoulder and took one last look around the house that I'd truly believed would be my forever home with the man I loved. And then I closed the door behind me.

The Council library was hidden beneath a massive forest preserve a couple of hours north. The drive was quick, and I kept the music blasting the entire way, not wanting a moment of silent reflection for myself right now. By the time I hit the offramp, I was belting Halsey at the top of my lungs, windows down and drawing stares from passing cars. I wasn't tone deaf, but I was close.

Most of the roads going into the national forest were two-tracks, maintenance roads only. Without an ATV, you weren't getting far. I left my car, well hidden, several feet into some brush, and got to walking.

These woods were always different, more wild. I welcomed the peace here, no matter what my state of mind, because I was guaranteed to feel better. I took my time strolling, enjoying the changing colors of the leaves, the bird trills, the deer that moved without concern for the intruder in their midst.

The library is only accessible on certain days and times, sometimes disappearing for months on end. It's hidden in a realm that appears at the whim of the heavens, particularly the planet Mercury and the constellation Gemini. When those bodies form certain alignments, you're in. Provided you have the key, of course.

The Council may *claim* ownership. They defend it and punish anyone who misuses it, but in reality, the library is a world in itself.

My mage Sight was the only way to see the trail that led to the front door. I tuned in when I got close. A natural path wound through the trees, but only if you looked very close did it look deliberate. When I stepped onto it, the air got warmer, the woods a bit quieter. My boots crushed through deadfall, snapping twigs, kicking rocks. I wanted the guardians to hear me coming.

Two proud birch trees stood side by side in a small ring of oak, rowan, and hawthorn. As I approached, I felt eyes on me, and two figures melted out of the bark, reforming their shape into armored warriors and drawing swords against me.

I halted and held my hands up, dangling the key from my right middle finger. It was a bronze coin, stamped with a figurehead that neither human nor Stranger history would be familiar with. Not anymore.

Bound in red thread and strung on a leather cord, I moved my hand, so the item swung back and forth like a pendulum.

Both guardians fixed their electric blue eyes on the item, relaxing their posture. They sheathed their swords and melted back into the trees without a word. The space between the birch shimmered as the doorway activated and I stepped forward as magick pulsed and undulated, crackling for a brief instant before snapping into reality.

The library itself was in the Strangefells, but there were several doors, just like this one, all over the world. This one was shaped like the tree of knowledge, limbs spreading across the entire top half of the doorway in intricate bronze detail. A tiny crow perched on a bend of the tree. I held the coin out to it and the bronze figure sprung to life, taking the coin in its beak and disappearing as the door creaked open.

I entered, and the crow flew past overhead. Even though the library was in an underground cavern, it was always bathed in sunlight. The stairs wound down, the open "sky" above me lighting my way.

When I reached the bottom, the hall opened out into a massive space. Blue skies shone overhead, fluffy clouds scudding in an imaginary breeze. The crow dropped the coin into a fountain with a basin resembling a white lotus and flew back to its post. Magick sparked, and the fountain gurgled to life as I waited for the librarian to appear. From the waters stepped an elegant woman in an ornate sari, her long black hair flowing over her shoulders as her blood-red lips twisted into a smile.

I bowed my head. "Lady Saraswati."

"Thought you'd forgotten about me," said the goddess of knowledge and wisdom, handing me back the coin.

"After the way we parted last time I was here, I figured it was a good idea to steer clear for a while," I said.

"As long as you don't plan on causing trouble, I'm happy to have you here." The smile turned into a knowing grin. "And that is all water under the bridge." She winked. "I didn't revoke your key, did I?"

I was about to answer, but her eyes narrowed. "There is something different about you." She studied me and then she backed up a step in shock. "I think you have some things to explain."

Lady Saraswati motioned me after her and led the way to a cozy little reading nook, inviting me to take a seat.

"How long have you had the power?"

My brow knit in confusion. "What power?"

"You can control the æther?"

"Solomon's gate gave me a connection to the ether that's still hanging around. It caught the attention of the wrong monsters and is actually the reason I'm here."

"It is not just ether." She waved her hand dismissively. "That is a byproduct, something sorcerers hedge their bets on. It only takes, never gives. The æther"—a wondrous look crossed her face—"is a source of creation. It is where we got our name."

"Am I hearing that differently? Æther?"

"Yes."

I gaped at her. "I don't think I understand. Are you saying that it's the same kind of power that the gods use?"

She inclined her head. "Yes, and no. Most of the Ætherim can't access it as such. Not anymore. It is too volatile to harness without great risk to us in our diminishing states. But being woven into Solomon's gate, dying, and coming back alive... it must've found you there."

"I've only been able to tap into it once, to avoid complete catastrophe," I said, remembering the anger and helplessness that drove it forward as we were on the doomed train speeding toward apocalypse. I never would've imagined that most of the people with me on that mission would be dead or missing just a few months later.

"Why didn't the Council recognize it when I showed them?" I asked.

"They would not have had reason to know. To them it would appear as plain ether. Unless Atum saw it too?" Her suspicion suddenly became uncertain, and she leaned forward in her chair.

"No," I said. "He wasn't at the meeting."

She nodded, satisfied.

"Is it something I can access at will?" I asked.

She shrugged. "You will grow to understand it. It will make sure you do."

I gave her a deadpan stare. "Can you give me a little more information than that?"

Saraswati shook her head. "That is something I cannot teach, but must be learned on its own."

That wasn't what I wanted to hear, but I gave a resolute nod. "I guess that brings us around to why I'm here."

The goddess got to her feet and motioned for me to follow her. "I already know why. That terrible business with your familiar."

"You know about that?" I asked.

Her eyes glittered. "I wish I could take credit for being all-seeing, but in fact your friend Morgan was here."

My hopes lifted. "Did she find anything?"

"Not yet. But we've been narrowing down sources."

We turned a corner, and before us were several tables laden with stacks of books. "Here we are."

"All of these?" My hopes lifted even higher. So many potential answers. I could find him. I *would*.

"Any suggestions on where I start?"

"Where *we* start?" she corrected.

I turned to her, surprised. "I will gladly take all the help you can give me."

"Perfect. Then I suggest you take that pile, and I will take this one."

It was a full day of poring over texts, Lady Saraswati peppering me with questions as we worked. She was eager to find out more about the æther, Adrian, and the sisters, and I was more than happy to talk with someone who could give sound advice on all of it. She was the keeper of this library for a reason, her wisdom unmatched.

The woods were dark by the time I left, and I lit a small ball of mage fire to keep me company. The little orb bounced at my side, illuminating only a few steps around me at all times.

When I reached my car, I only thought briefly of heading to Wolfe's, but that thought was quickly replaced. I knew exactly where I needed to go.

Chapter Six

"I'm still waiting to find out how you became a silent partner in this club. Geoff Ranzick doesn't seem like the kind of character you'd want to give money to."

Ivan gave me a pained look. "You have no idea. He may be insufferable, but this place is what I was interested in. I enjoy coming here and being anonymous. Just another extremely handsome face." He grinned when I rolled my eyes. "I can join in the fun whenever I want or disappear to a room all by myself."

"That only raises more questions," I teased. "That you want to be anonymous implies your face is well known somewhere. It's certainly not here."

"Ouch," he said, hiding a smile. "You didn't come here tonight to mince words."

"So spill."

"I am a member of Finvarra's court."

"Right. You mentioned you were Unseelie."

"No. I mean I have standing in his court."

"Oh," I said. "A noble?" How did I keep winding up in the presence of nobility? I couldn't be less politically minded and I hate all the drama, but once again...

"Low ranking, but yes. Enough of one to be annoyed by it. My family's doing, not my own. I bought into this partnership looking for escape."

"I can understand that," I said.

Ivan traced his fingertips along the back of my hand as it rested on the couch. I watched his fingers as he brushed my knuckles, wanting to pull away but still finding myself comforted.

"You know we've met before?" he said, his voice husky.

I looked at him, doubtful.

"During that nasty business with Ulfric and Finvarra. I was decently high up in the court, at the time, but Ulfric was a friend of mine."

"Oh," I said, not sure where to go from here. I was sitting next to Ivan on the couch, but this new revelation had me easing back a bit, turning my body so I could face him.

Ivan chuckled. "You don't need to look worried. Quite frankly, I think Ulfric is much happier now that he's been banished from court."

"You still speak?"

"On rare occasion. Usually when I need something sharp." He smiled. "But don't worry, I don't have retribution in mind. I know Ulfric doesn't hold anything against you either, in case you were wondering."

"It had crossed my mind," I admitted.

Ulfric was my inside man, helping me in a scheme that the fae queen had hired me for before I decided to go after her heart. It was one of her many bids against the king of the Unseelie.

Now that I'm older and wiser, I realize that those two are always sniping at each other and using various go-betweens to do their dirty work as one big game that they've been playing for thousands of years. But I had a job to do, and Ulfric had a bone to pick. So we teamed up. It all fell to pieces and Ulfric ended up being punished severely by the king himself, being banished and having the tips of his ears cut off.

When I ran into the dark elf last year, we seemed to resume our friendly terms. The master smith returned the torque my father gave me, altered in ways that I still wasn't sure of. The only thing I know for certain is that it helped me survive Solomon's gate, providing a refuge for a small spark of my life force to hide within until Tristan could call it back. But I'm sure it still held many more secrets.

Ivan steered the conversation back to where he wanted it. He motioned to me. "Our meeting was just in passing, but you left an impression. Ulfric would tell stories about you, and I've been keen to meet you since."

"Right. That's not creepy at all."

He tilted his head. "Perhaps a bit." He gave a self-deprecating grin. "Can you blame me?"

I took a sip of my drink, not answering, but I'm sure he saw the smile in my eyes. He resumed the delicate tracing along the back of my hand.

"So because of a few stories and legends, you just had to meet me?"

"That, but also because of your recent break up." He grinned with a sultry heat, leaning toward me. "I saw an opportunity and I took it."

My smile evaporated, and he pulled away, brow furrowed. "Did I misread the situation?"

"I've recently worked things out with my familiar."

"Ah," he said, retracting his hand and hiding his disappointment. "My apologies."

He draped his arm across the back of the couch and might've changed the subject, but he could sense my unease. "Is there more to that story?"

I chewed on my lip. Here we were, heading into personal territory again. But I felt better the last time I spoke to him. Only one way to find out if that would hold true a second time.

"Adrian was taken. Abducted. He's being kept in a location that we can't find."

Ivan's disappointment turned to concern. "I'm sorry to hear that. To be unable to find your familiar, they must be hiding him well."

"Too well. I'm trying everything I can think of to find him."

"Can you tell me more about the circumstances?" he asked, turning and resting one knee on the couch so he could face me completely.

So I did. I laid it all on the table without delving too near the bits that involved the DIWR or the Council, Solomon's gate, or my newly discovered abilities with æther.

"I wish I could offer you some advice, but I've never heard of anything like this."

I shook my head. "Nobody has. I just appreciate being able to bend someone's ear." I faltered. "In light of what you were hoping for, though, I'd understand if you didn't want to continue... whatever we're doing here."

He waved me off. "You're splendid company, even if you aren't available." He chuckled. "I'm not a petty man."

I cocked an eyebrow, and he smiled sheepishly. "No more than my brethren, anyway. But in matters of seduction," he said, that heart-stopping smile returning, "it's always just a matter of time."

"Who is this man?" asked Derfael.

We were sitting at the breakfast table. I'd be heading to the library again shortly, but breakfast together had become a nice part of our daily routine. He could moan about all the dumb customers he'd have to deal with today, and I could keep him updated on where I was at in the search.

"According to him, he's a fae noble just looking for a good time in a club that he partially owns."

"And you trust him?"

"Not even a little bit. But whenever I speak with him, I feel better. He takes away some of the stress for a while. I'm not sure if he's trying to mine information from me, or if it's some kind of magick he possesses, but I'm not complaining."

"That seems like a risky choice," he said, finishing the last of his pancakes.

"I'm not spilling all my guts. Just the stuff that's safe for him to know." I grabbed another couple of pieces of sausage and three more pancakes, dowsing them with syrup. The good stuff. Tristan was a great cook, but nobody could beat Derfael's pancakes.

I dipped the sausage in the maple and speared a bite of pancake before shoving it all in my mouth.

"And there's no chance that he's extracting other information you're not aware of? It is somewhat of a specialty of theirs." The warning tone was heavy in his voice. He had enough dealings with the fae to last several lifetimes, and he never failed to pull a story from his list of experiences that would harrow anybody who thought they were on equal standing with those particular beings.

"I've been shielding myself thoroughly. Glamoury doesn't work on us. I'm not sure what other magick he could be pulling out of his ass, but I'm not sensing any kind of intent from him."

Derfael brushed some crumbs out of his beard and tossed his napkin down on his empty plate. "Just be cautious. I don't need to tell you that you can't be trusting anyone's motives. Especially not now." He considered me. "But I do have to admit that you seem to be pulling yourself out of the slump you were in."

"Slump?" I asked, already offended.

"You were hitting the edge of a spiral, Talulla. Don't pretend otherwise."

"Cut me a bit of slack here. I've kind of been going through it."

"I wasn't condemning you for it," he said gently. "It is entirely under-standable. I just want to make sure you don't try to run from it, or pretend it's not happening. This Ivan fellow isn't the only person you can talk to, you know?"

"Sometimes it's just easier to talk to people you don't know."

"That's what worries me. And don't forget that he knows you."

And with that mic-drop of a statement, he excused himself from the table and headed down to the shop.

"Do you think I'm totally out of line here?" I asked, paging through a fresh tome. I'd almost made it through my second row of books.

"I'm sorry, I missed the part where I was a relationship coach?" said Saraswati, looking at me with a perfectly sculpted eyebrow raised.

"You've always got sage advice to hand." I shrugged. "It was worth a shot." I gave her a sideways grin and went back to my book.

"Yes, well." She, too, continued to scan the pile of books in front of her. Saraswati may have been the goddess of wisdom and knowledge, but even she didn't have every book in this library memorized. She sighed and looked back up. "Everyone needs someone to listen to them. But like your druid said, you need to be cautious."

I nodded. "Heard."

We lapsed into silence after that. I pulled out a green leather-bound book, the gold foil on the cover so worn I couldn't even read it anymore. The pages were a thick vellum and even though it was centuries old, time hadn't had much influence over the interior. After flipping through the first few pages, I stopped dead when I reached an illustration. Two huge serpents coiled around a village while it burned. The illustration had a cross section of the snake bodies cut out and each of their stomachs was full of people. It looked like they were being dissolved and broken down, releasing swirls of energy as they did so.

Underneath the woodcut illustration was one word. Lamia.

"Find something?" asked Lady Saraswati.

I turned the book so she could see it, and she moved over to my side, skirts rustling. The fine gold chain leading between her nose ring and earring jingled as she leaned forward. "Lamia."

"I've always known lamia as mythical creatures. Something more akin to a mermaid, or a faun. I never pictured them as giant beasts."

She shook her head. "I'm not sure that's exactly what they're referring to." She paged through a few more sections. "Here." She pointed to a rough sketch of a lineage tree. It was a breakdown of other creatures and where they were thought to have originated from. The archetypes that birthed the rest. "This is Ameris's work. He got his start as a scholar in Alexandria before dedicating his life to studying magickal creatures. He wanted to find their origins. Especially the most problematic ones."

I huffed. "Problematic is one word for it."

"Ameris's best working theory was a diminishing-return principal. That almost all creatures today are descended from chaos."

"And by chaos, you mean—"

"The primordial crucible."

"Great. That again." Every step of the way, it was just one reminder after another of all the damage that Moreno's plan had done. And was continuing to do. "Atum already mentioned that some of these things could be waking up, now that the Ancients shook up some cosmic dust."

"He would be correct. Solomon's gate opening put a ripple effect into the universe. There's no telling how deep they will go before they cease to be felt. Unfortunately, we may still be seeing a lot more things like this cropping up. All of the dark secrets that my kind tried to hide or control all coming back to bite us in the ass. There are many things we did that we are not proud of. At least, most of us aren't."

"Then why not try to correct them sooner?" I said, rubbing at my tired eyes. "All due respect, did you just cross your fingers and hope that this day would never come?"

Saraswati sighed. "You must understand, the world was a different place. Wild, untamed. *We* were different. The Ætherim were young and feeling invincible after we won our battles against our makers. There is always the risk of continuing to justify actions, even after the war is over. Things done out of desperation become dirty secrets that we sweep under the rug rather than confront. It was easy to excuse at the time as... necessary. To save the world and everyone in it. And after that battle, we became the most powerful creatures in this world." She smiled wistfully, her eyes focusing on somewhere far distant. "It is a heady experience. Add human worshipers to the equation. We became gods. All powerful. We could do no wrong. We had done no wrong. And that is how it stayed. Until last year. Every nightmare we sealed away and swept aside came back to remind us of our failures. And to remind us of just how much power we have lost. How fast we are fading."

She took a deep breath and released it slowly, closing her eyes. "There are a lot of things that we will need to deal with. These sisters are the first. They will not be the last."

"If people keep piling all of this great news on top of me, I might just explode with joy." I frowned.

"It may not be the best news. But I for one have already bound myself to service of solving these problems. I will not stand by and watch other people fight our battles for us anymore." She drifted back to her seat.

"So can this help us at all?" I asked, turning my mind back to the immediate problem. "Their connection with chaos? An infinite space needs some road signs to navigate, right?"

"And you want to follow them back to their lair?" Saraswati nodded, tapping her chin. "Give me a minute."

She trailed her fingers over the piles of books. Frowning, she stood and disappeared into the stacks. She was gone for about ten minutes and when she reappeared, she was holding a massive volume in her arms.

"Thought it could hide from me," she said, a triumphant smile on her face. "It always wants to play hide-and-seek."

"It's sentient?" I asked, but now that she said it, I did notice a faint thrumming of power from it.

"Oh, yes. It contains live charts of the stars. Not necessarily the road map you are looking for, but it may hold some answers."

I cleared some space on the tables, overrun as they were with my scribbled notes. The book made a heavy thunk as it hit the table and I eagerly opened the cover, gasping as I saw what was inside. I had flipped it open to a bird's-eye view of our galaxy.

The tome drew a little more power as it fired up and the galaxy moved, winding up individual components into their orbits and rotations. Each new page held wonders even farther out into space. The second half of the book was for Strangefells skies.

I remembered the mysterious stained-glass window in the houses of healing. When I visited Percy shortly after she was injured in the battle with the

Ancients, Frankie escorted me upstairs and the window was at the top with an unknown constellation. She knew nothing more about it than I did. Would it be in here?

"Fascinating, isn't it?" asked Saraswati. "I could look at this for hours. And I have. But what you are looking for is back here."

She flipped all the way to the back, perhaps the last quarter of the book. These charts weren't nearly as defined. It was more swirling essences in vague patterns and shapes.

"There are underlying currents that flow through space, massive bands of power. The same power that created the universe. They ebb and flow, not as predictable as an ocean tide maybe, but there are general consistencies."

"So we use these, to look for patterns," I said, nodding as my brain worked around the problem. "But how do we tell what's related to the sisters? Is there any way of altering these maps so I can overlay these patterns and see how they're interacting with our world?"

In response to my question to Lady Saraswati, the map before me shifted. There was a quick zoom, like a lens focusing in, and suddenly there was our planet. From this close-up perspective, the currents of power left shadows over Earth's surface, covering a wider swath than any eclipse I'd ever seen.

"Wow," was all I could say. My eyes went wide. "Can I borrow this?"

She looked at me, reluctance etched into her features. "That is a big request. This book is clearly one of the kind. If something were to happen to it..."

"Isn't there a safeguard? Some kind of tracker?"

"There is. But if I were to activate it, it would kill the bearer before it returned the book to me." She gave me a sideways smile. "Do you want to take the risk?"

"If you have to activate it, I clearly won't have it anymore anyway."

"Perhaps I should clarify. It would kill whoever bore it out of the library, as well as whoever took it."

"Okay," I said. "I guess I'm guarding it with my life."

She clasped her hands together in a mandala. I felt just a touch of her magick reach out, a quick needle prick as it locked on to me. "Indeed."

Chapter Seven

Book buckled into the passenger seat, I was on my way back to DIWR headquarters, plotting out my infiltration on the drive. The intelligence network was set up on a lower floor, so I wouldn't have to get past the guards posted at every main entrance. The paths to the lower floor were mostly protected by high-tech security. Harder to circumvent than flesh-and-blood guards. Units would be ready to mobilize, but they would need to be triggered first. All I had to do was avoid detection.

I'd "consulted" on this particular security set, pointing out the flaws that Strangers could exploit. And, of course, I left a few back doors along the way.

Staking out the entrance was the easy part. I waited until I saw one of the techs leaving the building, car keys in hand. The beaten down look on their face was visible from a distance. They probably had the entire team working overtime and then some.

It was a chilly day with a biting wind, so nobody looked twice at someone with their hood pulled down over their face. As the tech passed me, I bumped into them, grabbing the lanyard hanging off their pants pocket and casting a quick hex to make sure they'd forget all about it.

Moving quickly through the lobby didn't raise any red flags. If you act like you belong there, people think you do. Head bowed to my phone, I gave a wave to the security guard, keyed in with the stolen passkey, and headed directly for the back corridor. Thirty seconds later, I was stepping into the main hallway of the intelligence center. Spoofing the cameras was easy enough and deactivating the other tech with the magickal kill switch I'd installed made this a walk in the park. It was kind of sad. Even with a threat level in the red, security around here hadn't changed.

Throwing a cloak over myself as I marched along to Greene's office ensured no human eyes would spot me. I peered around the corner into the office. The handful of desks were empty, but there was a mug of still-steaming coffee on Agent Greene's desk. Approaching footsteps made me back up into a corner, but I was relieved to see Greene move into the hallway.

Clutching the book tightly to my chest, I waited until she stepped inside and closed the door behind us. Greene spun, not yet seeing the reason for it closing. There were no cameras in here, so I dropped my concealment. The instant she registered it was me, she gasped, backing up until she hit the wall.

I held out my hands. "I'm just here to ask for help. You have nothing to fear from me."

"Easy for you to say. You're public enemy number one around here. I should be reporting this immediately," she hissed. "They want your head on a pike."

"But you won't do that, because you know they're full of shit." I spoke with calm confidence.

She pursed her lips, still appraising me. "You're sure nobody saw you come in here?"

I gave her a baleful look. "What do you take me for, an amateur?"

She smiled. "I guess not." She tipped her chin in the direction of the book. "What's that?"

"Do you still have access to that fancy new toy that tracks signatures?"

She narrowed her eyes. "Yes…"

"I think I found a way to track those monsters back to their lair."

Her lips parted in surprise, and I could see a complete wash of emotions on her face as she determined her next move. I was asking her to risk her entire career. "Answering that question would be worth the risk, wouldn't it?"

"Thank you," I said.

"Follow me."

I threw my concealment cloak back around me as Greene led the way to the suite of rooms where they kept their top-secret tech. She used her key card, and the door slid open. I had to hurry in behind her, almost getting caught as it closed.

She went about her normal motions. There was surveillance in here, but it was internal. If worse came to worst and one of us slipped up, revealing ourselves, I could always rush to the security room and delete the footage.

I pushed the cloak a little farther out, so I had room to maneuver the book in my arms as she booted up the computer. As the program loaded, it took me a minute to study the patterns before I recognized something I could use. Never forget I was still pulling all this out of my ass as I went.

"Go back to the last event that we are positive was the sisters." I watched the date scroll back and when she stopped, I spoke the same date to the book. Her screen was just a mass of colors, streaking this way and that, flaring brightly in some spots that had nothing to do with the beasts' activities as far as we knew. Pinpricks of low-level activity were spaced in relatively even patterns, but I wasn't sure what those could be.

"Now center on eastern Europe," I directed. Greene complied without answering, still seeming for all the world like she was checking on a hunch of her own.

"Pan out."

I compared the two maps. "Now Asia Minor. Center the screen, two latitudinal lines to the left."

A pattern emerged, prickling in the back of my mind as I slowly put the pieces together. "Now Canada." All these places had the faintest thin orange line that cut through the other colors. Compared to the other noise, it would seem inconsequential. And each had pinpricks of red dots in the same clusters surrounding it.

"Central South America."

There again.

"Southwest United States."

Five more consistencies across the globe revealed themselves. "Can you flatten the map for the entire globe?"

She cocked her head slightly, brow furrowed, before she keyed in a command. The map flattened in the most accurate representation possible. "Now split it and overlay the eastern and western hemispheres if you can."

She made a small noise of consternation, and I smiled. Eventually, she figured out the workaround and my amusement vanished. "That's it. I've got it."

Greene closed out the program and rose to her feet, stretching, before leading the way back to her office. Two of her coworkers had arrived in the meantime.

After some pleasant small talk, Greene sat, reaching for a stapler as she shuffled some papers in her hands. "Oh, shoot. I keep forgetting to grab more staples."

"Just use mine," offered her coworker, a guy named Doug. I didn't know him very well, but he seemed like a wet-blanket type.

"If I don't do it now, I'll keep forgetting," she said easily. I followed her to the supply closet.

"Nicely done with the subterfuge," I said. There was enough space out of sight of the door that I could remove the cloak.

"What did you find?" There were pinched worry lines around her eyes.

"Good news and bad news."

Greene watched as I opened the book, instantly intrigued. "This is amazing," she breathed.

"So the way I see it, the sisters are using one, single current of energy. All of the points that they've struck have been in the path of this thing."

"And they all corresponded when I overlaid the maps," she guessed, trying to work out what it meant.

"They did. What I think is happening is that all of those points converge. Kind of in the center of the earth, if that makes sense. Basically, it's anchoring this whole swath of energy to our planet."

"I have a feeling we're about to get into territory that's a bit too heavy for me. Can you give me the TL:DR?"

"Big trouble."

She rolled her eyes. "Maybe a little more in-depth?"

"I think their lair is located within that current of cosmic energy. And they've attached to our planet like a barnacle. This is the same force that created our galaxy. Our universe."

"That sounds like it'll mess things up pretty bad."

I nodded. "I'll still need to confirm it."

"So does this help you find them? How can you even get into a lair in a place like that?"

"That's the million-dollar question."

A sudden alarm blared. I threw my concealment cloak back around me as Greene moved to the door. "I don't know what's happening. I don't think anybody saw us," she said. Panicked voices and running feet preceded a rush of analysts heading for the exit.

Greene grabbed the arm of a passing coworker. "What happened?"

"I don't know. We just got the order to evacuate."

A cataclysmic explosion tore through the upper floors, shaking the building like an earthquake and collapsing the ceilings. I pulled Greene back into the supply closet and threw a shield over both of us just as another explosion ripped through the lower floor. A fireball raced through the narrow hallways, followed by the screams of those caught in its wake.

She attempted to dart into the hallway, but I restrained her.

She fought to get free. "They need help!"

I felt it coming a fraction of a second before it hit. One final blast. I redoubled the shield just before the entire building came down on top of us.

"Are you okay?" I asked Greene, once debris stopped falling.

"What the hell happened?" she asked, staring at the tight pack of broken concrete and rebar surrounding us. We were completely encapsulated.

"Three explosions, by my count." I looked at her apologetically. "Probably not many survivors."

"How are we getting out of here?"

"Great question." My go-to in this situation would've been to push the shield upward and explode everything laying on top of us, but I didn't know how deep we were buried, nor if there would be any first responders in the way. There were enough casualties as it was.

Greene hesitated. "You didn't have anything to do with this did you?"

A reeled back a bit in shock. "You think I'd do something like this? Of course I didn't. Especially not with me in the building."

She shrugged. "You might've miscalculated."

My ears pinned back, eyes wide. "That's a bold statement to make when you're stuck in a bubble with me. Why would I have saved you?"

Greene begrudgingly admitted that I had a point. "If not you, then who? Would the Council have done this?"

"No, absolutely not." I was unsure of a lot of things, but I knew they wouldn't make such an overt declaration and take the first shots. Especially not without consulting me first. I shook my head, considering. "I wouldn't put it past the Known to do something like this. They'll probably try to blame it on us."

The debris on top of us shifted, groaning against my shield. We had to figure out a way to get out of here. I've made some great escapes in my time, but I'd never taken a human with me. I wasn't entirely sure what her body could take.

"Is there anything below us?" I asked. "A sub-basement, maybe?"

She nodded. "It's a small maintenance tunnel. I'm not sure where we are in relation to it though. It's on the east side of the building."

"There wouldn't be anything else, like a bomb shelter?"

Her lips turned down. "Maybe. It would make sense, but I don't remember ever seeing or hearing about one."

I put the mental map together, following our course through the building, as I tried to remember what side we were on. "If I'm right, we are also on the east side of the building."

"If you're wrong?"

"Then I guess we keep going until I hit an aquifer. Or the center of the earth."

"What exactly are you planning on doing?" There was a note of worry bordering on panic in her voice.

"I can't blast a hole without risking us getting severely injured ourselves. So we'll have to go through a different way."

"And that is?"

I bared my teeth in a grimace. "It's probably better if I don't tell you."

She was breathing in fits and starts, hyperventilating. "Jesus, Evyn, am I gonna survive this?"

I tamped down hard on my gallows humor and forced myself to give her an encouraging answer. "Yes. I won't leave you behind."

She took a deep breath and nodded her head.

"Okay. Take my hand, and don't let go."

Agent Greene hesitantly placed her fingers in mine, and I grasped them tight. I'd done this trick with a car full of people while we raced through the city after an Ancient on the run. Now I had to try it with a human while the crumbled weight of a building threatened to crush us. I thought about giving her a warning to tell me if it hurt, but figured that would just alarm her more.

Little by little, afraid to go too quickly lest my friend blast apart into a million pieces, I raised our frequencies.

"What are you doing?" she asked. Her words weren't strained or fearful, but she knew something was happening.

I ignored her, continuing to speed up the vibration of every molecule in our bodies, altering our physical forms into not-so-physical ones. When we sank through the concrete, Greene gave a surprised squeak. Before she could react further, we dropped through the carnage and into the sub-basement.

Before we could go through another layer, I cut the magick and both of us returned to normal.

"How did you do that?"

"Have you heard of ultra-terrestrials?"

She gaped at me. "You can do that?"

"I just did," I grinned, still clutching the book tightly to my chest. The maintenance tunnel had suffered effects of the blast, small cave-ins littering the path out as the emergency lights flickered eerily. We were intermittently plunged into complete darkness for a few seconds before they came back on. Everything was deadly silent except for the occasional creak of the weight still shifting above us.

An exit sign plastered on the wall clearly marked our salvation, and I rushed us in that direction. "Do you know if the entrance for this tunnel is inside or outside the main building?"

Greene looked hopeful for the first time since the alarm had gone off. "It's outside."

Sure enough, double doors appeared in view and small slivers of light peeked through. We ran into them at the same time, but they were locked; I could hear the rattle of a chain on the other side. Unsurprising.

I made quick work of it, aiming a hex at the padlock and shattering the chain, throwing the door open. Light and fresh air rushed in around us.

We came out onto a low slope, twin tire tracks long worn into the grass from decades of maintenance workers' trucks. This side of the building was still standing. Rubble littered the ground around us, and we moved quickly away, chewing up the distance beneath our feet until we got clear.

"Oh, my god," breathed Greene.

This wall was the *only* one still standing. The rest of the DIWR headquarters were demolished. Dust was thick in the air and small fires were burning. Sirens flashed in the distance, keeping a wide perimeter, but police and fire response had both walked in.

"I can't be seen," I said, throwing the concealment cloak back on myself.

"What should I tell them? I can't say that I just happened to be in the maintenance tunnel."

I gazed up at what was left of the structure. "Tell them you were able to get free and scrambled out one of the windows on this side. I doubt they'll ask too many questions. Not right away at least."

Greene was looking in the general direction of my voice. "Whoever is behind this, I'm sure it's not a coincidence they picked the day that you were in the building to make this happen. Watch your back."

"You too. Take care of yourself. And thank you for your help."

She turned and made her way to the small gaggle of survivors on the street as they waited to see if anybody else would make it out. They rushed toward her when they spotted her, surrounding Greene with open arms.

On the way back to my car—I'd never been more glad for the lousy parking on this side of town—my phone rang.

"Where are you?" said Percy.

A bit back a smartass remark. "At the location you're about to tell me about."

"The fuck are you doing at the DIWR? Did anyone see you?"

"No. What's up?"

"George wanted me to call you with the news, but I guess I didn't need to. We're already getting word that they plan to blame this attack on us. That it was our doing. Yards is gearing up for an announcement."

"What do you need?"

I finally reached my car, popping open the door and falling in to the driver's seat. I tipped my head back and leaned against the headrest, closing my eyes.

"Can you put us in touch with Lorraine Rollins?"

My eyes creaked open. "I am one hundred percent positive she does not want to work with you."

"I'm aware, and we've left her alone as long as possible. But now we need her. Her abilities are unsurpassed. Having a Seer—"

"Would be a huge boon, you're right. But she's been down this road before. It's why she keeps to herself."

"Can you at least give her the option of reaching out to us?" Percy sounded like she was trying to make a compromise, but if Lorraine refused, they would go to her.

"Things are going to get messy. She could help us avoid the worst of it. I'm sure we can work something out."

"You're sure of a lot of things," I murmured. "I'll see what I can do."

"Thank you," said Percy, tone clipped. "Meet us back at Council HQ when you're done."

She hung up.

Chapter Eight

The cozy Queen Anne-style Victorian with the poisoners garden planted all around it—courtesy of the eldest Rollins sister—was quiet when I approached the front door. Lorraine answered while my fist was still in the air, about to knock. "The answer is no."

"If you knew what I was going to ask, you know what they'll do if you insist on that answer."

She was furious, angry energy rolling off her in waves, and I didn't blame her one bit. I'd bent over backward to keep her safe from the DIWR, and now the Council was going after her.

She didn't invite me in, but crossed her arms and stood defiantly. "I have a pretty good idea. I'm leaving town."

"Is that going to work?" I asked.

The Seer chewed on her cheek, tapping her nails against her arm. "As long as I keep running, they'll never catch up. But that's the only way."

I hated myself right now. Why did I have to be the one to tear this woman's life apart? The resignation on her face as she prepared to give up everything and flee, and it had nothing to do with the war...

"Do you want to live like that?" I asked. It wasn't the worst thing in the world to be kept by the Council. She could work out a good deal.

"It's better than going back to what it was like before. I will not be held prisoner by another oligarch or dictator."

"I know it's less than ideal—"

"Do you? What *exactly* do you know about it?" she snapped. "You have no idea what I've been through."

"You're right. But I do believe the Council will offer you a deal. You'll still maintain your autonomy."

She sniffed. "As long as I do what they say."

"There is a certain degree of wiggle room," I said, imploring her to at least think about it.

"For you maybe. Not for a golden goose."

"Look, I told Percy I would deliver the message. And I have. If you decide to run, I'm not gonna say shit about it. You need to do what's best for you."

I handed her a number, scrawled on a scrap piece of paper I found in my car. "Give Percy a call if you change your mind." I paused. "The Council is… terrifying. But if they find something they want to protect, and you know how to play the game right, you could do a lot worse."

She reached out and took the paper, chewing her lip. I turned to walk away, but she stopped me. "Your quest to get Adrian back is going to destroy you."

I recoiled like she struck at me. "Do I find him?"

Lorraine nodded. "But he's not the same. And you won't be either. You will both suffer before this is over."

"Where do I find him?"

She shook her head, wrapping her arms tighter around herself. "I don't know. That part is blank."

"Do you know when this takes place?"

"After your first fall."

I blinked. That didn't sound promising. "First fall?"

She looked at me apologetically. "That's the best I've got. Like I told you before, reading anything around you is tricky."

"There's nothing else you can tell me? Even if it doesn't seem relevant?"

"No. I'm sorry." She stared down at the paper in her hand and I took that for a dismissal. "Evyn." Her eyes swirled gray as she read me in real time. "After the first round of shots, duck. Don't let their new weapons touch you. The bloodshed isn't done today."

I nodded and made for the garden gate, feeling her gaze trail me the whole way.

Percy jogged over to my car as I pulled into a parking space. "You're just in time. Yards is about ready to deliver his speech."

I nodded, slamming my door shut and following her quickly across the parking lot and into the building. "I already called Malcolm, he's getting the team assembled and ready to go. Every guard unit that I passed was getting twitchy and Lorraine said shit was going down."

"Evyn!" called George, waving us over. "Yards isn't wasting any time."

"Percy told me," I said, nodding.

"You were in the building?" he asked.

"My question exactly," said the Matron, appearing out of nowhere like a pissed off phantom.

"I was following a hunch," I said.

My aunt looked at me coldly. "And did you find what you were looking for?"

I inclined my head. "I did. Thanks for asking."

George's phone pinged, and he snuck a look in between nervous glances at me and my aunt. "Malcolm just arrived. They've assembled in the main chamber."

"Perfect," I said, grateful for portals and punctuality. He may not like me, but at least that perv was listening.

"Did you notice anything about the explosions?" George asked.

"If you're asking if they were magickal in origin, I'm gonna say no. They felt like regular old explosives that any human in the military or a militia would have access to. There were three separate bombs, all going off at different times, in different locations around the building. I was on the lowest floor with Agent Greene. There was less than a minute of warning before they went off."

George's eyes sharpened. "But there was advanced warning?"

I nodded. "They called for evacuation. Greene and I escaped through a maintenance tunnel."

"And you're sure you weren't seen?" asked the Matron.

"As sure as I can be. I was a little preoccupied."

Her nostrils flared. "Don't for a second—"

"Theresa," said George, placing a hand on her shoulder. "Please."

She huffed an angry breath, a rhino about to charge, but she instead turned and walked away.

"What happened to her?" I asked. "This isn't like her."

Percy and George exchanged looks that said they had plenty of suspicions, but no proof. "I wish I knew," he said. "A lot of people have been acting strangely on the Council. Out of character."

"Some people have even reported missing time," said Percy with a shudder. She actually looked afraid for the first time since she thought she'd lost access to her wolf.

I was going to ask why they hadn't shared this information, but I felt like a broken record. "And there's no sign of what's causing it. If anything," I said, resigned. I shook my head. "This has to be those snakes. All of this weird shit started after they showed up. They've got their tendrils in, all across the power hierarchy. Mind control wouldn't be a stretch." I remembered what happened when I "dropped in" on Cliff Tafford at one of his rallies. They had possessed him, and he had no memory of it when he came out of it. These creatures were so far beyond what I'd ever dealt with before. There wasn't even a way to tell how far embedded they were on both sides.

And to think that they could've even infiltrated my aunt's mind? The strongest woman I knew, the most powerful? How could anyone fight against that, if this woman that had seen every trick in the book didn't even realize they were influencing her?

"I'm going to go meet Malcolm. We need to set up forces outside the building, just in case." I looked at George. "You need to get to the safest room in this building and stay there."

He nodded and I saw Rami melt out of the shadows to make sure that George followed orders. Percy buzzed off to attend to something else, and I headed to meet my team.

It still struck me as odd to say that, a part of me still expecting to see my human team. Those impossibly brave and incredibly foolish warriors who agreed to follow me on an experiment. And their association with me cost them their lives. I know it was cowardly, but I hadn't been able to bring myself to check in on Briggs, Jaeger, and Pryor, afraid that I'd find out they were killed too.

"Alright," I said as I entered the chamber. "Here's where the rubber meets the road. I'm fully expecting this building to be surrounded and most likely attacked after Yards has a chance of blaming it on us before he gives the order to move in."

I quickly divvied out the positions and watched with satisfaction as my team mobilized into their separate groups, moving to take their stations. I had no idea what to expect, but it came to a firefight I wouldn't hesitate to fire back with everything we've got.

Malcolm joined me on the roof. It irked me to have to share space alone with this idiot, but it couldn't be helped.

"We're just waiting?" he asked.

"Just waiting," I confirmed.

He was silent for a moment, fidgeting, before he asked, "Why aren't we bringing the fight to them?"

I took a slow breath and released it, turning away from my lookout position to glare at Malcolm. "Why aren't we attacking them, unprovoked? Was that your question?"

"If we catch them by surprise, we have the upper hand."

I rolled my eyes. "We should already have the upper hand. This is our territory, we know it the best. And we'll have high ground." I turned away, and turned back to add, "You idiot."

"But—"

"No 'buts,' Malcolm," I snapped. "Things are bad enough without them accusing us of war crimes. If they bring the fight to us, we have every right to defend ourselves. If we attack them, on public land no less, that will give them every excuse to launch a full assault. We've been in a slow burn, and you want to turn up the heat to a blazing inferno?"

He grumbled something under his breath, and I ignored it. Malcolm lapsed into a blissful silence for another ten minutes.

"Do you see that?" he asked, nudging my arm and pointing across the way.

"Shit," I said. George's voice came through our line of communication, directly into my mind. Way more convenient than human comms.

"Yards just finished up his speech."

"I got that feeling," I said. "We've got military units closing in. Keep everyone inside, unless I call them out. I don't want any surprises."

"Got it," said George.

I tapped the plaque behind my ear and switched to the ground team on the east side. "You ready?"

"Copy," said Abeni. She was the second most senior member of the teams and a fierce elemental witch that could control fire better than anyone I knew.

I tapped the plaque again. "Team 3, ready?"

"Copy." Gio's brusque tone barked into the comm and I winced. He was a warlock with a penchant for necromancy, and I was looking forward to seeing what he could bring to the table.

The National Guard units rolled on toward us and I could just see news crews setting up in the distance on the rooftops. I don't know what Yards said, and I didn't care; I just hoped history would reflect that we stood down until they gave us no choice.

"Everybody hold," I said as a sea of green camo, tanks, and Humvees surrounded us.

A sergeant that must've drawn the short straw stepped up to the front of the ranks with a bullhorn in hand. It squealed as he turned it on and he almost dropped it in surprise. Once he got it figured out, he cleared his throat. "George Hardy, if you turn yourself over to us and tell your people to stand down, we can resolve this peacefully. We are asking for your surrender. Submit to a tribunal for your crimes and your people will be spared."

Malcolm growled beside me and took aim at the sergeant, but I stayed his hand. I placed my pointer and middle fingers against my throat and spoke a jinx that would amplify my voice, enough for the man below and the brass all the way in the back to hear, but it shouldn't carry far enough for the news crews to catch wind.

"Sorry, he's indisposed. You'll be dealing with me." I cut the jinx and tapped my comm. "Teams 2 and 3, move to the roof. Malcolm and I are coming down."

"What do you mean, 'Malcolm and I?' You can do the talking all by yourself."

"And have you shoot me in the back? No thanks."

"Babe, the only thing I'm going to shoot on your back is—"

"Finish that sentence and die," I said with a serene smile.

His mouth snapped shut.

"Either George surrenders or we enter by force and drag him out. We're not negotiating," said the sergeant.

"Let's go," I said, just as the two teams came through the roof access door. Without waiting for a response from Malcolm, I stepped off the ledge and jumped to the ground, purposefully doing the superhero landing. You know the one.

I popped back to my feet and strolled over to the sergeant, pushing the bullhorn down to his side. "He's not coming. Now clear off this property."

I heard the front door open and glanced over my shoulder to see Malcolm finally joining me. Through clenched teeth, I said, "Took your sweet time."

"I have a bad knee, that jump is impractical."

The amount of effort it took to school my expression was immense. This fuckin' guy.

Movement among the soldiers caught my attention, and I rolled my eyes as General Hicks appeared, pushing his way through the ranks. "Urquhart, get out of our way."

My pitying glance set him off guard. "Sir, no sir. I didn't listen to you when I worked for you, what makes you think I'll start now?"

His face purpled as he spluttered.

"Are you going to clear off, or not?" I asked.

"Absolutely not," he spat.

"Fine." I stepped back, Malcolm keeping pace with me, watching as every rifle and pistol was leveled at us. When I had a few yards of distance, I raised my hands.

Hicks smiled triumphantly, stepping forward and motioning to an MP to hand over his cuffs as his bald pate glimmered in the late autumn sun. I smiled and brought my hands together.

And everything erupted in flames.

Hicks screamed as the flames consumed him.

"Fire!" The order echoed to the soldiers and a volley of bullets ricocheted off the fire barrier. Lorraine's words immediately came back to mind as troops from the back of the line moved upward, brandishing odd-looking guns.

"Get down!" I yelled, dropping to the ground. Most of the team followed suit, but as this new round of weapons opened fire, the barrier just... fell. Two screams behind me had me wrenching around, keeping as flat to the ground as I could.

Payne and Tate were writing in pain, convulsing as some kind of strange light emanated from the impact point where they'd been shot. It glowed, following their veins as it worked its way into their body. They struggled to call their power, but couldn't summon so much as a spark.

"Rooftop, hit 'em with everything you got!" I ordered. "Give us some cover! And don't get shot! They have some kind of weapon we haven't seen before!"

A barrage of arms fire and magick rained down around us and the troops backed up, Humvees screeching in for cover. I motioned to the team members with me, ordering them back. I grabbed a hold of Tate and pulled him with me, motioning for Malcolm to do the same with Payne. To his credit, he didn't hesitate. Both men were still screaming, still fighting against glow chewing through their bodies.

The soldiers with the strange weapons popped off shots at our retreating forms before returning their attention to my teams on the roof. We barged through the front doors of the Council building and I slammed the door shut behind us, barricading it.

"Healers! We need healers!" I called.

A handful of people I'd only ever seen in passing ran from a site office where they'd been bunking down. They stopped short, staring at Payne and Tate in shock.

"What happened to them?" asked one of the women.

"I don't know. They got hit with some kind of weapon. They've been trying to draw on their magick, but haven't been able to."

I passed Tate into their custody. "Keep me updated if you figure out what the hell this is."

She nodded and I bolted off to the stairs, trusting my team would be following as we headed for the roof. I tapped my comm to connect to George. "You need to enact every physical barrier and fail-safe you have. They have some kind of device that blasted right through our fire shield."

"What? How is that possible?" he asked.

"No clue, but you cannot rely on magick. And don't get shot. Whatever this stuff is, it looks like it's capping our abilities." We reached the door to the roof and burst through it, my comm going dead as an enormous shock wave tore over us.

"Was that an EMP?" asked Malcolm.

"An EMP shouldn't have had any effect on our comms," I said, wrenching the plaque off my skin. It was burned and fizzling as the magick evaporated, but I still felt fine.

"The fuck is going on?" screamed Gio. "How are they doing this?"

Shit. Think, Urquhart. How do you fix this?

I ran to the ledge and peered over, ducking back as a bolt of blue light shot at me, leaving an arc burning on my retina. There's at least two weapons they're using that are counteracting our magick and I didn't want to find out until it was too late what other surprises they had in store.

But I also didn't want to give away my secret weapon just yet, at least not with the media bearing witness.

Abeni lobbed a massive fireball in the middle of their left flank, where most of the blue lights were coming from. It burst over them and dissipated, no sign that it had hit them at all. Out of the corner of my eye I saw the blue flash. I launched at Abeni as she conjured another wave of fire, taking her to the ground just as the projectile sailed an inch over her head.

Her eyes went wide as she realized how close she'd come to getting hit, chest heaving with the effort she'd been expending. "Thanks."

"Take yours and Gio's teams and head off those reporters and anyone else in the area," I said, motioning to the invisible line the media vans weren't crossing. "Take out every camera and knock out every witness. There can't be eyes on this battle. Check for drones, too."

Her brow stitched together. "Why?"

"I'm going to do something that nobody needs to know about, yet."

She still looked uncertain, but she nodded. "Okay."

"I'm serious. Not a single witness. Send up a flare when it's done."

Her lips pulled into a thin line, and she glanced at the battle one more time before forcing herself up and away.

"What the fuck! Where are they going?" asked Malcolm, creeping over on his belly to stay out of the line of sight.

"Trust me," I said, trying to psyche myself up and not wanting to take the time to explain, especially to this douche.

"That's it?" he huffed.

"Not now, Malcolm. Fuck off if you can't be quiet. When I give the signal, I just need the rest of you to cover me."

He wanted to object, but he shut his mouth and crept away. I took a deep breath and closed my eyes. I didn't even know if this would work or if it would just glance off their defenses like everything else had.

Five minutes felt like forever as Abeni and Gio organized their sweep and took out all tech and, hopefully, only knocked out the people. Seeing that fireball signal in the sky was a beautiful sight.

"Okay," I breathed. "I can do this." I caught Malcolm's eye and flipped him my middle finger. *That's your cue, asshole.*

He frowned but nodded, rallying the team still on the roof to fan out around me. I stayed low, and they crouched alongside as I dug deep. That roiling mass was never far away, but I reached for it and dragged it all the way to the surface, blue æther surging around me. The team stared at me, stunned, but as I slowly stood, they took up sniper positions at the ledge. For all their defenses, old-fashioned bullets still worked against the human forces.

As soon as I came into view, they opened fire. With a flick of my wrist, the æther disintegrated everything that came at me. They ceased fire, their fear visible as a thick haze hanging over them in the air.

"You have one chance. Leave."

Someone barked orders from the back and they raised their weapons again, firing a new volley of bullets, large caliber ammo, and the blue bolts. Nothing made it past.

I swept up my arms and sent a deluge of æther down on them, watching with detached fascination as the entire force disappeared within it.

"Evyn," said Malcolm. "What are you going to do with them?" Sweat beaded on his forehead.

I didn't answer. It was hard enough to focus as it was. I could send them away, make them forget, make them go back to their families and stay away from this war. All I had to do was—

Something shifted, and the æther boiled out of control, flaring up into an angry, tremulous thing. Screams rose into a chorus.

"What's happening?" hissed Malcolm.

I tried to pull the æther back, but it was slow to respond. With shaking hands, I attempted to rein it in, but the screams grew louder.

"Evyn!"

"I'm trying!" I snapped. Every fumbling attempt to regain control just seemed to make it worse. Then the screams stopped. The æther moved back toward me and into my body, leaving nothing but a red mist hanging in the air that swayed thickly in the wind before settling. Every trace of them, their weapons, and their vehicles were gone.

Malcolm's voice shook. "What did you do?"

Chapter Nine

The door slammed behind me harder than I intended, and I froze, wincing. I was clutching the book I'd taken from the Council library to my chest, grateful nothing had happened to it in the melee.

"Talulla?" asked Derfael, popping out of the kitchen. His face relaxed when he saw me. "Thank the gods. Are you alright?"

"I just got lambasted by the Council for an hour for trying to save their sorry asses. No, I'm not."

"Come," he said, stretching his arm out. "Dinner is on the table. We can talk while we eat."

"I'm fine. I'll grab something later."

"No, you will not." His tone was final.

I looked at him, eyes bleary with tiredness. "You don't need to take care of me."

"No, I don't. But I want to." He looked at me sternly. "You had a building collapse on top of you and an army try to kill you. I think that deserves a break. And maybe a chat."

With an inward shrug, I debated with myself which was more important. Solitude or food? My stomach growled in answer and Derfael steered me toward the kitchen.

"I made your favorite."

"No way," I said. Sure enough, as we neared the kitchen, I could smell the spices and the fresh bread. A grin spread across my face ear to ear. This was the best possible thing I could've come home to right now.

"Lamb stew." My excitement was palpable as I hurried over to the stove and lifted the lid on the pot. Derfael smacked my hand and waved me toward a seat at the table.

"Thought you could use a little comfort right now."

Bowls clinked as he ladled stew in generous portions and a bread knife sawed through the thick outer crust of still warm, fresh bread. The soundtrack to my heart.

When the steaming, luscious stew was set in front of me, I could've cried. "This is perfect. Thank you."

Derfael passed me a thick slice of bread, and I slathered it with butter before dipping it in the rich broth. The first bite was heavenly, and we didn't even speak for full minutes as we tucked in.

"Tell me about today," said Derfael, wiping his beard with a cloth napkin.

"It started well enough. I found a promising lead at the library. Saraswati let me borrow the book to look into it further. It's incredible, I really think I've got something here."

"And whatever it was could only be solved with a trip to the DIWR?" he asked, eyebrow raised.

"The tracking they'd been developing, that allows them to trace signatures, helped me find a pattern. I think I know where the sister's lair is."

Derfael looked up sharply at that. "That's great news."

I nodded. "Like I said, started off so promising. Agent Greene and I were trying to find a place to talk that was private, and then everything blew up. We had about a second of warning before the first bomb went off, then two more."

"And more than likely a false flag just so they could blame us and tip the tensions over into boiling."

"Probably," I agreed. "Percy called me almost immediately after it happened." I grit my teeth, still angry with Percy for what else she asked me to do after that, and that was before the ass chewing I'd just received. "The Council wants Lorraine, and they made me the errand girl to deliver the message."

The druid cursed under his breath. "Suppose it was just a matter of time. She's too much of an asset to leave alone."

"I'm not sure what she'll do. If she chooses to run, I hope that she stays ahead of them."

"You did all you could. The council already knew of her. Try as you might, they were going to do what they wanted regardless. At least you kept her off the DIWR's radar. I shudder to think what they would've done with that kind of advantage."

"They've got all kind of advantages, including weapons we didn't know about. They don't need Lorraine to be dangerous." I filled him in on everything that I'd seen, experienced, and… done… at the battle.

When I was done, the sound of consternation that rumbled from his chest was the epitome of anxiety. "And Saraswati is certain that it's æther?"

I nodded. "I really thought I had it under control, that once I was conscious of what I was doing, it would be a piece of cake. If I can stop a speeding death train, sending a bunch of people back home with no memory of what happened shouldn't have been a problem. But I—they were just…"

"Gone," he finished.

"I don't know how it went so wrong."

"When the feed cut on the news, I feared the worst."

I chuffed. "It was."

He was silent for a moment, and I glanced up at him. "No. It was the best outcome, all things considered," he said quietly.

My eyes widened in shock and he explained. "You saved most of your team and the Council. You showed them they aren't as prepared as they thought, and it might give the humans hesitation before trying something like that again."

"But if I hadn't been able to summon æther, this day would've ended very differently. We might've had to surrender."

"Mortals don't know that. Nor will they. I'm assuming the Council already bound everyone involved to secrecy?"

"Everyone who hasn't already sworn an oath of allegiance," I confirmed.

He nodded. "What was the Council's issue?"

"Mainly that it was reckless, and I could've just as easily destroyed all of us instead."

Derfael scoffed. "Ridiculous. They're overreacting. Everything went as you intended, other than the ultimate result."

Now it was my turn to pause.

"What?" he asked.

"I'm not entirely sure it didn't end exactly the way I wanted."

The druid evaluated me carefully. His spoon clinked twice against the bottom of his bowl as he absentmindedly tapped it in thought. "This is war. They were the enemy. To leave them alive would have been to invite future conflict. This was the only way to ensure they wouldn't continue to be a threat." He paused. "Am I close?"

I ducked my head. "My good intentions aside—I had no guarantee sending them away would work. But if they were gone, there would be no question. Maybe the æther sensed that."

"There are no easy decisions here. Whatever comes, we need to trust we'll make the right choices and live with whatever consequences follow. That is the only way." He gripped my hand. "What's done is done."

We finished our meal in silence as some of the tension eased away. He was right. All I could do was live with my choices.

"What else did you discover about Malea and Amara?"

I grimaced, recalling the cross-section illustrations in that book on magickal creatures. "Saraswati is confident they're original lamia."

Recognition dawned on his face. "I'd almost forgotten. But that makes sense. The progenitors are always more powerful."

"Atum was on the right track. He mentioned that some beings disappeared, once the Ætherim started to draw sides. Hid away, or created their own worlds." Derfael cleared the dishes, and I laid the book I'd borrowed on the table. "Then Lady Saraswati started telling me about cosmic energy, the real primeval stuff. How giant swaths of it are still floating around out there."

Derfael was picking up on where I was going. "They're using those to hide?"

I nodded, finding the right page in the book. "This band is currently anchored to earth, unless I miss my guess. The patterns of attacks all link up. Prevailing theory so far is that since æther is the same kind of energy the sisters forged their realm out of, they need that gate magick I'm attached to, to pass *through* to somewhere else. Earth is easy to get to, but they were shut out from the other realms when they chose to leave. Probably just the Ætherim being petty that they wouldn't play along. They keep mentioning retribution on old enemies and tried to assure me that they wouldn't stay once they got their vengeance, but—"

Derfael made a disgruntled noise. "Unlikely."

"Yeah."

"But if that is the case, Morgan was probably correct. They won't kill Adrian until they have what they want. A small comfort, but it's something."

"And in the meantime, they just want to keep making my life hell. What are they waiting for? If they wanted to trade, wouldn't they have offered that already?"

"Are you desperate enough yet? To give them what they're asking, knowing what it will lead to? Even to save your familiar?"

I thought about it, but it didn't take long to come up with an answer. "No."

After a few days, there was still no movement from the Known, and the government was tight-lipped about all of it. Nobody knew what happened that day, so speculation was rife. All they saw was the military move in, the news feed die, and the entire outfit disappear with just faint red stains on the pavement.

Derfael had been right. It had brought aggressions to a standstill.

I sighed heavily, eyes burning from dryness as I stared, uncomprehending, at the books splayed on the table. A piece of the puzzle was missing, the one little detail that would lead to the solution. I dug into my pocket and pulled out Solomon's ring. Ever since I'd emptied the cubby, I'd taken to carrying it with me.

It was warm as I held it with my fingertips, turning it to let the gold catch the light. I frowned, setting it on the table and forcing myself back to the books.

My eyelids felt like I had ten-pound weights strapped to each of them and I blinked back awake just before my face hit the table.

"Screw it." I pushed to my feet and grabbed my jacket, pausing at the front door and returning for the ring. Before I could overthink it, I slipped the ring around my left index finger and continued on my way.

Derfael may have had his reservations about Ivan, but the thought of speaking to him brightened my mood. He couldn't be all that bad, then, right?

Exodus was quieter than usual at the upstairs bar, and I made my way down to the blue room. When I found it dark and empty, just the ghostly runner lights illuminating the bar, my disappointment hit me heavier than I would've expected for some random man I only met a week ago.

"Ah, good, I caught you." I turned to find Ivan standing behind me, wearing a long coat and boots that were more casual than the fine footwear he usually wore. He smelled like the fall leaves and chill winds. "Would you care to take a walk with me? I need some fresh air." He held out his arm.

There was only a second of hesitation before I threaded my arm through his. All the comfort that I found in our conversation turned into a tangible feeling when we touched. "That sounds great."

"Excellent." He led the way up a back staircase to street level, and we came out in the brisk night air, the streetlights flooding everything with ambient yellow.

"It's still so strange to see it this quiet," I said, looking around at the all-but-deserted streets on a Friday night.

"Mmm," he hummed. "These tensions haven't been good for business, that's for sure."

I let Ivan lead the way, and he turned us toward the Riverwalk. The water rushed, flooded to the banks by recent storms. We crossed the exact spot where Jake and I had battled a kelpie Solomon's sorcerers had sent after me. Jake had saved the day that time, charging the elder fae and biting off a healthy chunk of flesh and hair that I was able to bind the creature with.

"An honest to gods kelpie? I'm usually kept up to speed on any of our more cantankerous brethren that step foot in the city." He seemed genuinely troubled.

"I wouldn't take it too personally. Moreno had everybody running around blind. We barely knew up from down at the time. Who knows how many things were hiding in that chaos?"

"At least you sent it back to where it came from. Quick thinking."

"I was highly motivated to not get eaten."

He chuckled. Up ahead was a small group of people and I could hear the distinct rattling of spray paint cans. The closer we got, the clearer the furtive whispering and mean-spirited snickers became.

"Maybe we should go back. I'm not in the mood for a confrontation," I said, pulling my hood up around my face.

Ivan put his hand over mine. "Nonsense. We'll be fine. It's too beautiful an evening to relinquish it to punks."

I chewed my lip before nodding. "Okay."

We continued forward, and I hoped they would ignore us. I shook my head to clear it as a buzzing sensation filled my ears, moving to press behind my eyes. Weird.

As we were passing by, one man looked up and noticed me. Recognized me.

"Hey! It's that Stranger bitch!"

I sighed. They really weren't that inventive with their insults. That alone was grating on my nerves. I wasn't worthy of inspiring some creativity with their vitriol?

"Don't start," I warned, coughing as a thick pressure built in my chest. It felt the same as when I channeled æther, but the ring wasn't pumping out any energy.

"I heard she lived around here," said another.

"Maybe we can get her to spill about what happened at the Council building. The news would pay good money for that."

"I'm right here, guys. If you're going to plot against someone, best practices say you shouldn't do it right in front of the person you're planning on attacking."

Ivan laughed softly beside me.

"Who's the dude?" said the first man, elbowing his buddy.

"Jeff Bridges," I answered. They looked at me like I'd just grown three heads. I waved my hand. "Never mind, before your time."

My companion visibly shook with laughter.

"You think this is funny?" asked a fourth man, the one holding the spray paint can.

"Extremely," said Ivan.

"You know, if I bring back a piece of Evyn Urquhart, I'll be a hero." He pulled out a knife from his combat boot and flicked open the switchblade.

I barked a laugh. "Did you guys take psychedelics tonight? Because you're living in a fantasy world." I turned away from them, Ivan putting his hand on the small of my back. "Have a good night, fellas."

The sound of running feet and jeers came up fast, and I turned, heart dropping as I noticed the blank, white eyes of the four men.

The world blinked out.

Chapter Ten

A scream cut through my daze, and I blinked back into reality. There was something warm on my face, contrasting, harshly with the icy wind blowing hard off the river. A steady drip, drip, drip, of some thick viscous fluid brought my attention down. I was holding a knife. I was covered in blood. My torque and Solomon's ring burned with equal ferocity against my skin.

A woman wearing a jogging outfit disappeared around the bend, continuing her screams for help. The halogen lights, buzzing overhead cast a harsh shadow over the bodies lying at my feet.

All four of the men that had been harassing us were dead. Cut to ribbons.

"Ivan," I called out. "Ivan!"

The scuff marks of someone crawling, dragging themselves across the ground, led away from the carnage and off into a low row of bushes that lined the walk. I hurried over, pushing through the dried branches to find Ivan laying on his stomach, his throat torn out. Sightless eyes stared back at me and the knife fell from my hand with a clatter.

I couldn't have done this. How did I not remember doing this? I've never blacked out in my life.

More running feet coming up the path, toward me this time. I picked up the knife and ran, vaulting the low railing and jump-stepping the entire way to Wolfe's.

I went around to the back door, trying not to leave more evidence behind than I already had. Did the trail have cameras on it? Bledsoe would be creaming his shorts at the idea of arresting me.

The back door stuck, and I had to lean my shoulder into it hard. It was seldom used, the hinges squealing loudly, a siren to give me away.

My movements were sluggish as I struggled upstairs, hanging onto the railing and almost slipping with all the blood coating my hands.

"Talulla, where—" Derfael broke off, eyes wide as he saw me coming through the door. "What happened?"

All I could do was stare at him stunned. "I— I don't know." My throat worked to squeeze down the bile that threatened to rise as I tossed my knife at his feet.

Derfael grabbed my wrist and held my hand up. The one with Solomon's ring on it. "Why are you wearing that cursed thing?"

Without answer, I pushed past him into the kitchen, turning the tap on hot and scrubbing my hands and arms in the scalding water.

He wasn't happy with that, but he let the subject drop for the moment. "Do you remember *where* it happened?" he asked instead.

"The Riverwalk. I was down there with Ivan." I grabbed a small vegetable brush and used it to get my cuticles. "There were these four idiots trying to pick a fight. But I walked away, I know I did. I wasn't going to engage. And then next thing I knew they were dead at my feet, I'm covered in blood, and there's a knife in my hand."

"Were you seen?" He took a few steps toward me, studying my face.

"Probably."

He swore.

"There was a jogger. She was screaming and running away. I'm not sure if she saw me as much as she saw the bodies."

"But there were still witnesses," Derfael spat. "And you honestly don't remember any of it?"

"No," I said, desperate. "The last thing I remember is Ivan putting his hand on my back." I snatched a towel off the bar. "We were walking away," I insisted.

"Is Ivan dead?"

I nodded. Nausea rolled over me, not stopping. I bent over the sink and retched, my already empty stomach cramping painfully. Derfael grabbed a bottle of water from the fridge and handed it to me.

"Why can't I remember?" I asked, gasping for air.

Derfael was at a loss. "I'm not sure, Talulla. I need to call the Matron. If there is even the slightest chance you were seen..." He gripped my shoulder, and I nodded shakily as he went to find his phone.

I grabbed a change of clothes and headed to the bathroom, the meticulous cleanup process a muscle memory after over a hundred years of practice. As

I was coming out of the bathroom toweling my hair dry, the doorbell for the shop downstairs rang.

Derfael got to his feet, motioning for me to stay put as he went to answer it. I stood at the landing, listening.

"Evening," said a familiar voice. "Derfael is it?"

"Aye."

"Ryan," I muttered. "Of course it's him."

"Is Evyn here?" he asked.

Derfael gave him the runaround and for a moment I thought he would actually be able to convince them to leave. Then there was a pause in the conversation, and my phone rang. Loud.

I yanked it out of my pocket, noticing Detective Ryan's name on the screen. "Fuck."

"Come on down, Evyn," he called. "We need to talk."

My steps were measured as I attempted to be nonchalant. Ryan and Bledsoe were at the door, the latter detective looking as giddy as I thought he might. I put out some feelers, but couldn't sense any other officers in the area.

"What's the problem, fellas?"

Bledsoe took a tiny step forward, licking his lips as his beady eyes narrowed on me. "There was a pretty nasty quintuple homicide on the Riverwalk. The person who called it in mentioned they might've seen you."

"I'm kind of like the bogeyman these days," I said, shrugging. "A lot of people see me where I'm not."

"Evyn," said Ryan, meeting my gaze. There was a look in his eye that was hard to decipher. He didn't want to think that I could've done something like this, but at the same time he was warning me not to cause trouble and tell the truth. "Why is your hair wet?"

"I'm sure you know what a shower is, Detective."

Whatever doubt he was willing to afford me disappeared. His look became cold, detached. Betrayed. "I think you're gonna have to come with us, Ms. Urquhart. We've got some questions that are best answered at the station."

"Allow me," said Bledsoe, pulling out his cuffs.

As he stepped toward me, Derfael blocked him. "Sorry about this, lads." There was a flash of light, and both men fell to the floor.

"Shit," I hissed, crouching at Ryan's side. His pulse was steady, and he was breathing fine.

"I just knocked them out for a bit. They'll be fine. They'll wake up in their patrol car somewhere else." Derfael growled, pulling me to my feet. "You need to go. Get to one of the safe houses. Leave your phone here. I'll tell Theresa to use other methods to contact you."

He fished keys out of his pocket and tossed them to me. "Take my truck."

"But—"

"Go!" he barked. "This isn't a debate!"

I took a shaky breath and took much quicker steps back up the stairs. I picked up my go-bag and the book I'd taken from the Council library before grabbing the keys.

Derfael's truck was parked around the corner. As I stepped out the back door, I pulled my hoodie up close around my face. There were traffic cameras on this side of town to worry about, but not much else. I stuck close to the shadows regardless. As soon as the engine roared to life, I sped off toward Belknap.

The overlook was a public park, but it was largely deserted most of the time. I drove the truck up the winding road, some of the curves cutting back sharply. I parked just off the small lot at the top of the hill and got out, grabbing my bag and putting a concealment and repellent barrier on the truck.

I walked in, sticking to the path until I saw the old fence post marked up with a barely visible sigil. The moonlight faded away until it counted for nothing among the dense foliage of the trees. The pines grew close together, and the old goat trail had become overgrown. I pushed ahead, moving deeper into the off-trail sections of the park.

There was very little sound to keep me company besides the *shush* of my shoes on the deadfall. The occasional lonely, late-season cricket would give a plaintive chirrup, or a bird would rustle in its nest, but otherwise, I made this trek alone.

It had been several years since I'd been to this particular safe house. We had a few hidden all over the city, and the Council had hundreds all over the country. This one was built long before Grand Rapids became the city it was, but I'd kind of called dibs and made this one my own.

The small, one-room cabin was far back in the park, almost at the boundary. It would appear like a thick crop of trees to anyone that wasn't allowed to see it and those trees would do their damnedest to be so uninteresting that people's eyes slid by without giving them a second thought.

I had to switch my vision to Sight to see it in the gloom. "It's sure seen better days," I said, regretting not taking the time to bother with upkeep over the years. Shit, there probably wasn't much food or supplies left either. Fuel for the fireplace would be easy enough to get, and hopefully the sleeping bags I'd stored were still good. Even if you put something in a bubble to keep it fresh and clean, time still took a toll on it.

Before I even entered the cabin, I reinforced the wards around the place. Those too had worn down, but it was a quick revitalization as all the framework was still in place. Once I was finished, I stepped up to the door and placed my hand on the frame, willing magick into it, reminding the cabin who I was. The lock switched open on its own and I moved inside.

The air was musty, but there wasn't any dust or critter activity. For off-grid scenarios, mages developed our own portable generators. There was a spire made of soapstone and quartz standing in the corner, about two feet tall and as big around as my arm at the thickest point. I touched my fingertip to the sharp point, pushing down enough to draw just a small amount of blood which absorbed into the spire. A warm hum of energy awakened, newly fed, ready and waiting for me to pour my magick into it.

It didn't take much to prime the charge, and in short order there was an electrical source ready to go. I flicked on a lamp and surveyed the place. It was exactly as I'd left it, probably forty years or more ago.

The woods were quiet as I set about gathering some firewood and kindling. I loaded up on fallen branches and twigs, grabbing some super dry pine cones as well. A dull glow cut my attention, and I turned to find an orb floating up to me. I grabbed one last handful of kindling and headed back to the cabin, the orb following close behind.

It floated gently along and I held the door open for it, closing it behind us. I continued about my task building a fire as my aunt's voice floated through the sphere.

"How are you doing?" That anger that was a constant presence with her now was only barely subdued.

"Pretty shitty, how about you?"

She sniffed. "Not much better. You've really gotten yourself into a pickle this time. The media is already gearing up their stories about this. After what happened at headquarters, they're desperate for a good story on you." She paused and I could almost feel her fists clenching as she reined in her anger. "You sure gave them something to talk about."

"It wasn't intentional. I have no idea what happened."

"Derfael says you don't remember anything?"

"The last thing I remember before I woke up covered in blood is running feet and the four men's eyes had turned solid white. The only other time I've seen that is when Malea and Amara were possessing someone."

The Matron cursed. "Great, their involvement is just what we need. What were the other times?"

"My run-in with Cliff Tafford. And a fight I had with Tristan. Our memories diverged completely and at the time I thought I'd been imagining his eyes flashing white for a second. I chalked it up to stress." I huffed a laugh. "They warned me they were gonna make me pay. Make me suffer for denying them what they wanted. Taking Adrian from me wasn't enough. They have to rip everyone else away from me too."

"Could they have possessed you? Is that why you blacked out?"

"No," I said, confident. "I don't know." My stomach sank. "Maybe. Were there cameras at the Riverwalk?"

"I'm afraid so. You were just out of frame, but there was plenty of footage of you and that man heading in the direction of the murders."

"Don't call them murders. If anything, it was self-defense," I said. "Of that, I am confident."

"Who was he?" she asked, showing no interest in my statement.

"I only met him a week ago. I knew him as Ivan." My stomach clenched with worry, a sensation I was really getting sick of. "He was a noble of Finvarra's court."

"What! Evyn, what have you done! Are you going to say that was self-defense as well?"

I pursed my lips, nostrils flaring. "No. I don't think he would've hurt me. He'd become an odd kind of friend. He just... listened."

"How much have you been telling him?" asked Theresa, her voice dangerously cold.

"Nothing. It was all personal shit, gripes, frustrations."

"A small consolation prize, considering you've probably sunk our relationship with the Unseelie Court in one fell swoop."

"Sure, that's all on me. Why not? It's not like he's an impossible prick to work with and won't ever be happy with anything. No. It's *my* fault if Finvarra cuts ties with the Council." A thought occurred to me. "Why don't you just ask Lorraine? She'll tell you exactly how it went down."

Theresa made an angry sound. "Lorraine never took us up on our offer. She's gone, and we don't have the resources to track her down right now."

I was relieved that she was still living on her own terms, but I was sad that it had to come to this. My tone was much less sharp when I asked my next question.

"Did Derfael take care of Ryan and Bledsoe okay?"

There was a long pause, and I thought the connection dropped. "They were very confused and showed up at the shop again, looking for you with an inexplicable sense of déjà vu. But they don't remember you being there."

"Is Derfael—"

"I've already told him to clear out. He's on his way to another safe house."

I nodded, relieved. Stacking a small handful of kindling underneath the logs I'd built-up, I conjured a small flame and lit it. The kindling caught fire, licking at the logs until they eventually gave in and started crackling. The glow was a small comfort, and I huddled near it, desperate for warmth.

"The Council will be convening to figure out what to do about this. We expect they'll be releasing the footage any time now." Another pause. "I don't need to tell you what this will mean. Fears are already high enough after the encounter with the military. People know you're responsible, but don't know how. Now this? The stalemate is going to boil over by tomorrow if we don't do it."

I couldn't bring myself to turn and face the orb. I stared resolutely into the flames. "I'll be excommunicated. I understand."

There was a pause. "I'm not sure what happened out there. For what it's worth, I believe you when you say it wasn't on purpose." Her voice had softened, and I could almost believe I was speaking to the same aunt I'd been able to have heart-to-hearts with just a few months ago. "But this is how it has to be."

"You don't have to worry about me. I'm good at disappearing."

"You don't have to disappear outright," she corrected. "The Council has plenty of places you can hide, ones that are still close by. I don't want you to leave the city."

"So you can keep an eye on me? Or so you can mitigate risk for the council?"

"That's not fair."

"But it's true though, isn't it?" My voice sounded hollow and lifeless even to my ears. "It's nothing personal, I know. It's just the way it has to be." I jabbed the burning logs with the poker.

"The excommunication won't be official, it'll only be to calm down the mortals. We'll say that we're dispatching teams to find you, I'm sure humans will be demanding it. But you don't need to worry about it. Just stay concealed."

I was silent, still staring ahead and lost in my own thoughts.

"Evyn?"

"Yeah." My voice was barely audible over the crackling, the logs fully consumed now. "I don't have many supplies. Can you send someone by?"

"Of course."

"Thanks."

I waved my hand and banished the orb.

Movement at the edge of my wards had me peeking between the slats of the shutters, gun in hand. Part of me expected—hoped—to see a familiar face. While I had seen the man waiting for me hanging around Council HQ before, I didn't know him better than that.

He gave me a small wave when I opened the door, several bags at his feet.

"Thanks," I said as I approached. "I appreciate the help."

"No worries." He watched as I looked through the bags. It was nice assortment of food, toiletries and a small portable television, although I was pretty sure I did *not* want to watch the news right now. And—I snorted. "Activity books?"

He smiled. "Couldn't resist. There's a puzzle in there, too."

"Great." Just one thing missing. I chewed on my lip, debating if I should send him out. It was the last bad habit I should be turning to, but given the circumstances...

"Do you have time to run back out and get something else for me?"

"Sure. Name it."

Thirty minutes later he returned with my requests. He gave me a sad smile as he set down the rest of my supplies. "Take care of yourself, Ms. Urquhart. This will blow over."

"Sure." I picked up the box and gave him a nod as I walked back inside, watching from behind the shutters as he disappeared back into the trees.

I flipped open the flap on the box and grabbed a bottle of whisky, grabbing a blanket on my way to the couch. I huddled up in a cocoon and began my descent.

Chapter Eleven

I opened my eyes blearily. Someone was knocking on my door. I threw off the mountain of blankets I was under, immediately shivering in the cold. I hadn't bothered to light the fire again since I got here a few days ago and the generator for electricity was almost depleted.

The knock came again, and I stumbled to the door. After a couple of unsuccessful tries, I opened it to find my aunt on the other side.

"What are you doing here?" I asked, wondering for a brief moment if I was dreaming.

She recoiled somewhat at the look—and probably the smell—of me. "What have you been doing?"

"Absolutely nothing," I said, giving her a defiant smile.

"Just feeling sorry for yourself?" She eyed the pile of discarded empty bottles. Her jaw worked in irritation, but she shook it off. "That's not why I'm here."

She moved farther into the cabin and wrinkled her nose in disgust. She moved to the spindle and poured some of her own energy into it, revitalizing the generator so the lights were bright enough to actually see my face. "Where is the TV I sent you?"

I pointed, flopping back down on the couch. I couldn't even find the energy to ask her what was wrong now. She plugged it in and waited for it to connect to a tower before finding the channel she wanted. "We have a very big problem."

"It's only been a few days, what else could've gone wrong?"

She shot me a baleful look, disappointment etched in every line on her face. She turned the TV to face me. It was a news anchor, looking stressed. Nothing new there.

"What—"

"Keep watching," she snapped.

It flashed to Senator Yards, doing his usual fire-and-brimstone style speech. Some B-roll footage of crowds amassing and more National Guard troops being deployed.

The news anchor came back on. "The search continues for Evyn Urquhart. Both human authorities and the Council have been searching for her tirelessly since her attack on the DIWR and a brutal attack just a day later that killed five more people."

"What!" Suddenly I was wide awake.

"In case you missed our warnings, this footage is difficult to watch."

It switched to black and white surveillance footage of me, sneaking around the DIWR headquarters. "I was cloaked! How the fuck did the cameras see me?"

They had me inside and outside the building, then the explosion, and then a picture of Agent Greene and I as we left the maintenance tunnel. "Shit, is she—"

"She's dead." My aunt said it so matter-of-factly that it stunned me into silence. "Shortly after this picture was released, she was beaten to death by a mob. For being in cahoots with you."

My mouth gaped open helplessly.

"Detective Ryan is also dead."

Nausea rolled over me, and I buried my face in my hands. "How?"

"His partner, Bledsoe, shot him in supposed self-defense. He said Ryan turned on him while they were hunting for you."

"That's bullshit," I growled. "They wanted him dead because he was working *with* me. Trying to find peace. Trying to help people."

Theresa said nothing in response.

More surveillance footage, me and Ivan traveling down the Riverwalk. An apparent scuffle right off screen is the jogger comes up on us, screams, and runs away. Then footage of me darting down another street, covered in blood and carrying a knife, looking half out of my mind. Then cellphone footage of the actual attack. I could barely watch it. I looked crazed, like my hold on reality had broken and I was in a blood frenzy as I hacked—

"This woman is extremely dangerous. If you see her, do not approach her. Report it immediately."

My aunt clicked the TV off, fury etched on her face. "Since you've been in such a pitiful state," she said, "I'm sure you aren't aware that several other nations have since followed suit declaring war on Strangers. Add that on top of countries that were already in an unspoken war with us, and the entire world is embroiled in conflict. And your face is at the center of it all. You are the most vilified Stranger of all of us, and because we employed you, the US Council is taking the brunt of the anger from the global Councils. As far as they're concerned, your actions have become the rallying point for mortals across the world to call for upheaval."

"What can I do?" My voice cracked. I was fighting just to keep myself from screaming.

"You stay hidden."

"But I can help!"

"You are the most wanted person in this country and probably every other. Anywhere else you go, humans or Strangers alike will gladly make a display of your corpse to curb further conflict. The Defense Department has been working on some very interesting weapons." For the first time a smattering of fear worked its way into her voice. "What we've already seen are just the tip of the iceberg. It seems as though our worst fears of the sisters whispering in the ears of leadership weren't far off. They know what weaknesses to exploit, and these weapons will make it easier. Our power, our magick, might count for nothing. It could be the difference that wins them the war."

"Don't cut me out," I pleaded. "Let me fix this!"

"There is no fixing this!" she screamed. "What don't you understand! You are the catalyst that tipped the world to war! Seeing what ONE Stranger is capable of, all the destruction you've caused, made the decision easy for them. They won't stop until every Stranger is wiped off this earth or banished to the Strangefells! You've done more than enough already."

She swept toward the door, boots thudding heavily across the dry pine boards. "You are no longer affiliated with the Council. As long as you stay hidden, we won't send hunters after you. But if you show your face that will change. You are officially excommunicated."

After she left I turned the mobile TV back on, watching with horrified fascination as the world's ending played out before me. Was this really all my fault?

Guilt chewed away at me. I guess now I had permission to disappear. Nobody was going to bother me anymore or pull me out of hiding. My purpose was fulfilled, and I was used goods. I truly had nothing left.

My blanket cocoon provided a small amount of solace as I wrapped myself back up tight. I was on my fifth bottle of whisky when I started to see a haze in the peripheral of my left eye. I wrote it off, but when the haze became darker and took on shapes, I thought maybe I was losing my mind. That's fine. Another bottle would be enough to make me oblivious to the heartbreak. Now that would be a blessing.

The cabin was overtaken completely by the darkness and voices whispered to me from mouths that didn't exist; a seventh bottle didn't make it go away.

"What fresh hell is this?" I asked, maybe to myself, maybe to the voices. I'm still not sure.

Vague whispering was the only reply.

I stood and the whole world lurched under my feet, sending me tumbling to the floor. I crawled, the floor a roiling sea, the old pine wood cracking and splintering around me as it was forced into movement it was never meant to make. Everything around me slipped into complete darkness.

My heart was in my throat, my chest painfully tight. I felt real fear then. From under where I knew my bed to be, the chasm underneath it yawned wide with an even deeper dark and multiple pairs of red eyes that stared at me. One of them winked and I caught the flash of bright white teeth. I clawed at the floor, trying to find my way back to the couch, to my blankets, tears starting to spill from my eyes in panic. A boney hand wrapped its fingers around my ankle, and I shut my eyes, not wanting to see whatever it was reaching for me. I couldn't even fight, paralyzed by my terror as I was dragged across the floor with agonizing slowness. What was the hurry? Nobody was going to save me.

Then the bottom dropped out of the floor and I fell, screaming, into nothing.

I woke in a room absent of all light, my heartbeat loud in my ears. Panicked, shallow breathing, that I soon identified as my own, bounced off hard walls. It sounded like I was in a small space, and when I tried to move, I found myself bound to cold stone underneath me. Moving what little I could, my fingertips found the edge of the slab. I was on a table. Maybe an altar.

I concentrated on my senses, trying to calm myself. My eyes refused to adjust to the darkness, no difference at all if they were open or closed. It was cold, and damp, a musky smell thick in the air. The stone under my fingers was rough. The edges felt chipped and there were pockmarks hacked out of it from sharp tools.

"Hello?" I called. Opening my mouth left a coating of something bitter on my tongue. Ash-like.

Had I died? I wanted oblivion, not death. Although maybe this was for the better. With no sign of life around me, my eyes drooped and I slept.

A sound broke through evil dreams. From underneath a million miles of water, I broke the surface to find myself staring into dimly glowing eyes. After so much dark, that little bit of light made me squint at the brightness of it. It glinted off the faintest hint of sharp teeth as the thing in front of me smiled. A croaking rasp bubbled up from its throat, some kind of purr.

"What new toy has the Nyx granted us today?"

"Nyx?" That couldn't be right.

The Nyx was only talked about in legend. A place people never returned from, if they ever actually went there at all. The Strangefells existed on a separate plane of reality, running parallel to the mortal world. The Nyx was something else entirely, something concocted and held together by nightmares.

"Helpless? Feeling lost? Did you just... give up?" it asked. A boney finger stroked my cheek, and I pulled away. Those same fingers wrapped around my neck and turned my head back to it. The face leaned in and hot, rank breath blew in my face. "Answer the question."

"I don't know."

The creature blew out a puff of air. "It lies." The thing stepped away and I could hear large feet slapping on a bare floor. Sounds of metal clashing together that took me less than a second to identify. I'd heard it many times.

Tools. Of the torture variety.

It stalked back over to me and stopped. "I'll show you what happens to liars."

A sharp blade cut into my chest. It was so cold, searing every nerve ending as the icy chill spread from the wound until my whole body burned like I was frostbitten. I gritted my teeth against the pain.

The thing hummed thoughtfully. "Strong. This will be fun."

"What do you want?" I gasped.

"The truth. Simply that."

"Fine," I hissed. "All of the above."

Its growl was different this time, like it was disappointed. "That's all right. We'll get those answers. We've got all the time in the world."

"You know how to make this stop," it said. Every torture session started with these words.

"I told you the truth. I'm a coward. I gave up. I turned my back on everyone and got lost in my own self-pity."

The knife dug in, and I howled in rage. "That's the truth! I don't know what else you want," I said desperately.

"Then we continue."

And it did. In a haze of wash, rinse, repeat. Sleep was the only respite.

"Get up," growled my captor.

I struggled to open my eyes past the crust of grime and blood. There was no way to tell how much time had passed but I'd been strapped to this table for the extent of it. Apparently, you didn't need food or water in the Nyx. Your body just seemed to function in some kind of stasis.

Nothing ever changed except for the pain.

The usual, dimly glowing eyes were staring down at me with their casual disregard, like they had every day since my arrival. This was a boring job for him, just going through the motions.

"Your new accommodations are ready," it said in a mocking voice.

I licked my lips, tasting more blood, long dried and bitter. Words came out in a harsh garble, my throat not used to producing anything but screams for the last untold number of days. "Where are we going?"

The bonds holding me tightly to the table disappeared, the sudden weight released from my chest inspiring a heaving gasp, sucking in lungs-full of air. My captor's clawed hands circled around my arm, yanking me off the table. The minute my feet hit the floor, I stumbled, but his grip tightened and held me up.

When the door creaked open, there was still no light. Judging by the sound alone, I determined we were in a narrow hallway. My feet slid helplessly along the ground as I was dragged, the creature not even giving me a moment to get them under me.

The air in the hallway was thick, that constant coating of ash on my tongue joined by a rancid, rotten-meat taste. Another door opened and he hauled me through. Blood rushed in my ears as my fear notched up a few paces.

"What's going on?" I asked, but my question went unanswered. There was a squeal of metal hinges, and I was tossed forward. I hit the ground and rolled before coming to a stop against something hard. A metallic clang echoed loud enough to make me wince as the door slammed shut and the large, heavy footsteps retreated.

I crawled around on my hands and knees, finding only solid walls and the seam of the door closed tight. I followed the door up with my hands, searching for any kind of opening and found a small slit, not wide enough for anything to pass through but plenty big to keep an eye on the prisoner.

I pressed my ear to it, hoping to hear someone, anyone else there. Silence. "Hello?" I called.

My question echoed a few times and faded. There was no answer. I tried a few more times, but the results were no different. Finally, I hunched up in the corner and fell asleep.

Only to wake at the sound of multiple voices outside my cell.

They were speaking in hushed tones, but it sounded like some kind of debate. They came to a conclusion, and the door swung open. This time there was a scuttling sound as another creature moved into the room, picked me up and hauled me out.

I tried my usual round of questions, mainly "where are we going?" but received no answer.

We traveled down a long hallway and it took longer for sounds to bounce back as it widened. A heavy door opened and I clenched my eyes tight as the first light I've seen since I got here blazed with a searing brightness.

Blue flame, that in normal circumstance would provide hardly any illumination, was enough to momentarily blind me. As my eyes adjusted, I got more details of the people I was with and the place I was in.

But I really wish I hadn't.

My usual torturer was on my left. I recognized the eyes and the teeth. The rest of him was sallow, his skin hanging off his frame like he was melting. Putrid sores festered all over his body and he was covered in some kind of slime. There was no nose, and his ears were just small flaps. Somehow seeing his whole face made that giant maw even more terrifying. A black tongue wriggled in his mouth like it had a mind of its own. To my horror, I realized it did. It flicked out between his teeth and looked at me with three beady eyes before darting back in.

The creature on my right was, to put it simply, a giant-ass spider… about the size of Jake. Sadness twisted my heart. Of all the things I was mad at Tristan for, separating me from Jake was the most painful.

The thing had at least twenty eyes and instead of mandibles for a mouth it was a flat slit in its face full of several rows of teeth. On its back was an appendage like a scorpion tail, but it ended in crab-like pincers. It pushed me forward when it caught me staring at its tail, hissing.

A large figure, backlit by the blue light so I couldn't see any details other than a shadow, stepped around a desk. As he moved closer, I made out a barrel chest, arms that were too long, legs that were too short. Some kind of scaled armor covered his body, but his face remained occluded. I could only tell he was peering down at me because his eyes were lit with the same luminescence as the others.

"How did you get here?" His voice was so deep, I felt it more than heard it.

"I'm sorry?"

He leaned down and turned his head to acknowledge each of my companions. That gave me just enough shift in the light to see that his face was almost human, barring the forked tongue that snaked out of his mouth.

"She's an interesting one, sir," said my jailer, ducking his head in deference. So we were indeed in the presence of the boss.

Fingers clasped my chin and raised my face. His skin was smooth and warm, but hard like an exoskeleton. "I asked how you got here. It's a simple question, requiring a simple answer."

I shook my head. "I was really drunk, and I heard voices in the shadows. Something appeared under my bed and dragged me away. I woke up here."

The creature's nostrils flared, and his lips pressed into a thin line. "You were fully conscious of this?"

"As well as I could be. Like I said, I was really drunk." Keeping up my disaffected tone was a challenge, but I wouldn't show this creature any weakness.

"But you must've been in distress?"

"Things had gone... sour in my life, yes."

"But you didn't harm yourself?"

"In a way. I just wanted to forget, go somewhere else."

He released my face. "Mission accomplished." He stepped a few paces away. "How is it you're able to withstand the tortures so easily?"

For the first time since my arrival here, a laugh threatened to bubble up. "This isn't my first time at the rodeo. I'm a mercenary by trade. Sometimes I get caught. The end result's the same."

He hummed. "What caused your life to fall apart so badly that you wound up here?"

"A lot," I answered simply.

His eyes narrowed. "Arriving here in a living body is rare. We usually find ourselves playing host to people that splintered. Lost parts of themselves somewhere, usually through their own carelessness or hubris, playing with magick they weren't ready for. They become trapped in their own minds, bodies elsewhere, but their souls are here. If you ever wondered what happens when madness takes you," he gestured around. "This is it."

"And you just keep them? Forever?"

He chuckled. "We make them stronger."

"I'm sorry?" Clearly, I'd misheard him.

The creature appraised me. "You really haven't figured it out." He opened his arms wide. "Welcome to the dark night of the soul. If this doesn't inspire you to break free from your madness, nothing will."

"You think you're doing a service here?" The dried blood itching on my skin begged to differ.

"Not everyone's experience is the same as yours, I assure you. The chamber you woke up in formed itself into the punishment you thought you needed most." He splayed his hands. "It's really all up to you. We're just following your lead."

"Bullshit. There's no way I'd choose this for myself."

"But you did." He leaned toward me. "I suggest you think long and hard about what brought you here. Because until you do..."

He backed away and motioned to the creatures on other side of me. The claw-like appendage of the spider-thing grabbed my arm and dragged me off.

When I arrived back in my cell, I did exactly what he suggested. But I didn't come to any new conclusions. I was angry and bitter and lost. That was the long and short of it.

My torturer collected me from my cell multiple times a day to continue the same work. Several more days or an eternity passed in this fashion and even though my body didn't need nourishment to survive here, I found myself flagging. I was exhausted, it took me more time to heal, and I just felt empty.

"Please," I begged. "I've told you everything. I hate myself and everyone that made me like this. I'm still a monster, but I'm not the worst."

"Closer," said my captor thoughtfully.

I screamed as the blade drove in, piercing upward through my intestines and curving toward my heart. The exact same way that Richard had tried to eviscerate me with his bare hands when Tristan and I had fought the Briste and his brother William. Also twins. I seem to have terrible luck when it comes to multiples.

The icy tendrils spread through me, cold fire that I never adjusted to no matter how many turns I'd taken in this chamber.

"You know how to make it stop," said the creature.

"I don't!" I yelled. "You're never happy with any answer I give you! I gave up, alright? It's true, I hate everyone for turning their back on me. They left me alone and broken, with nothing! After everything I gave them! I have dragged my soul over hot coals trying to give you the right answer, but nothing is ever enough!"

A growl of pain turned into a roar as the tip of the knife appeared through my chest.

"This isn't my fault alone!" I screamed, struggling against my bonds. "You think one person is capable of sending the entire world into madness? You can't put that all on me! I had help, motherfuckers! Lots of it!"

Pure, animalistic fury broke from my throat as the thing stabbed another knife into my femur, like I was a godsdamn pincushion. "This all started millennia ago, when the Ætherim didn't clean up their mess," I spat. "It continued when Moreno picked up the charge, and hurtled the messy events of a cosmic power struggle toward their inexorable conclusion."

My breaths were coming in short and shallow as my anger overtook any pain. "I was just a small piece of that puzzle. A pawn." I growled. "I've only ever been a pawn." The heartache in my voice was plain even to me and that only made me angrier. "A tool for people to use, one way or another. Whether it was the Council, using me to control people by fear, or Moreno, using my body for a portal. Or for unscrupulous, black-ops fuckers in league with giant snake monsters to frame me and use me as a catalyst to declare war."

Tears streamed down my face now, chest so tight from holding back sobs even as the icy pain of the knife lodged there became exponentially worse. "I wanted to change things. Make things better. Correct all of the mistakes I've made, or at least try to make something right. To make something good out of all the bad I've done. That's the truth. But all anyone tries to do is draw me back in to the old ways. It's easier just to go along with it."

My torturer tugged the knife from my chest and a sob tore loose as I waited for it to plunge into my heart for a final time. "I let myself become so tied up in Tristan, I thought he was the only reason I was holding onto that empathy and in my weakness, I spiraled out of control." I drew in a shaky breath. "I loved him. I still love him. And I'm pissed he's not here. But he's not the determiner of my life."

The other knife was pulled from my leg.

My sobs turned into a croaking laugh. "Nobody is."

The chains fell away, and I cackled. "I'll show them all!" I screamed.

Then, the hell that should have been my tomb spat me out into the confines of my cabin. But reality didn't return, not yet. I giggled, staring around me with joy and relief, tears streaming down my face as ghostly arms drifted down from the ceiling before lifting me into bed. A disembodied sea of hands tucked me in and stroked my hair until I fell into a deep sleep.

Chapter Twelve

Fingernails drummed on the side table. My eyes opened slowly to find a woman peering at me, lounging across the side table looking bored. Her sharp, well-manicured fingernails dug into the table, the other hand propped under her chin as she regarded me.

The room was cast in cold dawn, but I could see enough to know two things; her beauty was that of some ancient Babylonian goddess, and there was evil in her eyes.

Recognition finally hit me, and I sat up with a struggle, looking for the other one. She was lying on her side next to me, leaning on one arm, a leisurely smile on her face. She moved to a sitting position, her bell-lined skirts softly ringing. The veil covering her hair fell to the side and an ebony waterfall cascaded over her shoulder, the smell of orchids and belladonna wafting over me.

"Amara, the poor thing is exhausted from her trip, and you woke her."

"What did you do to me?" I asked thickly. I could barely think of the words let alone form them with my mouth. Every movement felt like I was in thick sludge.

"Nothing," said Amara, leaning on the side table, the very picture of innocence. Both of them laughed.

"We wanted to pay you a visit," continued Amara. "Seeing as how you're in such a troubled state. Do you give up yet? Did the Nyx give you the proper motivation? We never imagined you'd fall that far, but—" She made a noise of surprised delight.

"Your concern is touching," I mumbled, tongue thick and still coated in whatever remnants of hellfire and ash were in the Nyx. "But I'd like you to leave."

"But we can help," said Malea. "We are ready to release you from this torment."

"At what cost?" I asked. I felt more strength in me now, my words not slurring near as much. I flexed my hands, waking them from sleep.

"Give us the æther. We'll return your familiar, and we'll leave you alone." Malea moved slowly, languidly stretching before leaning over me and resting her head on my chest. She tapped a finger in the rhythm of my heartbeat.

"My, you're not even scared anymore. Does that mean we have a deal?" She caressed my face with a taloned hand.

"Prove to me that Adrian is alive."

She gripped my chin, and her nails dug into my skin. I could feel blood trickle from the pinpoint punctures. "You are in no position to negotiate."

"I'm not going to give you this power for you to use it carte blanche. As much as I want Adrian back, I can't trade his life for millions of others. I couldn't live with myself."

Both sisters growled and moved in on me, claws digging into my skin. "You will not live at all if you don't give us what we want!" hissed Amara.

Malea growled in agreement. "We asked nicely. Then we demanded. Then we took everything from you."

"Your lovers, your livelihood, all of your friends, your allies, your home. We've turned the entire population against you. Unless we tell them otherwise, the first people that see you will tear you to pieces, so great is their hatred," Amara said.

Lovers? Plural? "What did you do to Tristan?"

"Put a little ear-worm in his head. You'd both be better off if he left you."

"Is that all?" I asked, not believing it. As many times as they twisted behaviors and memories...

"He may have wanted to reach out," said Amara.

"He may have actually done so," said Malea. "But you know how things happen. All those messages got lost."

Amara turned my face roughly to her. "But if we need to give you more incentive, we could outright kill him if that would drive the point home."

I smiled. "You won't."

Their eyes narrowed. "What?"

"You won't kill him. You won't kill Adrian."

"Bold claims," said Malea.

"You should't have pushed me so far. The Nyx taught me a few things."

They looked uncertain now.

"I'm nobody's tool. Neither you nor anybody else is going to use me. Not ever again. I will fight like hell, and I will win. And I will bring down every ounce of vengeance and fucking fury I possess on your heads."

"Talulla." The name was barely audible, more felt than heard.

The sisters whipped their heads toward the source, their façade finally cracking. I watched as their glamour dissolved, revealing scales for skin, elongated jaws and yellow eyes. Their tongues lolled out of drooling mouths, forked at the ends.

"Talulla, come back," Derfael called, a firm command.

The creatures hissed as I felt the world around me breaking apart, light permeating the darkness. The sisters screamed banshee howls and Malea grabbed my throat, crushing down on my windpipe until I choked. She leaned her hideous face close and opened her massive jaws impossibly wide. "You dare—!"

"Talulla!" Derfael shouted. A hand descended from nowhere and punched a hole through the creature's chest. She screamed again in outrage before shattering into glass. The hand grabbed the front of my shirt as Amara lunged for me, yanking me free of their spell.

I came to on the floor of the cabin, slamming my eyes shut as soon as I tried to open them, the sun piercing into my skull. I rolled over painfully to see Derfael crouching over me.

"Talulla, thank the gods." He sat back on the floor with a thud, exhausted from whatever magick he'd done to get me out of that pseudo-reality.

"What are you doing here?" I asked. "The Matron said she told you to lay low." My voice sounded raw, unused. I sat up, feeling every ache and pain as I tried to ignore the healed scars crusted with ash and blood.

"She did. But she refused to answer questions about you and wouldn't let me reach out. I got suspicious."

"They excommunicated me. Officially."

Derfael swore.

"How long has it been?" I asked.

Derfael hesitated. "Since everything went sideways? Three weeks."

"What?!" I croaked. "What's been happening out there?"

Derfael helped me to my feet and got me to the couch. "Things are looking dire. Our forces are taking heavier losses than we anticipated. It's all ground assaults and guerrilla tactics. Entire cities have been shut down and evacuated, taken over by battle."

"Shit. How are—"

"Your friends are still safe, as far as I know. They've been keeping a low profile. What happened to you?" he asked.

"I was in the Nyx."

His gaze sharpened. "The Nyx?" He reached over and gingerly took my chin, moving my face around in the light. I could feel the dried blood cracking with the movement.

"I'd wager you were not alone in that place," he said, his voice tinted with sadness.

I shook my head. "No. It was... an experience."

Derfael went to the kitchen and got a glass of water, pressing it into my hands and closing my fingers around it. "Drink." He waited until I'd drained the glass and got me another before sitting next to me.

"I am sorry, Talulla."

He looked it. I'd grown up with this man and he had the emotional range of a chicken nugget. He was always either angry or indifferent. Sure he'd changed a little in recent years, but the look of sadness on his face now hit me so heavily.

"I'm not."

Derfael blinked. "What?"

"It wasn't pleasant, but it made me see a few things in a different light. I needed that." To emphasize my point, I got to my feet, heading to the kitchen and grabbing the remaining bottles of whisky. One by one, I dumped them all down the drain. Meanwhile, Derfael broke into the food stores that I hadn't touched in favor of my liquid diet, putting together a decent meal that tasted like heaven.

"What are you going to do?" he asked, pushing another plate at me. I ate it without a fuss. I'd need my full strength for what was ahead.

"I'm going after them."

A faint trace of concern flashed across his face, but he nodded, resolute. He couldn't dissuade me from it if he tried.

My running and hiding was done. Kowtowing to the Council or the DIWR was no longer a concern. I was a free agent. And I was pissed. The sisters made a grave mistake, and I would teach them that lesson on their own turf.

Let's see how much they liked it when I came knocking on their door.

The haze and aftermath of the Nyx was hard to shake off. Even once all the scars had faded and I'd scraped the dried blood out of every nook and cranny it was hiding, it didn't stop the memories of that place. I'd come out stronger, sure, but it was going to haunt me for a long time.

Derfael chose to stay with me at the cabin. Theresa was less than pleased when she found out. Multiple messengers, bearing dire warnings that she wouldn't protect him from getting caught in the crossfire if anyone came for me were met with the blustering fire of an angry druid. I don't think I've ever seen anybody speak to her that way.

As soon as I felt my strength was returned, it was go time.

"Can you get a message to Morgan?" I asked one morning. "Have her meet me at the Council library?"

His eyebrows rose. "The Council library? That's a bit risky."

"I don't think Lady Saraswati is going to choose sides quite that easily."

"And if she does?"

"I'll cross that road if it comes to it. But if she really wanted me dead, she could've called this book back." I patted the book of celestial maps. "I'll need both their input if I'm going to figure out how to break into that realm."

He sighed. "Aye."

Now the real question was, would Morgan meet me? She had far more to lose than I did if she was caught fraternizing with an excommunicated member of the Council's enforcement team. The two-hours-plus drive to the library was an eye-opener. I hadn't been outside the confines of the park since the war kicked off.

Driving through the city, I found only a ghost town. Evidence of battles fought and moved on, buildings destroyed or peppered with shrapnel. Spray-painted graffiti declaring allegiances or the names of those who had fallen. Even in the aftermath of the battle with the Ancients, it hadn't been this bleak. That battle had destroyed the city but brought it together. To rebuild. Now there was no allegiance between neighbors.

Surprisingly, most of the residential areas had been left alone. Some stores here on the outskirts were still open for business. Many houses stood empty, but there were quite a few that were occupied. Windows closed, blinds drawn, but there were signs of life.

As I hit the interstate, it became less obvious that there was a war going on. There was a lot less traffic, but there were fewer scars of battle to see.

"Fuck," I spat. As I neared the Osceola county line, a roadblock stared back at me. It was too late to pull off or turn around. They had scout trucks ready to chase me down if I did.

I've never been that proficient with glamour magick on the fly, but I was highly motivated to get it right in this moment.

Several men wearing the insignias of the Known's militia group surrounded my truck as I came to a stop. I recognized some of the same men that had attacked the press conference, and my blood boiled. Did they even try to punish these assholes for what they'd done?

I rolled my window down, taking note of the weapons they carried and their positions, figuring my strategy of attack if it came down to it.

"Hey, how you doin' there?" I asked, giving them a bright smile. If my glamour was working properly, I would appear to them like a small older woman with curly gray hair.

"Are there any passengers with you?" asked the man at the window.

"Oh gosh, no."

The man peered past me, regardless of what I'd said. "Where are you headed?"

"The family's got a camper. I had to make a medicine run for my grandson. None of the local pharmacies had any inhalers left."

The stern look on his face softened a bit. "He's all right, I hope?"

"He will be. Soon as I get back to 'em."

He exchanged glances with the other men, none of which had found anything. "All right then. Safe trip the rest of the way."

"Thanks." I patted the side of the truck with my hand. "You're doing good work here, fellas." The last of the suspicion eased off their faces, and they motioned for the roadblock to move back.

There were no other obstacles before I reached the national forest grounds.

I pulled my truck off the road, hiding it in some brush. With more people moving out to the country, I didn't want to take the risk of someone coming upon it. Even with the cloaking over it, if someone ran into it, they would realize it was there.

I was halfway down the path toward the library when I heard a very fake *ca-caw*! A smile crept across my face and I swept my gaze over the trees to locate the source.

Morgan stepped out onto the path. My excitement at seeing her faltered a bit as I noticed she was dressed in full battle gear. Close fitting black outfit, knife belts, a holster on each hip.

"Are you here to duel?" I asked, trying to make it sound like a joke. I really didn't wanna have to fight my best friend.

"No," she said, a tight smile on her face. "I don't go anywhere unprepared for a fight anymore. I got caught up in a small skirmish last week. Almost didn't make it out."

"Shit. Whereabouts?"

"Monroe Center of all places. Small bands of humans just happened to run into Council forces as we were moving into a position farther uptown. I'd been running an errand for Frige and stepped right into the middle of it. If it hadn't been for the resistance fighters showing up—" Her face was drawn just at the memory.

"Resistance?" I asked.

She nodded. "Unassociated Strangers. The Council, for some reason, isn't taking the volunteers into their forces. They want to enlist, to fight for their people, but they're being turned away all over the county."

"That's... not smart," I said. "Their forces are already limited and spread thin."

"I've been hearing rumors that bands of citizen resistance fighters are forming everywhere, taking in anyone who wants to fight." She fidgeted uncomfortably. "It's ugly out there, Evyn. I'd say you were lucky to have missed it, but considering where you were..."

"Derfael filled you in on what happened I take it?"

"He did." Morgan approached, giving me a tight hug. "Gods, I'm sorry I wasn't there for you. The Matron wouldn't tell me where you were. I told her I didn't give a damn if you were excommunicated or not."

"It's alright. Just hearing you say that means a lot."

Morgan gave me one more squeeze and let me go. We fell into step, side by side down the path. "I only know what I've seen on news coverage. Derfael has a few contacts in the Council willing to talk to him still, but he doesn't know much beside the basics."

"Every unit we come across has had at least one of those power-sapping weapons that we first saw at the Council standoff. Most of the time it's not permanent, but in the time it takes for the effect to wear off..."

"It renders them absolutely vulnerable," I finished, shaking my head in disbelief.

"The only thing that gives us hope is that they seem to need a charge in between each use. They always guard the gunner, but our forces have taken to always having someone with the gift of flight on hand so we can get to them before the next burst. We've already lost so many people. I never wanted it to come to war, but I also never thought they'd have a chance against us, you know? Does that make me terrible?"

"No. There was never any reason to believe otherwise. In the past, our conflicts were always solved with treatises. Mortals quickly realized they wouldn't stand a chance and surrendered. Weapons have improved, tactics have gotten more refined, but it still shouldn't have mattered. This already should've been done with, the humans grumbling about it but otherwise submitting."

"Do you think they would ever submit? Really? In their eyes, they probably expect us to take them as pets, servants, or playthings."

"Because it's what they'd do," I said, shaking my head. "Same reason humans fear being probed by space aliens. Because whenever mortals find something interesting, they put it in a cage and poke it with sticks."

"So they're projecting?" she asked with a grin. "Thanks for the psychological breakdown."

"That was always Tristan's specialty. I guess it rubbed off on me." I sighed. "The best we can hope for is going back to an uneasy truce. If not, most of us will return to the Strangefells and they can have their realm all to themselves."

Morgan snorted. "Without us around, I think they'll find it a much different place. Not for the better."

We reached the doorway between the trees. The sentinels poked their heads out and nodded acquiescence as Morgan and I showed our keys, the door appearing before us. We went through the same procedure, descending into the main cavern where Lady Saraswati met us. She held out her hands for the book and gave it a loving caress when I returned it to her.

"Thank you for bringing this back in one piece. I was worried when you hadn't returned. I was just debating how much more time I should give you before pulling the trigger."

"Thank you for the hesitation," I said with a grimace. "Although I'm not sure if it would've affected me or not. Could that spell reach me in the Nyx?"

Saraswati's eyes sharpened to laser focus. "The Nyx. How did you end up there?"

"A lot of alcohol. And depression."

"So you needed your dark night of the soul?"

"I—wait. You know about that?"

"Of course. Now I think we have a little more understanding of what the lamia want from you. This must be what they were orchestrating the entire time."

My lips peeled back in a sneer. "This was their doing?"

"Come. Let us sit. We have much to talk about and not a lot of time to do it."

"So let me get this straight," I said, struggling to wrap my head around everything I'd just learned. "The Nyx is some kind of constructed dimension that the Ætherim used to give their own people a timeout and a mental reboot. You lost control of it, and it took on a mind of its own, becoming that hellscape that I was trapped in. That realm is also made of æther, which I just happen to have recently acquired the ability to use."

"That is correct," she said.

"Malea and Amara tore apart my fucking life just so I would be vulnerable enough to wind up there, solidify my connection with æther, and now I've theoretically become a walking portal/master of creation? Am I getting that right? They engineered this whole thing ever since the Ancients woke up and reminded them to seize the day?"

"If it makes you feel any better, they've probably been planning this for millennia. You just happened to provide the perfect set of circumstances for them to take advantage of."

"It does not. Not even close. Please try again."

Morgan had been sitting there the entire time, speechless. "But this should be a good thing, right? Now you can easily breach their realm and take them on."

"No." Saraswati's tone was sharp, and we both looked at her in alarm. "They are stronger than you, and they have far more experience using these powers than you. It would allow them to wrest the æther for themselves. In the blink of an eye, it would give them everything they wanted. You cannot use it. To have the æther acting through you, unable to control it, it would look for direction, someone to stabilize it. Create with it. Æther doesn't like to be left out. If you summon it, you must use it immediately. Otherwise, it would take matters into its own hands. Right now, you are just a vessel."

"And you're a cheery ray of sunshine," I snapped, regretting it immediately. "I'm sorry. This is the second time in a year that some masterminding monster has used me like a fucking puppet for their own ends. When I just had this huge, meaningful breakthrough that I wouldn't allow myself to be used like that ever again."

"You still don't have to let it continue," said Morgan. "Going forward, make this all on your terms. Show them what a mistake they made."

I smiled at her. Talk about a hypewoman. "Even if I can't use æther, there has to be a way to get to them. To take them on."

"It is far too dangerous to—"

"I don't care!" I barked, slapping my hand on the table. Saraswati's lips pulled into a terse frown, but it didn't deter me. "I need to get my familiar back. It's *not* optional."

My two companions shared a look. Morgan was chewing on her lip and Lady Saraswati shook her head. But whatever Morgan was deciding on, she seemed to ignore the goddess's wishes. "I haven't given up on finding answers. In my spare time, I've still been doing a little digging."

"Do not even tell her," said Saraswati, forgoing any attempt at subtlety. "It is forbidden. You may be excommunicated now, but doing this will get you executed."

"What are you talking about?" I asked.

"There's a ritual—"

"Morgan, don't."

"If you won't let her tell me now, she'll just tell me when we leave," I said. Saraswati's nostrils flared with anger, but she gave a sharp nod. I was suddenly glad I didn't have any outstanding borrowed books on my tab.

"Fine. But once you listen to her, you will listen to me list all the reasons why you should not do this. Why it is foolish, and you shouldn't even know of it in the first place."

"Fine," I said, turning to Morgan. "Spill."

"I was taking a look into the Brotherhood of Levi. Several of my current resident spirits used to belong to that sect."

There were already so many questions swirling around in my mind, but I let her talk.

"Way back before the different realms were... solidified, and the boundaries between worlds were much easier to traverse, they started experimenting. To see the depth of the realms. How far they could go. Searching for dimensions across time."

"I just want to interject real quick and ask you to make me a reading list," I said, my natural curiosity going crazy. I thought I'd read all their works, but apparently not.

She gave me a sideways smile and continued. "It turned into some real Lovecraftian shit. Some of the creatures they talked about seeing..."

"There was a reason most of them were mad," Saraswati interjected, crossing her arms over her chest. "But apparently you want to end up the same way."

"They weren't of this world or any other. Even with their penchant for the unusual, they knew they couldn't allow access to those realms by just anyone. So they sealed them. Of course, the brotherhood wouldn't do anything without being able to undo it. They just made it undesirable. I had to dig deep to find any record of their rituals in this particular regard. There's only one copy remaining that I'm aware of, and I had to call in major favors to get access to it."

"Who has it?" I asked.

For the first time I could remember, Morgan got real cagey and avoided my gaze. "Nobody you know. Leave it at that."

She obviously had to know I wouldn't leave it at that right? I might leave it until later, but...

"Since using æther is out of the question, this actually fits perfectly."

"Almost like the sisters are still playing you, so maybe you shouldn't do it," Saraswati said.

"The only other way to open a gate that will cut through to their realm is to use the foundation of one of the super cities. Underneath Babylon, Karnak, the Forbidden City, and so on. Those sites are sitting on top of the original super cities, but the power is no less potent. Just harder to get to."

"Or Göbekli Tepe," I said.

"Yeah," Morgan sighed. "Or that one. Which would be the easiest because it's the least built over by human cities. Once you've tapped into that power reserve, you can open the gate. But you also have to feed it."

"I'm guessing chips and a beverage aren't going to do it?"

"Souls," said Morgan glumly. "You have to power it by feeding it souls."

"That is problematic," I said, rubbing my chin. Working with souls and spirits is a basic tenant of magick. But using a soul to power something was a whole different story. You have to draw spirits from the Dark and upset that balance, feed them to the meat grinder, and watch them be broken down into their base energy. Where they would then cease to exist. Poof. Gone forever. They would never get a chance to continue through to reincarnation, potentially affecting generations of living people to come. It was extremely forbidden, and Saraswati was right. If I did this, I would be facing execution. For a minimum.

"Don't stop now. Tell her what else she might do."

I blinked out of my thoughts and looked at Morgan who was frowning at Saraswati. "Nothing indicates that it could actually happen though."

"The rift is already there. I wouldn't put anything out of the realm of possibility."

"Can you share with the class?" I asked, my gaze bouncing back and forth between the two.

The goddess crossed her arms in front of her chest. "If it goes the wrong way, you could reopen Solomon's gate and give the Ancients another crack at freedom."

Chapter Thirteen

I couldn't sleep. Not for lack of trying. I had returned home—or to the cabin anyway—and gone straight to bed. Derfael was gone, but before I could worry, I noticed he'd left a note. Theresa had called him up for something, but he wasn't sure what.

If I didn't hear from him soon, I'd need to go looking. I didn't trust my aunt, not right now. Derfael was one of her oldest friends, but that wouldn't preclude her from using him as some kind of tool if she needed to. Or felt she needed to. War always brings out the worst in people, and people like my aunt can get very nasty indeed.

I went back to my restlessness, tossing and turning, willing myself to at least doze. I needed to look at things with fresh eyes I couldn't do that while I was this exhausted.

Morgan had explained in detail everything I would be risking, with Lady Saraswati reinforcing the doom and gloom. All the dangers, everything I would be risking, not only for myself, but for the world. Logically, I should've put the thought out of my mind entirely. Kept looking. Found another way there. But I just couldn't. I was aware of how selfish contemplating doing this was. But what if there was no other way?

If I couldn't use æther, it was my only chance to break in to the lamia's realm. If the goddess of knowledge couldn't find any other answers, then, despite all the dangers I'd be facing, I wasn't ruling it out.

I had just drifted off, my eyes finally heavy enough to drag my racing thoughts into submission. It was probably a fool's errand to run any of this by Derfael, as he would no doubt side with Morgan and Saraswati. But getting his seal of disapproval was often my go-ahead to do something. It gave me that extra bit of motivation to get it right and get it done.

A sudden thrill zipped up my spine to the base of my skull, blossoming into a headache and fading just as fast as it had come on. I shook it off, annoyed that I'd have to start trying to fall asleep all over again. Thirty seconds later, it happened again, and then I remembered what it was.

When I was young, still learning my powers and under Derfael's care, we'd come up with an early warning system to use in case we were separated and needed to tell the other to run and hide. I was far too inexperienced to protect myself then, and the people who had murdered my family and kidnapped my siblings were unknown and out in the world somewhere.

My power had taken longer than the average Stranger's to reveal itself, so it would stand to reason that if they found out I wasn't mundane they would come after me too.

And that's what was happening now. Wherever Derfael was, he was warning me to run. I rolled out of bed, not wanting to stand and make myself a perfect target. I hit the floor on my hands and knees, creeping over to my go-bag. I did a quick scan to the perimeter and cursed. There were at least fifteen magi gathered outside, within the perimeter, but far enough from the wards that they wouldn't set off any alarms just yet.

Theresa must've called Derfael out of here to eliminate the additional threat he would pose while they came for me. Were their orders to kill me or capture me?

I snuck into the kitchen, stuffing a few more rations into the bag before fitting it snuggly to my back and buckling it at the waist. I made sure all my holsters were in place around my body; hip, thigh, and the backup at my ankle. I double checked my knife belts, satisfied.

There was a hatch cut into the floor in the far east corner and I pulled aside the table that was set overtop of it. It creaked with a low growl as it opened, and I peered into the darkness below. A faint scuffle coming from somewhere deep in the tunnel caught my attention and I sent my feelers out again. Five more magi were heading my way, the crackling of their magick preceding them. The Matron wasn't fucking around. I didn't know if I should feel honored or not. Twenty magi for little ol' me?

The large numbers more than likely meant they were supposed to bring me in alive. But if I knew my aunt—which was debatable sometimes—her ultimate goal was probably to turn me over to the other side as a peace offering. Or a sacrifice, if you will.

Okay, I needed to think this through. If I went after the five in the tunnel, I'd be facing fewer opponents, but they'd still have the advantage. Tight quarters in a fight between magi becomes a powder keg real quick, a pressure cooker ready to explode.

If I took my chances outside with the fifteen mercs, I'd have much more open area to play with, but they were undoubtedly all loaded for bear and would unleash whatever traps they'd set the minute they saw me. But I could always go up.

I'd put a hatch out onto the roof just so I could sit up there and enjoy some fresh air and stargazing, but it's also well within easy reach of the tall pines. At the very least it would give me a height advantage.

I snuck up the narrow ladder to the roof and eased the door open, crossing my fingers that it wouldn't squeak. After an initial loud squeal, I paused and held my breath, listening for movement below. If they'd heard it, they were holding position. A silent muttered jinx was all it took to seal every door and window in the cabin. The walls were already reinforced so it would take a lot of battering to get through. The best bet for the team coming through the tunnel would be to go back out the way they came and trek back to the main team.

The trapdoor was silent the rest of the way open, and I scrabbled onto the roof, peering over the edge and straining my eyes in the darkness. One by one I picked out the faint shadows of the mercenaries lying in wait among the trees. I didn't recognize any of their signatures but one.

Malcolm. That prick.

I appraised the jump I would need to make to the nearest pine. Chances were good that they'd see me. I'd used the trick before, jumping between the treetops to gain quick ground when I was hunting down an elemental in the Alaskan wilderness.

I'd gotten way more than I bargained for with that one. Two elementals for the price of one, and I'd almost lost my life to a massive fish living in a frozen-over lake. Damn thing swallowed me whole after the water elemental trapped me underneath the ice. But that's a tale for another time.

A beam of pure energy shot straight at me, followed close behind by a blast of fire from a secondary source. I leaped off the roof as the cabin was rocked by the magick. I caught the branches of the nearest tree and dropped to the ground, my plan blown.

I threw up a shield as I ran directly at the mage in front of me. Her eyes widened only briefly before resoluteness and calm took her. She crouched back into a defensive position, throwing up a shield even as she conjured a blade of condensed air. I had to utilize my Sight to see it. The second I was within range she struck, slicing the blade down toward my shoulder, aiming to take my arm clear off.

As long as I was alive, I guess they didn't care what state I was in. I dodged to the side, ducking back within her reach and crowding her so she couldn't swing. Now I had a choice to make. Did I try to incapacitate them? Or did I kill them? They wouldn't stop unless they were out cold, or out permanently, and I was far too outnumbered to take the risk of them waking up and trying again.

My knife was to hand on automatic reflex. I palmed one of the small push knives, stabbing her repeatedly in the kidney. Another blast of energy from another merc went wide, just missing me. The mage stumbled back, and I drove the knife into her larynx, angling up so it caught her at the seam between her neck and chin. With a quick twist and a wrenching motion, I sliced her neck all the way down. She fell, and I moved onto the next.

A trio moved in to surround me, still staying well out of reach. The others would stay back for now. If they all swarmed at once, they knew I'd be just as likely to use their numbers against them, friendly fire becoming the real threat.

Two witches and another mage. One witch attempted to distract me while the other coaxed tree roots to wrap around my feet. I hit the roots with a burst of flame, gathering up a rush of energy as I prepared to move.

This was no ordinary jump-step. I flashed outside their perimeter with such speed, not only could they not follow it, but I had to work to keep myself from vomiting when I came to a stop.

Before I could lose my advantage, I struck, throwing the push knife and guiding it with a small bit of magick right between the first witch's eyes. The second screamed in fury and charged without thinking. She summoned a ball of flame to hand as the mage came up behind me.

I smashed my fist into the witch's throat, dodged an attempted strike from the mage, shattered the witch's elbow, while I summoned my own blade of air. The second I touched my hand to her chest, the air exploded out the other side. Before the witch had even hit the ground, the mage engaged me in a furious round of hand-to-hand combat. We exchanged strikes at lightning speed until

I got the upper hand. I snapped his neck, reaching for my .45 and firing two shots to my left, about six feet apart. Two more bodies hit the ground, and I let the mage fall from my grasp.

A volley of energy bursts and bullets flew at me, the remaining group deciding the risk was worth it to open fire. I threw myself behind a tree, bits of bark splintering and blasting around me. I wouldn't be able to sustain a shield for very long against an attack this fierce, but I threw one up as I darted toward the next tree over. I repeated this several times, making my way slowly toward my truck while also attempting to draw them out into the open.

A rush of air passed by me and the next time I blinked, Malcolm Finny was standing in front of me. "Come on, sweets. Surrender. Our orders are to bring you in alive."

"And then what?" I asked.

A slow sneer crept up his face. "Only one way to find out."

"I'm sure it's nothing sinister." I could feel some of the other magi working their way around the perimeter. They were shielding themselves, but not very well. Amateurs. Maybe the Matron didn't think as highly of me as I thought. Especially if this dipshit was in charge. "Are you leading this team? Kind of a demotion, isn't it?"

His lip curled. "We don't want to waste any real talent when they're needed on the front."

I sighed. "Insulting yourself again?"

He paused, eyes flicking back and forth as he tried to figure it out.

"Are you a glutton for punishment?" I asked.

He latched onto that one. "If you're the one doing the punishing, baby, sure. I'll let you take a crack at me anytime you want."

"Your overconfidence and perversion never cease to amaze me, Malcolm."

"What do you say? Give up?"

Without taking my eyes off Malcolm, I popped off five shots. Four more bodies hit the ground and a fifth cried out in pain. Malcolm and I exchanged glances before he charged me. He knocked the gun out of my hand, and we grappled, falling to the ground.

Shit. He wasn't a whole lot bigger than me, but there was enough of a strength difference that this was my weakest position. Malcolm wrapped his arms around my torso and threw himself back so I was just kicking my feet in the air. He pinned my arms to my sides, and I remembered my scuffle with

Briggs all those months ago. Was he still alive, or had the sisters gotten to him, too?

Malcolm tried to dampen my magick with a spell of his own, but I'd long ago learned all the workarounds for those kinds of bindings. I wouldn't need magick to take him out anyway. He stuck his face in my hair and sniffed, making a low groaning sound in the back of his throat.

"Gods, you smell delicious even when you're covered in sweat and blood."

I threw my head back, smiling at the satisfying crunch of his now broken nose.

"Bitch!" he spat.

"Next time you pin someone's arms to their sides," I said, fingers grasping the handle of another push knife and drawing it out of the belt, "make sure they don't have knives in easy reach."

As anticipated, instead of taking a stab in the outer thigh—painful, but far less dangerous—he flinched and released me, trying to scrabble away. I plunged the knife into his artery along the inside of his thigh and sliced down. He might heal faster than he bleeds out, he might not.

I jumped to my feet and froze. A warlock was coming up behind me, the hum of magick indicating he was ready to hit me with everything he had, as were the remaining two magi still standing from the main team. The other five from the tunnel hadn't made it back around yet.

Deep breaths, Evyn. This is gonna hurt.

On my exhale, I twisted and threw the knife into the warlock's kneecap while simultaneously throwing the strongest shield I could manage around me. He screamed, unleashing the blast mere feet from me. The others took their shots, and I was flung backward from the concussive force as the entire section of the park was leveled.

I landed in a heap, my shield breaking as I made contact with the ground. The first couple of attempts at getting up failed. Damn, that rung my bell hard.

When I finally got to my feet, my footsteps were staggered, and I kept running into trees. I tried to clear my head, heading for the truck. It was close.

I didn't look behind me as I finally shook off the dizziness and ran full tilt, running right into the truck and bouncing off it. The keys were still in my pocket, right? I grabbed the door handle, and the truck unlocked, a sigh of relief gushing from me as I hopped in. A cloud of dust was the only thing left behind as I sped away.

Chapter Fourteen

I had to charter a private plane out of Canada to get me to Turkey. So far it was one of the few countries that had resisted entering the war. I couldn't risk traveling through the Strangefells. Even if word hadn't made it to the Council yet of their team's failure, which was unlikely, someone was bound to notice an excommunicated mage's signature traveling between realms.

The Matron's attack on me had only hardened my resolve. I was going to Göbekli Tepe, and I was doing the ritual. I was getting Adrian back.

The pilot had to land us on a private airstrip, hidden away in the desert. I couldn't risk being seen. I disembarked, my backpack the only safety net. I was immediately taken by the hot, dry air, a wind whipping up and sending granules of sand into my eyes. I cursed and tried not to rub at them.

"You gonna be okay out here?" asked the pilot. Unless I missed my guess, this man was involved in a lot of shady dealings, maybe even black ops. I can't imagine he would've had a legitimate reason to know of this airstrip otherwise.

"I'll be fine."

He put his hands on his hips and looked at the nothingness that surrounded us. "And you don't want me to hang around?"

I shook my head. "Nope. You can takeoff whenever you want."

"Look, I don't know exactly what's going on here, but—" He had the air of a man concerned he might have transported someone to some kind of suicide mission.

"And you don't need to. You've got your money, I've made my intentions clear. You can go."

He might've argued a bit more, but a rising dust cloud in the distance caught his attention. "Shit." The pilot reached into the cabin and grabbed a couple of bottles of water, tossing them to me. "Safe travels."

I gave him a sarcastic salute, and he hopped back into the plane, cranking up the engine. By the time the caravan that had come to investigate reached the airstrip, both I and the plane were long gone.

Traveling in the desert is much easier if you can jump-step most of the way between those long stretches of scorching hot sand. I was taking a breather in the shadow of a large, rocky outcropping, sipping from one of the water bottles. I'd only touched down in Turkey about an hour ago, and the airstrip had been a few hundred miles from my desired destination, but I was already halfway there.

Jump-stepping did take a lot out of you though, energy wise. I decided to have a snack and wait until I felt back to normal strength rather than rush it. I had no idea what kind of security they would have at Göbekli Tepe. Moreno may have been long gone, and all her underhanded dealings buttoned up, but this was still the site of a super city, and there could still be more artifacts hidden here. They couldn't risk leaving it exposed.

Once I got a better grasp on what safety measures they'd taken, I could go about disabling them and clearing out any potential interference from guards or passersby.

It wasn't unbearably hot in this little shady oasis, and all my energy expenditure and lack of sleep were catching up to me. My eyelids drooped, and I slept.

Stay away. The darkness of a dreamless sleep rolled back to reveal the sisters' hideaway. I was in the same dimly lit chamber as the dreams before, but this time Adrian was fully conscious and staring at me with complete recognition. There was no fear, only resoluteness.

"Stay away," he said again. "You can't save me." He gave me a sad smile and for the first time I found that I could move in this dreamworld. I stepped quickly toward him, crouching down in front of him and putting my hands on his face. He was covered in scars and dried blood, but no fresh wounds.

"I can save you. I'm not leaving you here."

Adrian leaned into my touch, still bound to the stone chair. The shuddering sigh of longing that rumbled out of his chest broke my heart. "You have to. Even if you make it here, you can't get me free. They're too powerful. You're walking right into their trap."

"I have to try."

"Evyn—" he began, but a heavy sliding sound echoed from far away. Panic returned to his face. "Get out of here. Don't come for me. I mean it."

"I—"

"Go!" he yelled, lashing out with what force of will he still had and ejecting me from the dream.

I woke with a start.

"Dreaming about Adrian again?"

My eyes closed in a slow blink, and I hissed out a breath. "How did you find me so fast?"

Morgan smiled down at me. "It's not that hard, hate to break it to you. Not for me anyway."

She took a seat beside me. "I didn't figure I'd managed to persuade you, but it hasn't even been twenty-four hours. You couldn't have given it a bit more cool-down time? Really think about the death penalty offense you're about to commit?"

"You know I can't. If there is a solution in front of me, I can't ignore it." A shred of doubt from the dream I just had must've flashed across my face.

"Did you see something?" she asked.

I might as well tell her. There were no outward indications she was planning on stopping me, but I owed her honesty for the trip she made.

"Adrian told me not to come. It was a trap."

She stared at me. "Duh," she said, rolling her eyes. "Wasn't that a given?" She turned so she could really study my face.

"Are you not here to stop me?" I looked down at my feet and noticed the encroaching sunlight. It was beginning to creep toward noon and once we didn't have any shade anymore, I was genuinely concerned that Morgan might burst into flame. She was just so pale.

"The Council has no idea that I'm here. Or what you're up to." Her brows pinched together. "If I'd known the Matron was sending a team after you..." She shook her head. "I can't believe she did that."

"Our relationship has always been complicated. If it's between the greater good and her own flesh and blood, she'll always choose the greater good."

Morgan wasn't convinced by the answer. "When Malcolm made it back—"

A noise of disgust broke from my throat.

She laughed. "Yes. I'm sorry to tell you, he survived. Along with only a handful of the people he left with."

I couldn't say I was genuinely sorry, but I did have regrets about my actions. "He shouldn't have brought amateurs for a job like that. That dick always underestimated me, even though I always beat him."

She nodded. "He's all brawn, no brain. And he's the best we could do to replace you."

"Well, it is *me* we're talking about. It's not often creatures this extraordinary come around," I said, laughing.

"When he hobbled into the chamber, it was the first I'd learned of the Matron's attempt. I think that was the first *most* of us learned about it. She seems to have gone a bit rogue."

I cocked my head. That was unexpected.

Morgan continued. "I was pretty sure I knew where you would go."

"If Derfael hadn't warned me, they might've actually succeeded in capturing me."

A look alighted on Morgan's face, realization dawning. "That's why he was there. The Matron had him under guard, but I didn't know why."

"She was getting him out of the way. Twenty magi against the two of us wouldn't have stood a chance." I was starting to see my friend with new eyes. "Did you really abandon your post to come find me? And not because you're planning on turning me in?"

Morgan hesitated for a long moment, gazing out over the desert. The sun was finally starting to reach its zenith and she pulled a hood over her face, a light silk wrap. "The job isn't what I thought it would be. I didn't really have a choice but to take it. But lately, some of the things I've been witnessing... on both sides..." Her gaze went distant again. "I don't approve. And I'm not sure I want to be a part of it."

We sat in silence with that. I had mixed feelings. Happiness that my friend was here with me. But guilt, because she was now committing treason, among other things. I guess they could execute us together. I allowed myself a moment of morbid curiosity about what her preferred method of death would be. The Council could get *very* creative.

"I think I might have an idea. How to get you to their realm without giving them what they want," she said finally.

It was getting uncomfortably hot, so I suggested we travel on and find someplace else to hide from the sun. She was happy to oblige. Even with the covering shading her face, there was still the beginning of a sunburn on her nose and cheeks.

We traveled another hundred miles or so, until we found an abandoned village that the desert had reclaimed for its own. Taking shelter in one of the structures that still had most of its roof intact, we continued our discussion.

"So you remember how I explained the nature of my magick?" she asked.

"The spirits that take up residence within you?" I asked.

She nodded. "It made me think about how this portal is powered. And how we might be able to control it." Morgan picked at her nails in a nervous tick.

"There are several spirits within me that volunteered to go into the rift we'll be creating. I'm hoping that if it goes as planned, they'll be able to help guide it. Make sure it stays well away from anything the Ancients might be able to utilize."

Some of the tension that had been a constant knot between my shoulders eased. It had brought me no comfort to think about the repercussions to the souls I would be sacrificing to this thing. "And they're fully aware of what will happen when they're in there?"

"Yes. I made sure. Most of them are about through with their reincarnation cycles anyway, at least by their best guess, and the others are just innately curious. I couldn't talk them out of it if I tried. They seem convinced that there's no way of knowing entirely what will happen to them once they're in there. And if they survive it, they'll come back and tell me."

"That's—" I didn't have words for what it was. Naïve? Foolish? Brave?

"There's no question they always intended this to be a trap. If they weren't confident you'd be able to get to them, I don't think they would've taken Adrian there. The question is how exactly they're planning to get the æther from you once you're in their realm."

"It's buried pretty deep. It took the threat of certain death to bring it out the first time and the second I only think it was easier because I was wearing Solomon's ring. And ever since I've only been able to summon small bits of it."

Her head bobbed as she thought. "I think I have a method that will work."

"You're not coming with me." It was a statement as much as it was a firm refusal. There was no way I was putting her in that kind of danger. She'd risked enough already.

"I know," she said, a grin quirking the corner of her mouth. "I wasn't volunteering to. I'll be there in spirit." She winked, and I couldn't help but laugh.

It faded quickly as I realized all of the other obstacles we still had to pass. "Do you have any idea what kind of security they'll have at Göbekli?"

She held up her finger while she rummaged around in her pockets. Finding what she was looking for, she triumphantly pulled out a list, hastily scrawled on an envelope. "I did a little digging before I... excused myself from work."

She made a vain attempt to flatten out the wrinkles before handing it to me. "Security shifts for the guards, any wards and hexes, and the one safe point of entry for lazy Council members who don't want to deal with the red tape of calling ahead."

"They put backdoors into the security on a site like this?" I asked, incredulous.

"People in power get lazy once they're comfortable. Most of them couldn't imagine that someone would use this against them. Nobody would dare."

"Except us. But after this, our death warrants are signed anyway." I looked at her earnestly. "Are you sure you wanna go through with this? I wouldn't blame you in the slightest if you didn't. Nor would I think less of you. I'm not happy about this either."

She took my hand. "I'm sure. True friends don't abandon each other once the end of the road is in sight. We have a chance at making a real difference. Striking these monsters a blow. It may not fix the damage that's already been done, but it should weaken them. And that should help everyone in the long run."

I squeezed her hand, so grateful that she was here with me. Such loyalty was not something I ever expected, nor thought I deserved, from someone who wasn't bound to me in one way or another. I'd never experienced true friendship before, and I was glad I got to before it was too late.

"Are you ready?" I asked.

She nodded. "Let's do this."

Chapter Fifteen

Even though she brought me the proof on paper, I still could not believe how easy it was to sneak into Göbekli Tepe. For gods' sakes, how careless can you be?

The perimeter was wide enough that we felt safe beginning the ritual in the middle of the main temple. The T-shaped pillars surrounded us as we stood under the open sky. They'd uncovered more of the temple, discovering wide stairs, descending in three concentric rings to a stone floor. As they investigated further, they found a hollow in the very center, concealed beneath a single, carved circular slab.

The Council had been quick to hush up whatever it was that was under there. The two of us lowered ourselves down, sending a light in before us just to make sure there was actually a bottom to the dark pit.

It was empty and open now, but I could feel the faint traces of magick lingering. Solomon's signature was all over it. It would be the perfect place to set up.

I pulled some chalk out of my bag and with Morgan's direction, we quickly drew the seals and sigils around the floor of the chamber. The light filtering in overhead from the oculus cast a harsh spotlight in the middle of our working.

"There's no way to tell exactly what will happen when the spirits leave me. I've never seen it from an outside perspective, obviously. But it might look—" She shrugged helplessly.

"Weird as fuck. That's fine." I've seen a whole of things, not many of which can surprise me anymore.

She snorted. "Just don't assume that anything is wrong. I'll let you know if I need help."

I gave a single nod and she took a deep breath, taking a seat in the center of the circle. "This whole thing will be anchored to me so I'm gonna need a little extra time to put down some roots."

"Of course."

While Morgan rooted her power down into the earth, giving herself a strong link to ensure she wouldn't run out of power halfway through and shut me in that realm, I wandered. Every inch of wall space was covered with art and pictographs, the human inhabitants of this site's attempts at explaining the ruins they must've found here.

Göbekli Tepe was built on the foundations, long razed, of Solomon's true kingdom. I've only ever heard legends told of what those places were like. There were only a handful of super cities in far ancient times, dating back to tens of thousands of years before the pyramids.

What I wouldn't have given to see those wonders for myself. As much as they were dangerous, they were also beautiful. Full of promise, magick, and breathtaking architecture. A common ground for humans and Strangers to live, even if the dynamics were skewed. In those early days, the Ætherim were just children. The Ancients and the Elementals were waning, but still immensely powerful. The rest of us were just a shadow of a potential future.

A terrifying yet exhilarating time to be alive. Now it was just terrifying. I wasn't even close to reaching my maximum age limit, which would probably top out around seven-hundred years, but already I was mourning the loss of wonder in the world. But to be alive before most of the world was even known and magick ran wild and rampant? Every day would've been rife with endless possibility.

I was lost in that reverie when Morgan cleared her throat. "I'm ready."

A lump worked its way into my throat, and I swallowed it down. This was it. There would be no going back. Whatever happened from here on out, there was only one possible way it was going to end.

"Give me Solomon's ring," said Morgan, holding out her hand.

I drew the ring out of my pocket, but I hesitated. "Why?"

"You have to trust me on this," she said, her face somber.

I nodded and dropped the ring into her shaking hand.

She was trembling so badly she could barely slip the ring onto her finger. I crouched in front of her, not wanting to touch her or disrupt whatever scaffolding she'd built around herself to anchor her power.

"Are you sure? You can still back out. I'll figure it out on my own."

She smiled at me, knowing and coy. "We're dealing in forbidden magick here. Of course I'm nervous, but I'm not backing out."

I nodded and stood. "Where do you want me to stand?"

She motioned directly in front of her. "Don't move from that spot."

I planted my feet, exaggerating the movement. "Got it."

"Do you have a knife on hand?"

"What kind of question is that?" I asked, reaching down to my boot and grabbing the four-inch blade strapped there.

"Good. When I give you the signal, we're going to feed the portal."

My stomach worked itself into knots as Morgan started the ritual. I was heading into the absolute unknown. Morgan would do everything she could to make sure we pulled this off and I was able to make it back in one piece, with Adrian in tow. But even the best intentions could go wrong.

Her voice wasn't her own when she spoke. It was deeper, more masculine, harsh sounding, coming from a body that wasn't meant to speak that way. The words were in a language that must've been long dead, because I didn't recognize any of it.

As I stood there, I watched her face closely. It had gone slack, no sign of any worry or hesitation, and her eyes had become opaque, like there were heavy cataracts in both.

Her voice rose in volume, and the first hint of blue light crackled from Solomon's ring. Unbidden, the memories of that night in the warehouse came flooding back. I'd been so certain that I wasn't going to last the night. When I jumped back into the gate, having said final goodbyes to Derfael and my friends, confessed my love for Tristan. Right before running from him to sacrifice myself.

I chuffed. That should've been all the warning I needed that our relationship wouldn't work out. The signs were all there.

As the magick consumed me that night, burning my body from the inside out, I'd had the briefest instance of relief. I had been glad that that was how it was going to end. By my choice. Doing something that would leave a positive legacy. Dare I say I could've gone down as a hero that saved the world?

And then of course, Death had arrived, we'd had our little chat, and the next thing I knew I was waking up in Tristan's arms, my body restored. Everything after that, well... it went how it went.

And here we were.

It would've been a lot easier if I'd died that night, but that wasn't my fate. I was finally coming to terms with the fact that some of us are just dealt a rough hand, not because we're being punished, but because we're strong enough to bear the burden. I'd almost given up. Finding myself in the Nyx was horrifying and I wouldn't wish that fate on anyone, but it had also bolstered my will to continue. And to be fair, people like me have seen so much, having a dark night of the soul requires a bit *extra* to really shock us to change.

Heat prickled over my skin and the loud crackling of electricity filled the space as a portal sprang to life in front of me. No turning back. Hesitation and uncertainty crept back into my mind.

We were about to sacrifice someone's soul, several someones more than likely. I wasn't sure if having the souls within Morgan volunteer made it less despicable. It was their choice, but how could anyone truly grasp annihilation? Some part of you, even as a consciousness floating in the universe has to have some kind of hope that it won't be the end. It could very well be that they figured, since nobody had ever come back and reported on this one way or another, that the bit about ceasing to exist was an exaggeration and they'd be just fine.

Although the air warped between us, causing an occlusion like melting plastic wrap, I could still see Morgan's face clearly. She caught my eye and raised her knife.

Following her example, I sliced my palm with the knife, the silvered edge shining coldly in the gloom. We dripped our blood along either side of the portal between us, and by the time the task was complete, my palm was healed.

A crack of lightning out of the blue sky overhead tour through the oculus and lit everything with a harsh white overexposure. The shock raised all the hairs on my body at the same time the portal flared, becoming solid and shining with a blinding light.

A wind picked up and tore at my hair, two more bolts of lightning striking the portal. The heat seared my exposed skin as the gate took on a density, settling heavier onto the ground to the point that cracks spidered out from the impact zone.

Morgan, in the center of it all, was calm and serene. The chaos going on around her didn't seem to touch her in the bubble she was in. Not a hair on her head moved. She was staring straight into the blinding light of the gateway.

The liquid lightning that the gate seemed to be made of coalesced into a discernible form. The kind of doors you might expect to find on the medieval castle appeared, ornate and heavy, shut firmly.

Morgan began to chant, speaking words harsh and ancient, a language better left forgotten. It made my skin crawl with every syllable she spat out. Sweat beaded on her face from the effort of wrangling the power. All around her, I could see the faint shadows of spirits gathering, detaching themselves from her body.

But they weren't the only ones here. I could feel the heavy presence moving in around us. I couldn't tell between human or Stranger, but it felt like the existing occupants of this temple were furious. At any moment I expected to feel the claws and teeth of hungry ghosts tearing at me.

As she spoke the last words a silence so deep fell around us that I could hear my heart beating, and every breath sounded harsh and out of place.

A low rumbling, more felt than heard started far below my feet and all around us the ground gave way, leaving our circle hovering over a dark pit. An island in a sea of black.

The doors, with a suspicious lack of handles or locks, vibrated like they were trying to get my attention. As I watched, doorknobs formed. The only thing left to do now was give it what it wanted.

One by one, the souls gathering behind Morgan stepped forward. A young man was the first to reach the doors. He floated into them with a determined expression. Our eyes met briefly before he was swallowed up through the keyhole without even a final sigh to signify his passing.

It was the same for the old woman and her husband who came next, and a young woman after them. Soul after soul disappeared into it, the doorway opening another fraction with every spirit it took. I was just waiting for an opening big enough for me jump through, and hoping there would be enough volunteers to make it happen.

Finally, I saw my chance. It was open just enough. I rushed the few short steps and shoved through the door, my shoulders scraping the edges as I squeezed through. The great doors slammed shut behind me with a reverberating boom that sounded like eternity.

My body was weightless as I floated through that chasm between realms. I had no idea what was waiting for me on the other side, not really. The dungeon

Adrian was in could be just a tiny portion of the world I was entering. It would all be worth it to get him back alive.

When my feet hit solid ground, the world came into focus.

Like a curtain of darkness dissolving into splinters, pinpricks of light turned to recognizable colors, then became identifiable shapes. Before me was a huge manor of polished stone, glinting in the eerie red light that emanated from a sunless, moonless, cloudless sky. All I could see were dark spots of black against the haze of red that I took for stars. The grounds stretched away as far as I could see on either side of me, and the manor itself was four stories high.

I was far enough away that anyone watching the grounds would be able to see me coming. Normally, that would've raised all manner of misgivings, but not here. I was an invited guest.

The trek across the grounds was uneventful. There was nothing in the way of elaborate sculptures or gardens. No outbuildings, distant forests, a wild shrub here or there. No winding driveway of crushed stone to welcome guests for illustrious parties.

It was just open and empty, as far as the eye could see. At least the grass was lush as I made good time crossing the lawn. As I approached the entryway, it did its job as the front door for an evil monster's lair. It was terrifying and imposing, standing three times as tall as the grandest doors I'd ever seen. It was more akin to the gates of Mordor than anything that belonged on a manor home.

I thought for a brief instance about knocking on the door with the heavy brass monstrosity adorning it, just to make a point of being polite. I quickly shrugged that idea off and pushed them open.

Beyond the door was nothing but darkness. With a double, triple check that my guns, knives and sword had all made the trip with me, I proceeded.

As soon as I set foot in the place, candles blazed to life, flame after flame igniting one after the other down an extensive hall that ran straight down with many archways and side halls as far as the eye could see. It was rather stunning.

My footsteps were amplified as they bounced off the marble, sleek wood, and iron. A winding staircase to my left curled upward and disappeared out of sight. Great porticos and elegant, carved murals in bas-relief surrounded me. I wandered closer to see them more clearly by the candlelight. Any curiosity was quelled the moment I got a good look at them. Countless scenes of pain and death, chiseled with such vivid detail it was hard to look at.

Designs in the marble and painted wooden decorations lined the doorways appearing every few feet that drew off left and right to unknown destinations. The salt-and-pepper marble floor echoed on all sides as my footfalls moved down the hall.

I paused, an awareness creeping in at the edge of my consciousness. Focusing on it, my heart lifted. Adrian was here. I could feel him again. I quickened my pace, the additional fear and lingering pain that came through our bond spurring me on.

Statues of mysterious creatures that lined the walls followed me with their eyes, then turned their heads to watch me walk by. The stone creatures gave way to mirrors as I passed through another portico. They lined the walls, more candles set intermittently against them. As the glow bounced off the glass, the light in this room was far more intense than the main hall. High vaulted ceilings were painted with black-and-white images, just as gruesome as the murals I had passed earlier.

Through everything was a pervading silence. The hallway ahead of me was dark, but the threat wasn't coming from there. It was all around me, from every direction. I'd never felt anything like it before.

I passed through that room into a narrower hallway that was twice as tall. Massive candelabras hung overhead, candles burning in their sconces and dripping wax in long frozen trails several feet long.

A light came from an open staircase ahead of me, its black iron railing inlaid with sigils and seeming to glisten with a wet sheen. Luckily, I wasn't meant to go that way.

My path led downward.

I turned right, a small offshoot of a hallway that seemed like an afterthought calling my name. A vase with a mix of dead flowers, the first sign of anything that had once been living that I'd seen so far, sat on a black spindle-legged lacquered table. Next to that was a large door. It was the only one on this stretch of wall.

And Adrian's signature pulsed behind it.

With a steadying breath I pulled it open, peering beyond into the gloom and waiting for my eyes to adjust. I was at the top of a set of stairs, but calling them stairs didn't quite do them justice. It was more like a spiral into nowhere.

I peeked over the banister and stared down into total blackness, the large chandelier hanging overhead only illuminating a small way into the cavernous dark.

There seemed to be a real theme going on here.

A gust of wind issued from below. A smell like a desert wind, hot and dry drifted upward with the undercurrent of blood and raw meat. A lump rose in my throat, and I tried to keep myself from gagging. I shoved my rising trepidation back down. That was where I needed to go.

I moved from the banister to stand in front of the first step. The stone stairs were pockmarked and scuffed, years of wear and tear showing. In the faint light of the candles burning overhead I noticed a stain that ran down the length of the stairs as far as I could see.

As I stared at it, a memory that wasn't my own snuck into my head. Countless victims, their bodies dragged, broken and bleeding down the spiral, thunking slowly over each rocky step. I growled in frustration and swept the thought from my mind as well as I could. Now they were just baiting me.

I steeled myself for the plunge and took the first steps down the stairs, continuing until the light of the chandelier faded and I was left in total darkness. I summoned a small ball of witch fire to guide the rest of my descent.

The sound changed as the walls drew in closer, the dank stone dripping with the same dark fluid as the staircase railing. A quick glance showed the top of the staircase far, far above me, a small pinprick of light that was almost imperceptible.

When I stepped off the stairs, I stumbled on the uneven floor, catching myself on the wall and grimacing as my hand came away sticky and hot. It was blood all right, so warm it had to be fresh. Under my feet was a pile of clothing strewn about the floor two feet deep. They were caked in blood, dirt and other filth and were disintegrating as I waded through them. I wiped my hands off on a tattered, half burned shirt, not letting my thoughts wonder about the person who had been wearing it.

I was in a museum of the damned. There was everything from modern-runway chic, to rotting and decayed Renaissance garb, tearing to rags under the heels of my boots.

The smell down here was overpowering, and every breath felt like I was breathing in a furnace. Sweat dripped down my face and along the back of my neck and my palms were just as greasy.

Another long hall lay ahead of me, and I shuffled through the cast-off rags toward the tall doors ahead. Something caught my eye, and I looked down. And froze.

"No."

I was surrounded by military uniforms, damaged, but new. Hundreds of them. How? Hadn't *I* been controlling the æther? How had those soldiers ended up here?

The doors, diminutive compared to the others with a simple wooden façade, opened invitingly. I raised my eyes, wary, half-expecting something to come through after me. When nothing appeared, I moved forward.

An inscription was burned into the lintel in that same mix of cuneiform and Linear B that I'd seen on the stone chair Adrian was tied to. Even though I couldn't read it, it was a safe bet it was something poetic and ominous.

He was here. I could still get him back. I couldn't worry about the disturbing connection I'd just discovered, not now. I pushed the doors open all the way and took a sputtering breath as a rush of hot air came flying into my face.

And then there was fire.

Chapter Sixteen

The flames burst up and around me before receding and leaving everything in a scorching dark. The flash of fire left me disoriented and my eyes screamed with pain, unnatural colors swirling in my vision and preventing me from adjusting. Even my Sight couldn't clear the blinding effects of the fireball.

I explored my other senses, opening them up fully but only became more frustrated. They were blocking me, keeping me from feeling anything. I could hear no more than I could see or touch. It seemed like a blanket was covering me, acting as a buffer between me and what lurked in the dark.

I took tentative steps into the room, my hands twitching over my guns but knowing I was just as likely to shoot Adrian as anything else in this state.

A tingling came over me and the deadening effect lessened as the door slammed shut with a bang. The sound startled me the rest of the way out of my senseless state. My vision grew clearer, and I saw dark shapes in the room, all along the walls. They weren't living things, I was sure, but that was all I could tell.

I heard small scuffling and heavy sliding at the far end of the chamber.

Another heavy sliding began right behind me, and I whirled to find nothing. I still couldn't tap into my Sight and my heart skipped a beat when I realized my magick was dampened as well. With sheer force of will, I forced my other senses to compensate.

Soon, I smelled blood and bile and fear, heard things moving in the dark, felt the occasional cobweb or wisp of breeze on my skin, tasted a horrible acrid burning and hot sand on my tongue. My sight blurred, dry eyes on fire and watering, the tears falling down my cheeks and mixing in with the sweat. It was so hot that my tears actually felt cool.

The gliding sounds got closer until I could smell something new. A wet rot mixing with a poisonous chemical smell. Dread pierced my calm and switched to fear as something brushed against me. Solid and muscular, rounded. I knew a giant snake when I felt one.

It breathed against my hand, and I went for my guns, but was hit with such force I was thrown off my feet, landing hard and skidding until my head banged against the stone wall with a sickening crack that sent stars through my vision and gorge to my throat. I tried to lift my head, but failed and lost consciousness.

When I came to, fire was licking at the walls and roiling around the ceiling, but after a moment I could see that it was intentional and controlled. I looked around from my prone position, checking to see if anyone was nearby before I raised my head and gave it away that I was conscious. Seeing nothing and no one, I sat up slowly around a crashing pain in my skull and observed my surroundings. There were deep reservoirs of liquid in a trench all around the outside edge of the circular room that fueled the fountains of fire that covered the walls.

The chamber was huge, walls at least two hundred feet high and a diameter that had to have been at least four football fields' worth. The heat was so intense now that I could barely tolerate it.

I stood shakily and did a small pat down, checking first to make sure all appendages were still attached and where they belonged before moving on to find, with no small amount of surprise, that all my weapons were still in their rightful places.

"We thought we'd let you keep those. They look so nice on you," said a familiar voice.

Malea and Amara were sitting right in my direct line of sight, but I hadn't even noticed them, sprawled together on a throne of hewn obsidian. Sharp edges glinted, but it didn't cut them.

They stood with sinuous grace and moved toward me. Tall and lithe, with sensuous curves, their black hair done up in ornate styles and dripping with gold and diamonds. But now instead of their usual skirts and bells they wore nothing at all, fully exposing skin that was gray and covered in scarred markings I didn't recognize. Iron rings were threaded through their skin in a pattern that started at their chest, ran down their sides and over their hips, resembling equal patches of scales. Iron nails pierced their nipples and gold chains were strung between their breasts, the frailness of the chain looking out of place against a backdrop of ancient evil. Matching chains were strung about their waists, low on their hips.

"Where is he?" I asked, cutting straight to the chase.

"So direct. Not even bothering with small talk," said Amara, discernible only by the long red slash over her left eye, trailing down her cheek. She blinked electric-yellow, slitted eyes at me and smiled.

"Very rude," said Malea.

"Could you cut the shit?" I asked.

At their sour looks I added, "Please?" I took a step toward them. "Now where is he?"

"She can't even see him right in front of her face," said Amara, continuing not to address me directly.

"What are you—" I began, but the words choked in my throat as I saw him at last. Just beyond the sisters, in the obsidian chair they'd just vacated, was Adrian's motionless, bloodied body. He was slumped to the side, and I couldn't tell if he was dead or unconscious. Any words I may have had made way for a wail of shock.

At the sound of it, Adrian stirred, barely, but it proved he was alive. I ran to him, and ran straight into a barrier that knocked me back a few paces.

"Adrian!" I screamed, battering against it.

The sisters only laughed. The two of them moved languidly toward him, draping themselves across his still body.

He twitched away, even in his unconscious state. I shoved my hands against the barrier and tried to melt it, threw energy blasts at it, tried to cut through it with an enchanted blade.

Breathing hard, I leaned against the invisible boundary, staring at Adrian in desperation. "You will give him back to me or I will tear you both apart with my bare hands," I said through gritted teeth, knowing the words didn't carry the weight I wanted.

"We're having too much fun with him to let him go," Amara said, brushing at some blood on his chest and licking it from her fingers.

"No, we won't let him go." Malea smiled, an exact replica of her twin.

Amara lifted Adrian's head, and I saw his face, mangled and torn. It was nothing but a sheen of blood covering a mess of mangled meat.

"Adrian, no," I moaned, choking back a sob. "What did they do to you?"

"Would you like us to catalog his injuries for you," the twins said together.

"Or would you just like to see for yourself," finished Malea.

My hands clenched, and I gritted my teeth. I beat my fist against the barrier in fury. What else could I do?

"Please," I ground out.

The wall disappeared from under my hands and I took cautious steps forward, keeping a close eye on the sisters as they moved back.

Adrian's flesh, from what I could see under all the blood, was carved and flayed. Runes and sigils were etched into his body, seals to bind his power and regenerative ability. There were a few engraved so deeply I could see bone glistening through the red. Those ones were runes of concealment, specifically tailored so that I couldn't track him down.

A chill stole through me, cold and relentless. When I finally reached him, I kneeled and peered into his face. His eyes were shut, but when I put my hand on his cheek, he opened them slowly.

A smile curved his lipless mouth, pained but relieved. "Evyn?" He breathed a sigh. "I knew you'd find me."

The words were so weak I could barely hear him.

"I did." My voice cracked as I strove to keep myself from crying. "It took me a little while, but I'm here."

"Thought you'd given up on me."

"Never," I said, carefully taking his hand and flinching. It was like holding a bag of loose gravel, small broken bits held together only by skin. I'd seen bodies dropped from sixteen-story buildings that didn't shatter like that. Slowly, the horror that I felt was being replaced by rage, pure and simple.

"It hurts," he said, trying to grip my hand back and failing.

"Once we get out of here, I'll get you fixed up good as new," I assured him, trying to clear some hair out of his face but it was stuck too firmly in blood.

His eyes widened and he moaned. "No. You can't be here. Why are you here? I told you to stay away. I told you this was a trap."

I cradled his face in my hands. "It's all going to be okay. I've come to take you home," I said gently.

Cackles issued from both sides. "You will do no such thing," said Malea. She waved her hand, almost an afterthought of motion, and I slid across the floor, away from him like a strong breeze throwing a paper doll around. Malea resumed her seat on his lap, her skin smeared with his blood. It oddly highlighted the carefully cut scars she wore over her entire body.

"Yes, I think it's time the mage says goodbye," Amara spoke while draping herself over his shoulders and he flinched visibly.

"I'm not leaving him!" I roared, jumping to my feet.

"Then give us what we want!" The sisters reared up and their tongues flicked out of their faces in simultaneous hisses.

Malea stalked forward. "The only way you two leave here is after you've given us the key for Solomon's gate." She pressed a finger to my chest, and I could feel the pull of a portal threatening to suck me back out of here. Just like that, all of Morgan's work might be undone.

I stared at Adrian and bowed my head, crossing my fingers that Morgan's plan—whatever it was—to keep the æther from them would work.

"Okay."

Amara narrowed her eyes. "Okay?"

I nodded. "Take it."

The sisters smiled duplicate smiles of victory. They circled me and murmured words of power that I could feel building up in a vortex around me. A wall of energy surrounded us, and the hairs on my arms stood up. I could smell a strong scent of ozone, and all sound was oddly muffled.

Their chanting swelled and I felt a strange sensation in my middle, a fluttering behind my sternum that kept growing stronger. It wasn't the æther. I had no idea what it was.

"Let it go!" Malea snapped. "Set it free!"

I focused in on it and visualized the pocket of sensation bursting free from my chest. A greenish light burst from me and into them and they lifted their arms, absorbing it all.

Just as suddenly as it started, everything faded back to normal. What the hell was that?

The vortex fell away, and the sisters stumbled back, looking slightly disoriented. Amara smiled venomously. "Thank you, Evyn."

The sisters turned back to Adrian and draped themselves over him once again.

"Say goodbye to your lover," said Malea with a malicious smile. She caressed one side of his face. "It will be the last time you ever see her." She kissed him lightly and turned to me, licking her lips and smiling.

Adrian shook, despair emanating from him in waves. "Evyn," he whispered, and the sisters cackled again, long and loud. "Don't leave me here."

I could feel myself being pulled away, a new gateway, different from the one that brought me here, opening and trying to pull me out. If I lost him now, I might never find him again.

"I gave you what you want!"

"Maybe if you hadn't made us ask so many times, the outcome would've been different," Malea sniffed, waving her hand in dismissal. The gate pulled at me, threatening to drag me away.

I screamed a war cry and grabbed my sword from its sheath, slamming it through the floor. It broke through the stone and sent a fissure shooting toward the trio where it cracked the throne in half and sent the sisters tumbling to the floor. Adrian was freed, but too weak to move.

Their concentration broken, the gate snapped closed and the force pulling at me disappeared. I pulled a .45 from my hip and, as Amara raised a hand with an incantation on her lips, I shot her between the eyes. She fell backward and hit the ground with a soft thud.

Malea screeched in a pitch that made my eardrums recoil and I hesitated. Before I could train my gun on her, she threw herself at me, pinning me to the floor and knocking the gun from my hand. Her fangs elongated, turning into saber teeth, and she leaned over me, her putrid breath making me gag. Saliva dripped from the tips of her fangs and burned my face like acid.

She reared her head back and telegraphed her move before she made it. She meant to rip my throat out, but I reached for the small knife coiled in my hair and rammed it up to the hilt in her eye socket.

Normally that stops things pretty well. You get a knife jammed in your eye, you're going to at least hesitate and rethink your life choices. Bare minimum.

Instead, Malea drove her now spike-like claws into my kidney, and I just barely managed to catch her other hand before she stabbed her nails through the underside of my jaw.

As she continued to punch her nails into my abdomen it was getting harder and harder to hold her back from making a killing blow. On the next swipe, I deflected the strike toward my shoulder and used my now freed hands to grab her hair and bring her close for a head-butt that made her eyes cross from the impact. I threw her off me and grabbed my other gun, but she tackled me again and I only managed to put a bullet in her chest. That only made her angrier.

Now Malea was so enraged all she could do was hiss and spit and aim repeated blows at my face, her fists like solid iron, shattering my nose, cheekbones and eye sockets. I could barely see her face, twisted and hideous with hatred, through the blood running in my eyes. She didn't want to kill me, not yet. She wanted to make me suffer first, take me apart inch by inch.

I was hovering on the edge of consciousness when she shrieked, and the flurry of attacks stopped. I wiped blood from my eyes to see Adrian standing above her with my sword somehow held in his broken hands, her head several feet from the rest of her body. I tensed as her body twitched, but then it stopped.

Adrian released the sword, and it clattered to the ground with him following shortly after.

I rushed to him and leaned in close. "I'm alive," he whispered. "Just really tired."

Surprised laughter burst from me, and I collapsed next to him. "Thanks for the assist."

I sped up the healing of my face, directing magick to it to staunch the bleeding while I waited for the other aches and pains to die down. Adrian's fingers brushed against mine and I twined my fingers carefully with his.

"Did you think we'd go down that easily?"

I jerked in surprise, jumping not so gracefully to my feet. The bullet wound in Amara's forehead was gone and she was holding the bullet itself between two fingers, taunting me.

"I think she did," said Malea, her head still far removed from her body. Amara picked up her sister's head and handed it to the reaching hands of her torso, the sight of a body reattaching its own head almost comical if the situation had been different. "Your demon must be taught a lesson in manners for beheading his hostess." She stood next to her sister, neither of them any worse for wear at this point. "After all we've done for you," she chastised him.

Adrian's chest heaved and he shook as he lay there, eyes closed tight.

"We aren't asking nicely this time. Leave," said Amara. The gateway reopened and the sisters threw their full power into shoving me toward it. Then they stopped, their eyes open wide as their bodies rippled with green light.

"What—?" said Malea, gripping at her chest. Both of them shrieked, throwing back their heads as the light burst from their mouths and eyes. Several of the spirits that had fed themselves to the doorway appeared, clustered around the two lamia, overwhelming them. They shoved the sisters toward the portal, which now glowed with an ominous red tint. Like they were stuck in quicksand, Malea and Amara attempted to fight back, but it did nothing to help them.

Amara went through first and the portal shuddered, the vortex picking up strength and sucking Malea in after her. The spirits disappeared with them, but the portal didn't close.

It pulled at both of us, and I grabbed for Adrian's hand, seeking for a handhold in anything as we were dragged along the ground. I found a tiny crevice that halted my movement, but our hands were so slicked with blood and sweat, he slipped from my grasp.

"Adrian!" I screamed. He disappeared into the portal. "Adrian!" I let go and pushed myself faster toward the portal, reaching for him. Then I was through.

The weightlessness aided my speed as I propelled myself toward him but just before I could reach him, he spun off away from me with a soundless cry.

And then he was gone.

I fought the against the pull, but it was no use. I blinked.

All I could see were stars. The heat and fire were gone, replaced by a chill so sudden my entire body spasmed from the cold. I had just materialized in the desert, and he was nowhere in sight. I couldn't even feel him.

I screamed, long and loud. The exertion caused a wave of dizziness that had me stumbling and crashing into the sand. I flipped over on my back and stared at the sky, the dull pain from my healing injuries proof of my failure.

Was he still with them? Or had he been taken somewhere entirely different? And if he wasn't with them, how would I ever find him now?

Chapter Seventeen

I squared my shoulders and fought off the hopelessness of the situation. A quick chart of the stars and I started north, hoping to find a village relatively close by. I had work to do.

Through the hot days and cold nights, there was nothing but sand everywhere I looked. There was no oasis, not one sign of life other than the occasional scorpion hurrying to do its business and burrow back into the coolness under the sand. If I wasn't a mage, I would've been dead by now, my bones the only thing left to tell anybody where I was.

This place was some kind of dead zone, so separated from the Strangefells it even curbed what little magick I had left. It would take forever to replenish my power in a place like this. I was too weak to jump-step, and every attempt to contact Morgan failed. I really hoped she was alright.

There was plenty of time to think as I walked. About Adrian, about how much trouble I was facing if my actions were discovered, if I would ever see Tristan and Jake again. How I really should have focused more on leg day at the gym because trudging through all this sand was killing me.

On the fifth day, I started to wonder if I'd wound up in another dimension myself where the entire world was a desert you could never escape. The sun was high in the sky when I heard camels braying and some kids laughing just over the next dune. I cautiously peeked over the hill and saw a caravan, a good-sized one, slowly moving on a path they'd probably traveled a thousand times, but their memories were the only permanent road the sands would allow.

I hesitated briefly and debated whether to show myself. They may welcome a random woman covered in dried blood stepping out of the desert... but my only other option was to continue wandering until even magick couldn't save me, so I had to give it a shot.

I stood and moved to the top of the ridge, and it didn't take long for one of the children to spot me and start talking animatedly as they pointed in my direction. The caravan stopped and I held up my hands, the best show of a white flag I could accomplish, and slowly approached. The closer I got, the better I could sense them and was relieved to find that they were Strangers. It was a faint aura, but it was there.

As I got within twenty feet one of the men barked something at me in a language I recognized to be Farsi. I know dozens of the current spoken languages, but my Farsi was a little rusty.

"Who are you?" he asked.

"A lost traveler. Glad to find herself among Strangers," I managed to cobble together.

They all looked surprised that I spoke their language, even if it was broken.

"You are American?" asked one of the women.

I nodded. "You wouldn't happen to be able to point me to the nearest village or airstrip, could you?"

There was silence for a moment and then some of the men talked quietly among themselves. The same man that had spoken with me first said, "It is two days travel that way." He pointed north; at least I was headed in the right direction.

"Thank you," I said. I began to move off, but the woman stopped me, catching up to me and touching my arm lightly.

"You need food, water," she said.

I smiled and looked beyond her at the rest of group that looked less than pleased. Given everything happening in the world right now, it was understandable that they'd be wary of any outsiders. One of the grandmothers looked like she'd be ready to cuss this woman out later.

"Thank you, but I'll be fine." I had two days left in me. Pretty sure. Almost 100% positive.

"We must insist. It wouldn't be right for us to let you go without it."

I hesitated. "I don't want to cause you any trouble."

"It would not be any trouble," she said, staring at her family.

A few gave relenting nods, and I smiled again. "That would be lovely, thank you."

I followed her back toward the line of pack animals laden with all their supplies. A couple of small children zoomed around us, having already grown disinterested with the arrival of a Stranger in their camp. As a little girl was running past me, she stopped in her tracks and stared. Pointing she said, "Blood."

That was a word I could say in every language known to man, but if a girl not more than four fixes you with a stare and says it that bluntly, it makes you pause.

"Jalila, do not be rude," said the woman, shooing the girl away. Jalila shrugged and ran off to join her friends.

"It's okay, I must look terrible. I was injured and have been traveling for five days since finding myself here so—"

"Five days!" the woman exclaimed. "You were out there for five days?" Now we had everyone's attention. "With no supplies? No shelter?"

"I can survive a lot when I'm motivated," I said.

"Survival is one thing, but you're walking, talking, planning on traveling at least two more days?" She stepped closer and appraised me with narrowed eyes. "What are you?"

"Wow, direct." That came out in English. I switched back to Farsi. "A mage." I inclined my head toward her in a polite bow. "My name is Elizabeth." They were already wary of me, no sense in seeing if they knew the name Evyn Urquhart and, if they had, if they were mad about it.

She didn't look all that convinced but returned the gesture. "My name is Hosni."

Hosni waved her hand at a boy, and he ran to join us. "Tell them to set camp. We are going to stop here for the night."

"Don't let me hold you up," I said.

"I insist," said Hosni. "We all do." And there was more than just rigid politeness in her tone. I was being commanded to stay.

When the tents were set up and the cooking fires roaring, everyone set about doing their usual tasks. I just tried to stay out of the way as they went about their routine, practiced hands performing the same jobs they could do in their sleep. Some of the grandmothers tried to enlist me to help with the cooking preparations but it was quickly discovered that I was a lousy candidate for that job, and they sent me back to staying out of the way with many a hand pat and look of sympathy that I would be such a lost cause.

The amount of luxury they unpacked from their saddlebags smacked of magick, plain and simple. There's nothing else that would allow for plush pillows, warm blankets, drapes, rugs, down bedding, and mattresses, low tables, tea sets, a couple of small settees, ornate lanterns and lots of candles to fill them, an enormous array of cooking equipment, and on and on to fit in saddlebags that normally would barely hold these things enough for three people, let alone thirty.

By the time everyone was settling around the communal tables with their smaller family groups to share in the evening meal, the mood was significantly lighter. Everyone engaged in small talk while digging into the amazing feast the grandmothers had prepared. I was glad they didn't let me help with it, because I would have surely blundered something and reduced the meal to less than the perfection it was.

After dinner came tea. As the evening wound down, people moved away to their own tents and their own pursuits, and Hosni finally turned the conversation to more serious subjects. Her large black eyes reflected the candle flames all around us.

"So, Elizabeth. What is your story?" she asked.

I smiled sideways and took a sip of tea, the mint cooling my body in the lingering heat. "We might be here for a while. Sure you want the whole thing?"

Hosni huffed lightly and cocked her head. "Let's stick to the highlights, then." The silk of her hijab caught the light in such a way that it looked like she had an aura about her.

Trying to stall wouldn't do me any good and changing the subject was bound to just earn me ill will among people kind enough to host me in the middle of a barren wasteland. "I was looking for someone. Things went a bit sideways."

"Did you at least find who you were looking for?" Hosni asked.

Unbidden, that last image of Adrian, our hands slipping apart, his ruined face screaming in silent horror, flashed through my mind. I flinched. Silence stretched on while I tried to wrestle my emotions under control. Wind was stirring up outside, the hiss of sand becoming more noticeable pattering against the canvas.

"Elizabeth? Are you alright?" Hosni gripped my hand, and I snapped back from my memories. I yanked my hand away, standing suddenly and overturning my stool. Hosni likewise rose to her feet, raising her hands and drawing quick symbols in the air, calling up a barrier between us. If I so much as sneezed right now, she was ready to battle to the death.

I slowly raised my hands, palms outward. "I'm sorry. You startled me is all." I swallowed thickly. "I did find who I was looking for." I wrapped my arms around myself, fighting off the sudden chill that stole through me. "But I couldn't save him."

Hosni dropped the shield and her eyes softened. "I am sorry. But if you don't mind my asking, where exactly was he being kept?"

"I'm not sure if the dimension has a name, but..."

A keen interest dawned in her expression. Hosni took a seat at the table again and motioned for me to do the same. There was a lilt in her voice that made me think she was asking these questions for clarity rather than curiosity. She knew something. "Who was keeping him prisoner?

"They called themselves Malea and Amara," I said. "I think they're original lamia." Just then a burst of wind pushed the canvas flap apart and a shower of dust and sand came with it. The grit stung my eyes as I jumped up to re-secure it. That seemed like ominous timing.

When I turned back to the table, Hosni was staring into her hands, like she was reading a book that wasn't visible to my eyes. Lines had appeared on her face that I hadn't noticed earlier. Her eyes flicked up to me and a ring of gold appeared in the black irises, standing out starkly in the gloom, but one blink and it was gone. Her gaze was piercing, sizing me up.

A slight pressure in my brain gave her away. She was trying to read my thoughts and dig up memories, but I'd long ago learned to keep intruders out. I had an impressive rolodex in my head that needed to stay securely there.

"What are you looking for?" I asked. "It's kind of a mess, I haven't had time to clean it up."

"Who are you really?" she asked. "Only very dangerous people or very old and powerful people are usually able to keep me out of their minds. It is my gift, and I am the strongest in my tribe. And you do so with practically no effort at all."

I shook my head. "Time for one of my questions. You know those monsters. Their names were familiar to you. What do you know?"

Hosni didn't like the turn the conversation had taken, but since I'd put her so off guard, she complied. "I have heard these names before, yes. Not for many years." She looked skyward through the small opening in the top of the tent that acted as a chimney. The stars out here seemed endless, away from any unnatural light to get in the way of the view. With the wind-driven dust it looked like every one of them was glittering, a sky full of diamonds.

"When I was a child of maybe seven years, we happened upon another Stranger, seemingly appearing out of the desert like an apparition. He didn't fare nearly as well as you. He stumbled into our encampment raving like a lunatic of two women and a dungeon of fire, of people eaten alive by giant snakes, piles of clothing the only things left behind. Endless screaming, and pain beyond measure. Half his face and body was little more than bones clinging together by thin muscle and sinew, the skin eaten away by an acid of some kind. He spoke of being in the belly of one of these snakes."

Hosni stood and walked over to the small chest of drawers, opening one near the top. She pulled out a small piece of paper that looked like it would fall apart if you looked at it wrong. Barely clinging together at the folds, she opened the page and handed it to me.

"He lingered for two days in that state. The only time he wasn't raving was when his pain made him pass out. Or when he was drawing this over and over again," she said, handing me the page. The scribbles were of various runes, some of which I remembered seeing on the sister's bodies. But in the center of it all in alarming detail was a sketch of eyes. Marred by a long slash mark across the left, all the way down the cheek. I'd bet every penny to my name that it was blood red in color when this man was face to face with the real creature.

As I stared into the eyes drawn by a man in fever dreams on his death bed, a piercing scream came from outside.

Even though I was closest to the exit, Hosni was on her feet too fast for me to follow and sprinting past me out the door, nearly ripping the canvas in her wake.

I followed right on her heels and was nearly blown backward by the strength of the wind. In the distance a giant wall of sand was moving toward us, a roaring sound rising above the wind. In the center of it, seeming to lead it like some kind of deviant drum major, was a cyclone twisting and spitting across the dunes. Lightning forked around the barrel of the tornado, illuminating within it a face that was little more than a skull. I rolled my eyes; apparently this guy had never heard of subtext.

I calmly walked out toward it, shielding my eyes as best I could to keep them from getting sand blasted like a rusty old fender. The rate of speed this thing was traveling at combined with the sheer size and spectacle of its display... I'd give it ten minutes tops before he ran out of energy. It was purely showmanship, all flash and no bang.

Hosni grabbed my arm and pulled me back, but I shook my head. "Don't worry, I'll handle it!" I shouted over the noise.

"Are you crazy! What do you hope to do!" she shouted back.

"It's probably here because of me anyway!"

She didn't argue with that. I continued toward it, raising my hands and drawing in energy, bright light surrounding me and a hex crackling at my fingertips that would put an end to the showboating and make it a fair fight. I aimed toward the center of the cyclone and unleashed the hex. It was like putting a finger on a spinning top, the hex driving a stake of power into the ground and pinning the cyclone by its tail. Its momentum vanished and the sand fell out of the air to form a new range of dunes, rearranging the landscape yet again.

The driving force behind it all went flying forward, landing facedown in the still-settling dunes. A djinn struggled to his feet and spat out a mouthful of grit. He raised himself up to his full height and summoned black flame that boiled around him like a living thing. He raised a dagger overhead and lightning struck the tip in a shower of sparks, lighting up his face.

"Naaji?" I questioned.

The djinn hissed. "Fuck. Evyn?"

I sheathed my sword and stood down. No need to be on guard with this one. "What the hell are you doing here? Someone pull some strings to get you out of eternal confinement? Or were the real demons picking on you too much and they sent you back?"

His answer started out sarcastic but escalated into shrieking anger. "I just missed your super funny jokes and came to the last place on earth that you should be to hear them again!"

"Calm down," I said. "I've got no interest in sending you back."

"Really?" His flames dissipated and suddenly I was just talking casually to an old acquaintance with ashen maroon skin and a smile wide enough and toothy enough to give you nightmares for days.

"How did you get out?" I asked. "You were imprisoned in the seven hells."

"The second one," he confirmed. "All I know is that some kind of tear opened up a week ago and created a portal. A bunch of us made a run for it and a fair amount made it through before the thing closed again." Naaji kicked at some sand, scuffing his feet absentmindedly and waiting for the conversation to be over.

Oops. Was that my fault?

Hosni had crept closer to us while we were talking. I couldn't blame her for being curious. This was clearly not the altercation any of us had been anticipating. I heard her sharp intake of breath as she caught sight of the djinn. She said a few words in Farsi that I didn't understand, and Naaji recoiled like he'd been slapped.

"Hey, calm down. I'm just minding my own business."

"That sandstorm was just minding your business? What exactly is your business?" she asked him.

Naaji scratched the back of his head. "I thought the skull in the cyclone made it pretty obvious. Do I have to get a skywriter involved to spell it out for you?" He looked at me for sympathy. "What is wrong with people these days?"

"Do you know this creature?" she asked me, crossing her arms like I'd just confirmed her worst suspicions about me.

Naaji spoke up first. "Yeah, Evyn and I are old *friends*." He snorted. "She sent me to the second hell, I spent every day there thinking about the many ways I could kill her and desecrate her corpse, and we catch the occasional game of canasta on the weekends. A tale as old as time."

Hosni really looked pissed now. "I thought your name was Elizabeth?" Her tone was deadly quiet.

"Elizabeth?" mocked Naaji. "Evyn, are you lying to these nice people? Afraid your reputation precedes you?" His smile was gleeful at the thought that he could cause havoc in *my* life for once. With a grand flourishing bow, he announced, "Ladies and gentlemen may I present the infamous, the notorious, the queen of the resting bitch face, Evyn Urquhart!"

"Evyn—" Hosni paled, turning and walking back toward the rest of her family.

"Oh, no," Naaji said, putting his hands to his mouth. "Did I just blow your cover with your hosts? Whatever will you do now?" he asked, chuckling.

"Send you back to hell if you don't get the fuck out of my face in the next two seconds," I said, my anger making him stop mid laugh. "One—" I said. Naaji disappeared.

I turned back toward the tents and the angry looking folks with crossed arms and hands on hips. Some of the men had weapons in their hands and some of the women *were* weapons, so they were already set to fight. When I was within easy speaking distance I said, "I'm sorry. I never meant to deceive you. My name tends to have a certain effect on people, and I'm not that person anymore. I don't mean any of you harm." Nobody said anything, didn't even move. "If you could remind me again which way town is, I'll be on my way."

Chapter Eighteen

When it seemed like I wouldn't even get a middle finger pointed in the general direction I had to go in, I set off toward what I thought I remembered a man pointing to earlier.

"Wait," said Hosni. One of the grandmothers completely lost it and unleashed a string of harsh words directed at the younger woman.

"There are things she still needs to know, grandmother," said Hosni. "And I'll make sure she leaves right after."

The woman threw her hands up and stalked away. "Evyn," Hosni said, motioning for me to follow her back to her tent.

When the canvas flap closed behind us I wanted to thank Hosni for the intervention but she cut me off with a quick slashing motion of her hand. "Save it. I'm not doing this for you." She moved closer and spoke lower. "If I'm right, you may be in a position soon enough where every bit of information against these beasts will help you defeat them. My people have had encounters with them and their descendants for hundreds of years. Nomads are easy prey for them. To have them gone would be a miracle."

She picked up the drawing I'd been looking at right before Naaji crashed the party.

"I stayed close to this man, helped my mother care for him. We did what we could, but he died. I never knew his name or anything else about him other than he suffered greatly before his death. And he was terrified that he would go straight back to that place when he died.

"That man was doubtless not meant to escape. You could smell the evil that the magick left on him, like a thick perfume that overpowered even the stink of his fear. I made the mistake of touching his hand, thinking to comfort him, and my mother couldn't stop me in time. A connection was made then. I didn't yet have even the barest of understandings of my abilities or the strength of them. I traveled to that place, saw the things that this man saw, and the beasts that held him there. And they saw me."

Hosni rolled her sleeve up to her elbow and showed me her arm. What looked like the imprint of scales, like a snake had wound its way around her arm and squeezed until it left permanent impressions. "This was my reward for spying on them. It took me months to heal." She rolled her sleeve back down. "But their cruelty also left that door opened just a crack, allowing me to sense them at times. And I've been known to have dreams of them and things that might be yet to come. Not two weeks ago I had a dream of a woman with chestnut hair and pale skin walking out of the desert. And along with that vision was the overpowering feeling that you were linked to those monsters, too. And that you possessed something wild within you." She shifted, stretching her neck from side to side as the stress crept up her shoulders. "Do you know what you are dealing with?" asked Hosni.

"Kind of. Ancient lamia, the original of their kind."

Her large eyes flashed as she stared at me. "In a way. But it is not so simple. How is your familiarity with chaos demons?"

My eyes drifted closed and I drew in a shaky breath. "That makes the most sense of everything."

Chaos demons, like Behemoth, Jormungandr, Leviathan—maybe Malea and Amara had been the creatures the Brotherhood of Levi had discovered on the far reaches that made them shut down access to those realms in the first place—were created at the same time as the Titans, if you believe the legends.

Immensely powerful infernal beings. Just a step below the Ancients, really.

Fuck.

"Do you know what their purpose is? All they'll tell me is that they have a score to settle."

Her face darkened. "They want to tear down the remnants of the Ætherim. The gods forced them away from the Strangefells with their petty squabbles and the lair they built for themselves became a place of seclusion and madness. Only when their realm aligns with Earth can they visit this world at all. And you've seen the result of those."

"And now they've anchored their realm to ours."

"What?" she asked sharply.

"They anchored here. I'm not sure exactly how, but—"

"If that kind of energy remains locked on us, that could cause far more problems than just those two being able to enter at will."

"Yeah." An uncomfortable silence fell between us. "Is their only vendetta against the Ætherim? Or are they planning something after that score is settled?"

Hosni looked surprised. "They intend to make this their home. They want a return to the old ways, of the far ancient cities."

"Of course they do. What is it with these powerful old fucks that want to destroy the world and rebuild it? They all want the same thing, every time. They're just power-hungry jerkoffs that can't accept that things change!" I ranted.

My hostess watched me with mild amusement.

"Sorry," I said, shaking out my hands as I paced. "That's been building up for a while."

"Indeed," she said, still with the ghost of a grin on her face. "It's true, regardless. This all had to come to a head eventually. After the Ancients were awakened, every other beast thought they would take their shot at freedom and power. A call went out that day, and I'm sure more will answer."

"Not the first time I've heard that rousingly positive speech," I grumbled.

She shrugged, unapologetic. "I truly hope you can resolve this."

As promised, as soon as our talk was done, I was shown on my way. Hosni gave me a small bundle of food and a water bottle. "More of a gesture, I suppose, since you lasted five days with nothing and it's only another two until you reach the village." A sideways smile, something I was coming to recognize as her hallmark. "I won't say you have an open invitation to return, but if you find yourself in our part of the desert again, I wouldn't be averse to sharing a pot of tea. Provided you come up with another alias that isn't later torn apart by some escaped demon." She laughed. "I am not sure if you noticed, but my grandmother really hates you."

"Thank you for your help and hospitality. I wish we'd been able to meet under different circumstances. And I sure hope the world doesn't end, because I'd like to take you up on that tea."

By the time I reached the tallest dune, Hosni and her family had already broken down their camp and were continuing on their way to whatever destination I had interrupted. The two days travel breezed by and before I knew it, I was arriving in a village. Now all I had to do was find a way back home.

If I'd ever forgotten how much I hated traveling overland the human way, getting home reminded me real quick. And once I reached home, I realized just how little I had left here.

I really hoped that Derfael was okay. I doubted the Matron would've let any harm come to him, seeing as he'd done nothing except keep me company after I returned from the Nyx. He hadn't aided my escape, other than giving me a heads-up. But I hoped she hadn't been able to figure that out.

I couldn't go back to my home, either one of them. They'd probably also look for me at Adrian's apartment and at Wolfe's. Maybe I would get lucky, and they would assume I just wouldn't come back, but it would be unlikely the Matron wouldn't take some measures to have my usual haunts watched.

Going to Percy or Ishani was out of the question. I didn't know where the majority of my other contacts or allies lived, nor would I just want to show up on their doorstep and ask to crash on their couch. There were a number of other safe houses around the city, but the council knew about all of them.

With that in mind, there was only one place that it made any sense for me to go. To the one place they would never expect to find me.

The warehouse on the river was even worse for wear than it had been the last time I'd seen it. The fence had been torn down, and all the makeshift memorials with it. It looked like tanks had rolled through here at some point and used the building for target practice.

I picked my way through the rubble, not looking for anything in particular except a good spot to set up as a makeshift shelter. The binding magick the Council had put on this place had worn off, and I hoped that also meant that any kind of surveillance they may have had on the area was no longer active.

There was a hollow in a corner that had been left standing even as the walls around it collapsed. A small section of catwalk still clung to the brick between the second and first floors. Piles of rubble shielded it from view from anywhere else on the property. It seemed as good a place as any to hide.

Now, I would just need to—

A scuffling noise made me pause. I glanced back over my shoulder, but didn't see anyone, and the noise stopped as soon as I moved. I slunk into the shadows, grabbing a knife and poising at the ready. My breathing instantly evened out, silent, even in the dead quiet.

Light steps, coming my way. I reached out my senses, trying to get a feel for whoever it was that was encroaching on my supposedly safe hiding place, but I cursed when I realized they were shielding themselves.

The steps neared, and I prepared to strike. I would have a fraction of a second to act as soon as the intruder appeared in my vision.

The new arrival moved forward at a steady pace, creeping closer. They would turn the corner any second and my knife would be the last thing they'd see.

A pale face with stark purple veins turned the corner, and my hand was already drawing back to strike, even as my brain caught up to my reflexes.

"Morgan?"

The geist jumped a mile in the air. "Gods!" She clasped a hand to her chest and realized it was me. "Evyn?"

I had already sheathed my knife, and she rushed forward, grabbing me into a hug. She was shaking, and when she pulled away, there were tears in her eyes. "I thought I killed you."

"What happened?" I asked. "After..."

Morgan wiped tears from her eyes and shook her head. "We should move. I've got a spot in a nearby building. They'll probably be along any minute now.

"Who?"

"The Council."

I huffed a laugh. "I don't think they'll be looking too hard, not right now anyway. Unless we become a problem, they'll leave us alone until the conflict lulls."

Morgan looked at me out of the corner of her eye. "I think you're underestimating how pissed they were when they sent Malcolm and his team to round you up. You are their bargaining chip. They need *you* in order to *lull* said conflict, and they won't give up on finding you."

Morgan led the way back to her makeshift camp in an abandoned building across the way, gaze darting back and forth as we hurried across the broken pavement of the old parking lot. As we climbed to the top floor, I quickly explained everything that happened after I entered into the lamia's realm.

Morgan listened to it all with increasing horror and when I was done, she rested her hand on my shoulder. "I'm so sorry, I really thought—"

Tears burned the backs of my eyes as I fought them down. I hadn't allowed myself to think about it overly much while I was trying to survive in the desert, but now that Morgan was here in front of me, a dark reminder of everything we'd sacrificed and gone through to try and save him, it was impossible not to come to a stark conclusion. With no way to track him... it might be time to admit he was gone. It had all been for nothing.

Morgan pushed aside a thin wooden door propped against the frame at the top of the stairwell. "Welcome to Chez Morgan."

"I like what you've done with the place," I said, looking around at the dilapidated space. The floor was covered in dirt and debris, old packing materials, and abandoned tools. Graffiti covered the walls and an old, scuffed up pentagram was poorly painted on a patch of concrete littered with plaster flakes off the ceiling.

"Are you hungry? I've got some food stashed."

"That would be great."

Morgan retrieved a box from underneath a pile of moldy cardboard. When she caught my expression, she gave me a wry smile.

"Didn't want anyone happening by and taking my stash. It's getting more dangerous to venture out."

The simple and true statement hit me harder than anything else had since I returned to the city.

We prepared a small meal on a propane stove and settled in to hash out the details of what we'd each been doing in the days since our failed attempt to rescue Adrian.

Just then there was the crackle of a portal opening on the outer border of the warehouse property. I looked at Morgan, but she didn't seem concerned, just moved to the window and cautiously peeked out.

"Council thugs," she confirmed. "Right on time."

I joined her at the window and saw three massive mages lumbering into the wreckage of the warehouse. They must not have expected me to still be there, because they weren't trying to be quiet.

"Should we—"

She cut me off before I could finish the question. "This place is shielded by my ghosts. They won't be able to detect us through the other signatures."

The mages poked around for a while before reappearing and walking back in the direction of the portal.

We settled back in and picked up where we left off. "So what happened to you?" I asked.

"The portal blew up in my face as soon as you were through and knocked me out cold, I don't even know for how long. It was dark when I woke up." Her eyes went distant as she remembered. "I tried everything I could think of to get a lock on you. I even tried to contact the spirits that sacrificed themselves, but you were gone. Completely off my radar." Her eyes teared up again as she looked at me. "I thought I'd never see you again."

I scooted over to sit beside her, but she waved off my concern. "Doesn't matter. You made it back." She elbowed me. "I'm starting to think you're unkillable."

"That's a theory far too many people are tempted to test lately," I said tiredly.

"I figured this would be the last place anyone would look for you, so I've been keeping an eye out. Just in case. I hadn't given up hope quite yet."

I smiled. "You're the real deal, Morgan. Never forget that. You could outpace half the chuckleheads on the Council without even trying."

Her cheeks reddened at the compliment, and she busied herself finishing her meal.

"So what do we do now?" I asked. "I hadn't thought the Council would be an immediate problem. There are some shielding techniques I can use, and your ghosts are always appreciated, but..."

She snorted. "They sure like having you around." A grin spread across her face, Mischievous Morgan returning. "We get into more trouble that way."

I worried my lip with my teeth. "I'll lose my mind without something to keep me busy."

Morgan appraised me. "There might be something." She set aside her plate. "Before I went rogue, I knew a few people who splintered off from the Council forces. They were sick of being used as cannon fodder."

"Resistance?" I asked.

She nodded. "But I understand if you're sick of the fighting."

"Of course I am. But it's what I do best." I looked at her, concerned. "Are you sure that's what *you* want? You have a really good chance of evading the Council and living a long life if you run."

"Don't be ridiculous," she scoffed. "After all this? I'm done being scared. It's time to fight back against all of them."

After a brief and restless sleep, we set out on the hunt. Morgan was confident they were hiding in one of the already hard-hit areas, but it seemed like the entire city fell under that classification now.

In the time we'd been away, the place I'd called home for almost two-hundred years had suffered catastrophic damage. Most of the outskirts had been demolished, and a large majority of the metro had been subjected to repeated firefights and artillery fire. There were still some poor souls stuck living here, but most daily life had ground to a halt.

The Council headquarters was still standing, in pristine condition, even though nobody was there anymore. They wouldn't risk losing their pride and joy, even though there are much better uses for their magick elsewhere.

The only people that roamed the empty streets with any regularity were marauding militias, looking for survivors to torment and anything of value to steal. Most of the military outposts that had been set up here had been removed or abandoned, the units being reassigned to other locations with active conflict.

It was the last place people would look for Resistance. Travel is easy with portals, and if they had even a moderate proficiency moving large numbers of people through them at once, they would have no reason to abandon their comfort zone.

The biggest question was, would they actually accept me into their ranks, or would they turn me over to the Council for a reward?

I laughed when I realized where Morgan was leading us. Belknap Park. There was a reason I had my safe house here, and the Resistance must've had the same idea. The overlook gave you a view of the city from a good height, and there were lots of high hills within the park itself to give a look out a huge heads-up if trouble were on its way.

Morgan stopped suddenly and I followed her lead, looking ahead into the shadow of a wooded area.

Five people in camo broke from the tree line, heading for us with weapons in plain view, but not trained on us. They stopped a good twenty feet away.

"Fuck, are you kidding me?" said a woman, angrily holstering her gun. She looked at Morgan. "You, I'm fine with, but her?" She cut her hand toward me like a machete.

I peered more closely at her and smiled. "Gina?"

She shot me a look before turning to her compatriots. "We're fine. It's Morgan and Urquhart."

Her companions stared at her, including a wide-eyed youngster, probably only a hundred-years-old. "How do you know Evyn Urquhart?" he asked.

"We go way back. Unfortunately."

"She's just mad because she washed out of the merc program," I said, teasing. I'd liked Gina a lot. She had great instincts, she was an excellent fighter. But she was soft. She could've been a perfect assassin if she hadn't let her feelings get in the way.

"What do you want?" she asked Morgan, ignoring me.

"To join you," said Morgan.

Gina and the others looked at us suspiciously. "Why?"

Morgan shrugged. "There's a war going on. We want to help."

"Last I heard, you were with the Council." Gina turned to me, a grin spreading across her face. "You on the other hand." Her rifle moved toward me, just a hair. "Excommunicated? We could hand you over for a hefty prize."

Dammit. That answers that question.

"I'm also on the list of the Council's least favorite people," said Morgan. "We're better assets to you on your team." She sniffed. "And do you really think the Council will give you anything but a bullet to the head for your trouble?"

Gina's smug smile withered and she drew the others a short way away. They spoke in whispers until they came to a consensus. "Fine. Follow us." She gave me a ghost of a smile, buried under her exhaustion. "There are others back at camp who will actually be *happy* to see you."

Chapter Nineteen

We were escorted into camp, a haphazard set of tents and other shelters of varying degrees of comfort scattered around. Depending on who set them up, and what magick they possessed, some of the accommodations were downright luxurious for a bunch of rogue fighters in the woods.

Gina stuck with us, but the others broke off to return to their posts. "You'll need to talk to Lyle first. He runs this outfit."

I nodded, looking around me as we went. A large figure caught my eye, and I did a double take. "Moshe!" I exclaimed, rushing toward the giant.

He turned with a confused look on his face that was quickly replaced with a huge smile gleaming through his bushy beard. "Evyn," he rumbled, sweeping me up in a backbreaking hug. "Just can't stay out of trouble, can you?" he asked, a humorous glint in his eye.

"Never," I said.

"Who's this?" he asked, motioning toward Morgan.

"I'm Morgan," she said, giving him a shy wave. "Nice to meet you."

Without preamble, Moshe swept her up in a hug that elicited a small squeak from her. When he put her down, she was bright purple in the face. He chuckled. "Any friend of Evyn's..."

Gina cleared her throat and Moshe glanced at her with just a slight roll of the eyes. "Shouldn't you be getting on with the patrol?" she asked.

"Sure, sure," he said, turning back me and Morgan. "I'll see you later. Come by my tent for dinner." He waved over to a large contraption of tarps. "Knock on the flap," he said, chuckling.

"Will do," I said.

"How do you know each other?" asked Morgan.

"We go way back," I said. "We were both training for Council enforcement positions, but he decided he didn't want to take orders from anyone. We still worked together often, and he was always like a big brother to me."

Morgan was staring at me curiously.

"What?" I asked.

"For all your talk of what a monster you used to be, you sure seem to be highly regarded by people you considered friends. Normally monsters don't get bear hugs and big smiles from people that knew them at their worst."

"I could also compartmentalize pretty well until the height of my awfulness."

Gina snorted. "For your friends, maybe. We all thought you were a bitch."

I looked at Morgan and jutted my thumb at Gina. "See?"

Morgan tutted.

We reached a hill that was buzzing with magick. All sorts of protections, alterations, concealments. Layer upon layer of security. Gina placed her hand on a large rock and a dull glow emanated from her hand before a tunnel into the hill appeared.

"Neat," I said.

"We try," said Gina dryly.

The three of us moved into the earthen mound, the tunnel entrance closing behind us. It was a short walk until we passed a couple of guards right before the tunnel opened into a cozy living space, warm with firelight.

A man was sitting in a green-tweed-upholstered chair, drinking coffee while he looked over a stack of handwritten papers piled on the side table and at his feet.

My first impression was of an English professor that went a bit off the wall and was forced to take a sabbatical. But when cold gray eyes flicked toward us and stared me and Morgan down with shrewd appraisal, I changed my mind. This man was dangerous and calculating.

"Lyle," said Gina, stepping in front of him. Her confidence wavered a little in this man's presence. "These women have an interest in joining us."

"Morgan?" he said, putting his papers aside. He cocked his head as he looked at me. "And Evyn Urquhart? An excommunicated traitor with a price on her head, and a deserter that the Council would also undoubtedly like to see returned to them?"

Apparently Lyle *had* gotten the memo about both of us.

"We just had this conversation with Gina," said Morgan. "I'll tell you the same thing. We're worth far more with the skills we're bringing to the table than anything you'd get from the Council."

Lyle sniffed. "You're not wrong. It's only a half million for both of you combined. Hardly worth it."

"That's it?" I asked, hurt.

Morgan patted my shoulder and kept a straight face when she said, "It's okay, sweetie, you know how cheap they are."

Lyle watched this interaction with mild bemusement. "Why should we take you in?"

I just blinked at him. "If I have to explain that to you in detail, we're clearly in the wrong place."

He stared at us for a moment longer before his face split into a grin. He splayed his hands. "Welcome to the family."

We'd only been there a couple of weeks, but Morgan and I quickly ingratiated ourselves to the group, building up enough trust that we were promoted in what ranks they had. There was a surprising shortage of strategists on the team, so that was where I made myself most useful. After several successful campaigns dealing harsh blows to the Known all over the Midwest, our outfit had become the bogeyman. We specialized in appearing out of nowhere, decimating the enemy, and disappearing just as fast, leaving nothing but confusion and chaos in our wake.

Morgan preferred scout duty. It gave her time alone to recharge. Every night we would meet back up in our shared tent, which wasn't as basic as it sounded. We managed to cobble together an impressive showing from the scavenged supplies that we found around the abandoned sections of the city.

This particular night, we'd just returned from another sneak attack on a contingent of militia that splintered off from the Known. These guys were the worst of the worst, only in it so they could cause havoc and pain. They searched for anybody still living in the city. If they appeared alone and vulnerable, well... let's just say, none of us felt bad about removing them from the equation.

The entire camp was celebrating, and we'd even broken out some of the remaining liquor we'd managed to squirrel away. Morgan and I were speaking with Lyle and Moshe when a woman rushed into camp, breathing hard, her cheeks flushed with excitement.

She spotted Lyle and made a beeline for us.

"I finally got word," she said.

Lyle's smile tightened and he motioned at me and Morgan. "Ladies, this is Veronica. She's our intel specialist."

"Spy, you mean?" I asked, raising my plastic cup in a cheers.

Veronica gave us a brief tilt of her head in acknowledgment before turning back to Lyle. "The nobles have decided to meet. They finally got the last two holdout families to join them. They're all going to be there at the same time."

I looked at Lyle, curious. "Why the interest?"

He didn't look me directly in the eye, already a concerning sign. He turned his full attention to Veronica and put an arm around her shoulder. "If you'll excuse us," he said, drawing them away. Veronica's smile faltered.

"What was that all about?" I asked Moshe, who was watching them with interest.

"I'm not sure," he hedged.

"You might as well tell us." I quirked an eyebrow. "I'll find out anyway."

He gave me a hard look, but realized there was no point in dissuading me. He sighed. "There was a plan at the very beginning, when we kept hearing about a gathering of nobles. Veronica was keeping an ear to the ground, hoping to find out more information on when it was happening. It's been so long since we've heard anything, I think Lyle was just about ready to give up." He cast a glance at their retreating forms. "It might be back on now."

"You're going to crash the party." It wasn't a question.

He nodded. "That's the idea. We infiltrate, hold them hostage for our demands."

My sudden reawakened worry for Tristan ignited a rush of fear in my chest, but I pushed it down. "Did I misunderstand when I thought we were fighting against the Known? Against the human threat? Why would they think going after the nobles would give them any kind of leverage for the aim they claim to have?"

Moshe looked suddenly guilty. "They have a dual purpose here. They want to eliminate the threat of the Known. But even though we're not Council loyalists by any means, none of us want the nobles to see the kind the power they used to have. It'll be a chance to make a statement."

"And what kind of statement are you trying to make?" I winced at my inability to keep the sharpness from my voice. "That despite the current dumpster fire, you're willing to make it all worse? That you don't care about finding stability as long as you get your message across? You don't have to like the nobility, but so far they've done nothing to display any kind of desire to resume their old ways."

"I know this is difficult to hear, what with the history between you and the chump—"

"Tristan and I are no longer a thing, haven't been for quite some time. And even if we were still together, I'm more than capable of keeping my objectivity. I'm no fan of theirs, and I'd be right with you in delivering some 'messages' to a few nobles in particular."

Sophia's face with her obnoxious smile swam into my mind and I wanted to smack that smirk right off her face. "But I still would never advocate doing what you're thinking of doing. If you want to go in somewhere and point guns in people's faces, why don't you aim that vitriol at Tafford and his cronies?" I shrugged. "Seems like it would serve you a lot better. Like it would serve all of us better. Maybe even give Strangers a morale boost."

"Evyn, I get it. We can't stand to see the worst in people we care about. But I'd bet you anything that they want to use this war as a cover to weasel back into power. This is our chance to ensure the Strangefells is ruled properly once this war is over. We can get a complete reset, without the bullshit politics or power plays."

"Do you not see the hypocrisy there?" I stared at my friend with new eyes. There had never been any hint that he felt this way.

"I don't know what to tell you, sis. If this plan works out, I'm going with them." An uncomfortable silence stretched out before us, and Moshe began to fidget. "Think about it, okay? If you come with us, you can keep the chump safe."

I inclined my head but said nothing, and he walked away.

Morgan's eyes were round with disbelief. "Are they insane?"

Several people looked around at us and Morgan blanched, leaning in and quieting her voice to a whisper. She drew us a few feet away. "I knew they favored some extreme tactics, but this?" She ran a hand through her hair and worried her bottom lip with her teeth. "What have I gotten us into?"

I shook my head. "It's not your fault. Gina never showed any sign of this kind of treachery when I knew her, either." I grinned at her. "If we hadn't joined them we wouldn't know about this. Happy accidents."

"So what do you want to do?"

"Whatever they think they're going to accomplish, I'm not going to let them do something incredibly stupid and risk everything falling apart." I caught Morgan's look out of the corner of my eye and pulled a face. "More than it already has."

Even as the thought formed, the butterflies in my stomach redoubled their mad fluttering. This was stupid, I couldn't just... but I had to. "I think it's time I paid Tristan a visit. There's just one small problem."

Morgan would've come with me if I'd asked, but I thought it would be too suspicious if both of us disappeared at the same time. I couldn't risk Lyle or any of the other leadership getting word of what I was going to do. Rumor was already spreading that I wasn't a fan of this idea, so everyone had become close-lipped about it.

I had no idea what their timeline was or even when the summit was supposed to be planned. But, since it took so long for Veronica to get intel on it, I'm guessing the only reason she got word was because it was happening soon. The closer an event gets, the more people become involved, and the harder it is to keep secrets.

Tristan could be anywhere in the world right now, but then I remembered my link with Jake. He was my guardian, we would always be connected.

I'd never tried to find someone, let alone a canine this way before, but as I found a quiet place to sit and focus, I fell into the magick easily enough.

An hour or two passed of my sending out a call and hoping Jake would hear it before I finally got a bite. He was confused, and then I felt joy blossom through the connection as it strengthened. Tears sprang to my eyes. It had been months since I'd been in the presence of that happiness. That pure, unrelenting, unconditional love.

Making the connection was the easy part, turns out. Even though the guardian inhabiting Jake's body was a higher being, I was still basically communicating with a really smart dog. His brain didn't work the same way, and getting a lock on the location through the images and thoughts Jake imagined would be most helpful really weren't.

But eventually, we got everything nailed down, and I hoped that Tristan wouldn't suspect. I didn't think he'd go out of his way to avoid me or keep me out, especially if the sisters were the ones that had been blocking his messages, but I didn't want to find out the hard way.

Jake loved to go for shorter strolls several times a day, so there was a good chance that would provide me a moment alone with him.

"Can we go over the plan one more time?" Morgan asked. It was late and we were both ready for bed, but I nodded.

"After you leave for sentry duty, I'll find an opening to slip away. I'll find a good portal to use and hope the Council doesn't sense it—"

She snapped her fingers. "That's it."

"What?"

"I was trying to think of a solution for the Council tracing you through the portal."

I raised my eyebrows. "What did you come up with?" Her ghosts had been occluding us so far, but that only kept me safe as long as Morgan was around.

She grabbed a bottle of water off the card table we'd set up in the "dining room" and motioned for me to roll up my sleeve. She sprinkled some water on her hand and drew a quick rune I didn't recognize on my forearm.

A few hushed words of power and the rune glowed briefly before disappearing. I didn't feel any different.

"What did you do?" I asked.

She smiled triumphantly. "I just gave you a temporary bodyguard. Mrs. Clements, if you're curious. She can be a bit much, but she's solid."

I felt a strong sense of ire wash over me, but they weren't my feelings. I looked at Morgan, my ears peeling back in discomfort. "So there's an actual ghost around me right now? And I can feel her emotions?"

She nodded, her smile brightening. "Neat, huh?"

No. No, it was not. It was creepy. Interacting with the dead and being bound to a ghost are two very different things.

Morgan waved off my unspoken concern. "It's temporary," she reminded me. "When you pass through that portal, your signature will be occluded and the Council will never know."

"Damn," I said, examining my arm with renewed interest. "Where have you been all my life?"

She flushed at the compliment.

The next day, I kept careful watch on the group that remained in camp, waiting for my opening. It finally came when Lyle and several of the other leadership disappeared into the meeting hall.

I snuck away and moved quickly to the second closest portal to our location. I didn't want to risk anyone following me. There were ways to figure out where a portal had recently opened to, and I didn't want to lead them right to Tristan's doorstep. Hopefully, they wouldn't even know I was gone, but why take the chance?

In the blink of an eye, I was gone.

Chapter Twenty

When I stepped out of the portal, I could see for miles around me in any direction, a breathtaking view. The manor up ahead had a distinctly medieval vibe to it. Tristan's family had built it, and he'd just recently reacquired it around the time we'd moved into our house together, but I'd never been.

I wasn't sure if it was just him staying here, or if others were here as well. I couldn't get that kind of information from Jake, at least not in a way that I understood it. For all I knew at this point, they could be holding the summit itself here, and I could be walking into a hornet's nest of nobles and their security, along with every ounce of the paranoia that ran rampant with those people. Although, the paranoia wasn't undeserved, especially with at least one resistance group after them that I was aware.

I was in a vineyard easily able to duck down among the rows of vines to stay hidden from the walls of the manner. There would still be several hundred yards of open space to cross before I reached the high walls of the property itself. It was a fortress, the high walls surrounding it clearly made for defense.

I appraised my surroundings and what I had to work with. It was already late in the day, so I wouldn't have much to lose if I hung out until dusk. Their security would undoubtedly be set to destroy any attempts at shielding, so the low light would make the crossing easier. A few adjustments to my concealment cloak and I could blend into my surroundings instead of trying to hide completely.

There was a small barn, more of a shed really, at the far end of the vineyard. I made my way over to it, keeping a wary eye for anyone that might still be hanging around. The workday must've ended already as there was no one in sight, but some of the machinery was still warm to the touch. It was dark, but only somewhat cooler in the shade of the barn and I hunkered down between two piles of straw to wait.

I must've dozed off, because when I woke, the sunset was in its last moments before it sank down beneath the horizon completely. The perfect time to cross.

The concealment cloak draped around me, and I altered it to shed light instead of neutralizing it. If anybody caught sight of my movement and really stared at me, it would look like a patchy blob of air bobbing around the field. It would be enough to raise suspicions, but at least it wouldn't get me caught outright.

After using my Sight to check my surroundings once again, I made my way in a quick but casual pace across the open field. The fortress loomed ahead of me, the walls a bloody red in the last light of the sun. I stayed close to the battlements as I traced my way around, reaching an imposing gate at the front. The heavy iron portico was raised, and I slipped through without incident onto a gravel drive that wound to an impressive entryway already packed with expensive cars.

"Shit." This must've been the location of the summit after all. Unless Tristan had truly changed that much and was collecting high-end vintage cars. I would need to tread much more carefully. If I got caught skulking around by a paranoid noble's security team, this was going to get messy.

I kept to the shadows until full dark surrounded me. Cheery lights clicked on one by one in the manor windows, warm and inviting. The front doors swung open and a small collection of people, laughing and chatting among themselves with alcohol-fueled excitement, headed toward their vehicles.

They piled into three cars of the dozen or so that were there, and I had to rush for cover as the headlights swung across the grounds. Once the sound of tires on gravel had faded away, and I could no longer hear the engine rumbling, I poked my head out of hiding and moved closer to the home.

It seemed like forever had passed since I'd seen Tristan, and the idea of meeting him again, especially under these circumstances, only added to my nerves. I didn't know what to expect, and I hated that. Malea and Amara had influenced the majority of our breakup, but I was still being a lousy partner. Maybe they really did only hasten the inevitable and getting my hopes up that all would be forgiven would only lead to worse heartache.

Guilt gnawed at me at the thought that Adrian was out there somewhere, after we'd rekindled our relationship, and I was pining after my ex. The moment

I thought I still had a chance to fix things with Tristan, I knew that's what I wanted to do. But how could I break Adrian's heart again?

Slow down, I thought to myself. *He may have moved on, and you'll just have to live with that if he has.*

Lights spilled out onto the grass and illuminated quite a bit of the yard. Brief glances inside as I skirted the square-window-shaped puddles of light showed mildly elaborate furnishings, leaning toward comfort over luxury.

The sound of a door opening above me made me freeze. Two voices were chatting lowly, the murmurs carrying across the dark grounds. I risked a glance and saw the glow of a cigarette, letting out a sigh of relief. Just a smoke break. I hadn't been spotted.

I waited until they'd gone back inside before I continued my trek to the back of the house, which was where I had it on Jake's good authority that Tristan mostly took him for walks. The gardens in the back were quite beautiful. Fairy lights were strung between the trees lining the main pathway. Roses were everywhere, along with arbors of climbing, flowering vines, the build of which reminded me of the one that had been destroyed at our house.

I picked a spot just out of sight of the trail that Jake had shown me. It was the one they most often traversed. Now all I had to do was wait.

And it didn't take long. Pretty soon I heard the click of a door opening, and the rush of sound from a party within before the sound of four paws prancing along the manicured pathways, accompanied by a set of dress shoes, met my ears. A sigh of relief slid between my lips that I wouldn't have to get rid of a certain countess.

Suddenly, my heart was in my throat, pulse pounding madly. What would he say? What would he do? He probably thought I'd cut him out of my life, same as I'd thought of him. Only to his mind, he'd been making every attempt to contact me, and I'd been ignoring him. That was so much worse than not reaching out at all.

Jake was hurrying in my direction, and I knew he caught my scent when he barked and took off running. Tristan called after him. Hearing his voice again took me by surprise. It hadn't changed except that maybe it sounded a bit more tired than usual. What hit me so hard was how much I'd missed it. Tears sprang to my eyes hearing that baritone again. All my sadness and heartbreak welled up like it had never faded and by the time Jake barreled into me, I was a blubbering mess.

Jake's keening, happy whine was music to my ears as I wrapped my arms around him, his dancing feet and tail making it very hard to hang on for a hug. He finally pulled me over, and flattened me under his weight, pinning me down as he licked my face.

"Jake, what are you—" Tristan's footsteps halted, and the sudden tension made Jake pause as well. I looked around to find him staring down at me, mouth agape, a mixture of hurt and anger on his face.

I tapped Jake on the shoulder and he rolled off me. As I got to my feet, Jake sat next to me, pressing into my legs for comfort as Tristan and I stared at each other.

"Hi," I said, offering a shy smile.

He didn't respond.

"There's something you need to know," I said. I hoped my tone came off soft and casual, but my heart was thundering so fast, I'm not sure what I sounded like.

Tristan's face slid into a smooth, expressionless mask. "I have nothing to discuss with you." He turned to walk away, but before I could protest, Jake barked low with warning. I've never heard him bark at anyone he knew in that threatening a manner before.

Tristan turned back around slowly, and Jake pawed the ground with an angry swipe, his message clear that the man better stay put. Jake's weight pressed harder into my legs, and I was grateful for the support.

"I didn't know you were reaching out," I blurted.

A flash of surprise crossed his face, but he quickly hid it.

"I've had multiple run-ins with the sisters since you left. They made it their mission to tear my life apart. They admitted they pushed you to leave, and they blocked all of your attempts at communication with me. I thought you'd just gone silent, that you weren't interested anymore." I laughed, thick with derision. "And I was pissed at you for not having the decency to tell me it was over. And furious that you'd taken Jake." My words were laced with obvious pain.

Tristan's anger faded and he took an involuntary step forward before stopping himself, his fists clenching at his sides.

"They took Adrian. They killed my team, they helped people destroy our house, and now I'm being hunted by the Council," I said, voice cracking. Jake whined and looked up at me. "I tried to save Adrian. I was so close, but we were separated." A tear escaped, despite my best efforts. In the last month I'd had to confront more feelings than in my entire lifetime, and it was just too much. What do people do with emotions like this? "I should've just given them what they wanted."

Tristan's resolve broke, and he stepped forward, wrapping his arms around me. It felt like coming home.

All my walls came tumbling down, and I sagged in his arms, sobbing. There was so much more I needed to tell him, and there wasn't much time, but I couldn't bring myself to leave the safety of his embrace.

He stroked my hair, whispering comforting words as I calmed myself, his familiar scent surrounding me.

"Is there somewhere we can go to talk?" I asked, finally releasing him.

He stared into my eyes, and I was hopeful at the spark of longing I saw there. He finally tore his eyes away and looked back at the house.

"They won't be expecting me for a little while."

He led the way to a bench hidden in a grotto. The night-blooming jasmine and moonflowers were unfurled and fragrant, and he waited for me to take a seat before following suit. He didn't sit at the very farthest edge, but he left plenty of space between us.

I nervously tucked a strand of hair behind my ear and leaned forward to pet Jake. If I just focused on him, I could ignore the fluttering in my chest and the preoccupation with Tristan's presence.

"How have you been?" he ventured.

I looked at him askance. "Do they not have news here?" I asked gently, somewhat hoping he didn't know.

"Yeah, we do," he said sheepishly. "I don't know why I asked that," he ran his hand through his hair. He hesitated, and I knew what he wanted to ask.

"I didn't do it. The DIWR attack. It wasn't me. And the murders on the Riverwalk…" I shrugged, helpless. "I don't remember it. Malea and Amara possessed the attackers, and that's the last thing I remember. I clearly did it, but I don't know how or why it turned that brutal."

Jake rested his head on my knee. I stroked his blaze, eyes tearing up again with how much I'd missed him.

"Who was the guy you were walking with that night?" He kept his tone nonchalant, but I had to tamp down the immediate bristle. Really? That's where you're taking this conversation?

"A fae lord. I'd met him about a week before that night. He was a great listener, and I had a lot of baggage to unpack."

Tristan nodded, and there was a lightening in the lines around his eyes. Was he asking out of genuine curiosity and not jealousy? However, it did open the door...

"I saw a photo of you at that gala." I searched around for a date. Time was still a little confused since the Nyx. "About a month ago. You looked well."

He gave a soft snort. "I hate those parties. Absolutely miserable, but necessary." He shot me a glance. "I'm guessing you saw Sophia with me?" He sounded... embarrassed.

"She is stunning, nobody can deny that," I said.

He groaned. "She's also painfully shallow and difficult to work with." Jake grunted in agreement and Tristan and I laughed. "But she's been instrumental in getting everyone onboard. It's out of duty, not enjoyment, that I attend these events with her."

Some of the pressure in my chest eased, and I nodded.

"Someone else did come into my life, though," he said, voice quiet.

I stared down at Jake, readying myself for the devastation. At least I hadn't lost him to Sophia.

"It started a lot like your relationship with the fae lord. We talked for hours every day. Then it turned into something more. But she left."

I started and looked at him. He took a sudden interest in his cuticles. "I think she could tell I wasn't ready for someone else. Not really."

I chewed my lip, able to relate to that wholeheartedly and feeling no end of guilt over it. One confession for another. "Adrian and I reforged the bond, right before..."

He stiffened but nodded. "I'm glad," he said, forcing a smile. "What you've been through, I'm glad you weren't alone."

I paused. "I wound up in the Nyx, Tris."

He inhaled sharply and Jake pressed against my legs, looking up at me with his soulful brown eyes. "What? How did you make it back?"

"I came to some hard truths." I swiped at a tear and barked a shaky laugh. "Wouldn't recommend the process." I sobered and Tristan placed a tentative hand on my back. "But I played right into the sister's hands. They needed me to pass through to the Nyx so my bond with æther was solidified."

"What?" he asked sharply. "Æther? Since when—"

"We have a lot to talk about," I said, holding up my hand to stay his questions. "And I will tell you everything when we have more time."

He slid over and pulled me to him, resting his chin on my head. "I never should have left you." Guilt wracked his voice.

I shook my head and pulled away, touching his cheek gratefully before letting my hand drop. "Yes, you should have. I wasn't in a good place, and I was dragging you down with me. You deserve to be happy, too." A lump rose in my throat. "This was going to happen one way or the other. If you hadn't left, they would've killed you. And I wouldn't have been able to do a damn thing to stop them."

"It wasn't even a week before I regretted it," he said. "Then when my attempts to reach out never got an answer—I thought the same thing you did. Only in my mind, you never cared at all."

A strangled cry caught in my throat. "You really thought that?" I asked, horrified.

"My thoughts were so scattered then. And the more I look back on those last few months we were together, the more I realize I'm missing big chunks of time. Memories are either gone or so fuzzy that they don't seem real. I'll look back at notes and my day planner and can't recall any of it."

I nodded. "The same for me with things like our anniversary dinner. Whenever you'd make plans, I *would not* remember it until it was too late. Stress was my go-to explanation, but I only ever outright forgot things when it involved us. And then I just figured it was my usual self-sabotaging of everything good. I tried so hard just to fail you again, and I hated the pain I was causing you."

Tristan rested his hand on my cheek and leaned in, touching his forehead to mine. I closed my eyes and put my hand over his, letting myself get lost in the moment. The breeze wafted the scent of the gardens around us and rattled the leaves in the trees. The tall grasses shushed.

"I need to tell you what I've discovered," I whispered. "I've probably already been here too long."

He sighed, pulling back and nodding, but he took both my hands in his.

"The summit you're holding?" I began.

His gaze sharpened and flicked back toward the house. "How do you know about that?"

"Word got out. There's an attack being planned by a resistance group I joined up with. They're going to attack and hold the summit hostage as a political statement. They want to press the reset button on our entire Council system. They'll try to execute you if you give them the chance. You have to call it off."

He shook his head. "That's not an option."

"Why?"

He chewed his lip, deciding on an answer. "It's not just a summit. It's a peace talk."

I blinked rapidly. "Peace talk? I thought the humans were confident of a victory?"

"It's not going as well for them as they'd hoped. Like I said, Sophia is the best I've ever seen at political maneuvering. She probably knew before the humans did that their momentum was fading fast. Superior weapons don't count for much if they don't actually succeed in killing the people they're aimed at. Our numbers are holding strong, despite everything."

I let out a burst of breath and smiled so genuinely, it hurt my face. "That's the best news I've heard in a long time."

"So you can see why calling it off isn't an option?"

My gaze ambled around at nothing in particular as I thought. "Then I'll just have to make sure the resistance can't get anywhere near here."

Chapter Twenty-One

Leaving Jake and Tristan was one of the hardest things I've ever had to do. As soon as I stepped out of the portal, I hurried back to camp. Everything looked the same as it had been. Nobody rushing around, no guards looking intent on finding someone.

The couple of people I did see as I moved through camp almost went out of their way to ignore me. *That* made me nervous.

When I reached our tent, Morgan hadn't returned from sentry duty. I thought about taking a nap, the exhaustion starting to overwhelm me along with everything else, but my thoughts were too rattled to let me sleep. The sinking sensation in my gut wasn't helping either. It was too quiet around here. Something wasn't right.

At last, I heard steps outside the tent, and Morgan appeared a second later. She paused when she saw me. "Back already?"

With a brief glance out of the tent flap, I said, "Let's take a walk." I didn't want to chance being overheard. Once we were deep enough in the woods and I didn't sense any sentries around us, I stopped.

I quickly filled her in on the pertinent aspects of my conversation with Tristan. We may have been close friends, but I wasn't ready to unpack my emotional turmoil with her yet.

She didn't even bat an eye. "What's the plan?"

I smiled. "When did you become such a bad-bitch warrior? The Morgan I first met was always so shy and reserved."

Some of her humor faded. "She's seen some things."

That, she had.

"Just stopping Lyle and Gina won't eliminate the issue entirely," I said. "I don't know what other networks they're connected to that might take their place. Do you?"

"No," she said, brow furrowing. "Can we redirect them? Or we could sabotage their portal. I've got a few spirits that would be more than willing to take on the job."

The last time her spirits had attempted to intervene with inter-dimensional transportation, everything went to shit and I wound up in the middle of the desert. Granted, it was going bad already, and they probably saved my life, but still... it was just too unpredictable.

"Maybe," I said, not wanting to completely shut down the idea just yet. Those circumstances had been less than ideal, and maybe with a little more planning, things could go smoothly next time.

"What if we—"

Morgan's head snapped to the side as her gaze homed in on something I couldn't see. "Did you hear something?" she asked.

I shook my head, listening. Nothing.

She studied the area for another second before turning back to me. "I could've sworn—" She stopped again, only this time she darted off into the woods.

I took off after her and we sprinted for about a hundred yards before she stopped. Morgan looked around her again, like she was trying to re-orient herself.

"What do you see?" I asked, still not sensing anything myself.

She held up a finger and I quieted. Morgan closed her eyes and focused. She turned, seeking without sight, before finding what she was looking for. She stalked forward with an intense purpose and I followed warily.

At the very edge of my consciousness, I thought I could sense...

Couldn't be, I thought, shaking my head. There was a faint sense of him, of Adrian. Far in the distance, I could just hear the faint shuffling of footsteps, stumbling through leaves and twigs. The steps would pause every so often before starting up again, painfully slow.

I sprinted off.

"Evyn, wait!" called Morgan, but I ignored her. I dashed through the woods toward the source of the noise finally spotting a figure up ahead. In my shock, I missed a tree root, catching my foot on it and sprawling onto the ground. I heard Morgan's sharp intake of breath behind me as she saw him.

"Adrian!" I shouted, pushing to my feet and jogging toward him. It was like watching a zombie. Every movement was jerky and unstable. His flesh was mangled and covered in blood. He fixed confused, empty eyes on me and then it was like the puppeteer cut his strings. He fell straight down, and I caught him just before he hit the ground.

I crouched down next to him and checked for a pulse. It was thready and faint, but it was there. Morgan helped me ease him down gently.

"I need to go check something out. Are you okay?" she asked.

"Yeah, go ahead." I nodded, all my attention on Adrian, barely even registering it as she moved off.

He was bleeding profusely from a wound in his stomach, and I ripped off my sweatshirt, pressing it down hard to staunch the flow while I evaluated his other injuries for anything else major.

The rest of his wounds that I could see appeared superficial, and a quick scan internally showed most of the damage in his abdomen. Moving the sweatshirt out of the way, I grabbed my triage kit off my belt and snatched the poultice from its baggie. I stuffed the wound full of it before laying my hands over top and chanting words of healing.

I repeated it until the wound knit itself together. Blood stopped gushing freely and I continued until it and the internal damage was healed enough to focus on the rest of his injuries.

He was covered in blood from head to toe and some of the sigils they'd etched into his skin were getting infected. For that to have happened, meant they must have blocked his healing somehow.

I pushed matted hair from his face. He was almost unrecognizable. I laid my hand on his cheek and his eyes opened a fraction. But there was no hint of recognition anywhere.

"Adrian?" I asked.

He tried to speak but his voice wouldn't come to him. Finally, he gave up and closed his eyes, and I felt him slip back into unconsciousness.

"How's it going?" asked Morgan, jogging back out of the woods. She stared down at Adrian in shock. "The sisters did this to him?"

"Yeah," I said, teeth grinding with anger. "There's a stream around here, isn't there?" I asked. "I can't see what I'm doing with all this blood."

"This way," she said, helping me pick him up. We hadn't gone too far before I heard the gently running trickle of water.

After we set him down, Morgan looked at the blood on her hands and held her fingers to her nose. "There's poison in there. It's degraded, but it's still strong."

I made a mental note to ask her later about how she could smell poison in blood. For now, I had to figure out how to solve the problem. "I've got salt in my kit, but it's not gonna do us any good with running water like this."

"Hold on a minute," she said, and she got that dazed look in her eye that I'd come to realize was how she looked when she communicated with her spirits. Getting her answer from her panel of experts, she knelt at the edge of the stream and placed her hands in the freezing water. Earth started to move, mounding up in ridges and forming a shallow bowl, about the size of a bathtub.

"You can move earth, too?" I could do something similar, but it always involved a shitload of kinetic energy, and I couldn't mold it nearly as neatly as this.

"Sometimes, if I let my spirits come forth and use my body, they can channel some of their abilities through me."

I guess that kind of answered my previous question too, but my mind still had a hard time wrapping around it. I removed the salt from my pouch and dumped it into the water, chanting a few quick words to heat the water as well as sterilize it, and to activate the cleansing powers of the salt.

I looked at Morgan, grimly. This next part was going to be ugly.

She nodded and helped me lift him once again. We stepped into the water on either side of the newly formed basin and slowly lowered him in. When his body made contact with the pool his eyes snapped open and he screamed, clawing at me to let him go.

I threw up a hasty bubble to prevent his screams from drawing unwanted attention. I gritted my teeth, glad that Morgan could pin his legs. He'd hurt himself thrashing like this. Steam erupted from his skin as the poison evaporated from the wounds.

After a couple of minutes he stopped screaming and fighting, quieting to small, pained whimpers. I nodded to Morgan and she released him, staying close just in case.

With gentle hands, I washed him, taking note of each wound and debating how to heal the damage. I didn't have access to my usual store of medicinal herbs, and I couldn't risk taking him back to camp.

The water was a murky red by the time I was done, the steam dissipating completely. Morgan swept clear a patch of ground before helping me lift him out again.

"What do you need from me?" she asked.

"Are you able to heal these surface runes?" I asked, pointing to the shallow cuts all over his body. Most of them were nonmagickal, just the sisters' way of leaving their signatures.

"Yes," she said, crouching down next to him and starting to work.

Locating the sigil that cut off his regenerative ability wasn't hard to spot. It was carved so deep against his ribs, it exposed the bone. Knitting together tissue was one thing, but this rune oozed a vile magick. I'd have to break the hex before I could remove it. Only then would his body start healing on its own.

I touched my hand to the wound and began to chant, throwing out stronger and stronger commands, but nothing happened. I drew up more power and pummeled the hex with every counter curse I knew. Still nothing.

"Evyn," said Morgan. She had finished healing the other runes already and was going to work correcting the broken bones. "Maybe you should try the æther again."

"What? I can't risk that," I said, shaking my head vehemently.

"It might be the only way. And you don't have to draw much." She pulled Solomon's ring out of the pouch she kept it in. "I think the only thing that went wrong is that you didn't use the ring as a focus. From the way you describe it, it sounded like you assumed it was an amplifier, or even the source. But it's supposed to help you channel the æther, and give you the ability to command it."

I stared at the ring. "There are so many things that can go wrong. He's already survived so much, I don't want to risk killing him."

"Understandable," she said with a small smile. "But I believe you can do it." She pushed the ring at me, and I took it with shaking hands. I placed it on my left index finger and some of that wildness and restlessness inside me that had become a constant companion, settled.

With a deep breath, I rested my left hand on his side and opened up that channel just a tiny way. Solomon's ring grew warm against my skin as I imparted my will upon it, ordering the æther to stay at a steady trickle as it flowed from my fingers and into the wound.

This time whatever was holding the sigil in place gave way and the wound glowed a bluish-gold. Adrian moaned and his eyes flitted around beneath the lids. The hex broke with a flash of light and the æther siphoned away all the remaining magick in it. The rune healed, sealing up and disappearing, like it had never been there.

The instant it was gone Adrian moaned loudly but still remained unconscious. I breathed a sigh of relief. His body was so desperate to heal itself that it did so faster than I'd ever seen.

Adrian's breathing eased and the tension in his muscles drained a bit. Just a small fraction, but gone nonetheless.

There was one final sigil remaining. As a fail-safe, they'd added a sigil that attempted to sever our ties, to hide him from me, no matter where he was. It was already starting to fail, since I had felt his presence before we found him in the woods. But as long as it existed, our connection would never be able to regenerate.

By this time Adrian looked almost normal again except for the gaping wound right over his heart. I leaned close to study it and I could see the bottom of the wound pulsing, just a hairsbreadth of tissue between his heart and the open air.

Morgan and I were both drained at this point, but I readied myself for the plunge.

I channeled æther into it, using the same procedure as last time. The wound gave off a foul black vapor and a bright red hue formed around the edges. Sweat was rolling down my face, the effort of controlling the æther getting more difficult by the second. I felt more than saw Morgan place her hand on my shoulder, channeling some of her own energy into me to keep me from passing out. My vision blurred as the sigil kept resisting my attempt to heal it. I guided more æther into it, faster now. The red light pulsing at the edges began to turn golden blue. Finally, the æther broke through and the foul smoke whirled up in a small tornado before it disappeared. The skin healed over, and I collapsed backward, taking Morgan with me.

The bond returned with such force that Adrian's eyes flew open, and he gasped before falling back into unconsciousness.

"That was impressive."

Morgan and I spun around, hands going to our weapons. Lyle, Gina, and a handful of others had snuck up on us. I crouched in front of Adrian, ready to defend him to the death if it came to it.

"Calm down," said Lyle. "You're in no position to fight. Can you even stand?"

He was right, but I wasn't going to tell him that.

Lyle smirked. "Just come back to camp with us. We're not gonna hurt you. We'll set you up somewhere comfortable so you can keep an eye on your boy there."

"Why?" I asked, beyond suspicious.

"I can't let you interfere with our plan, but you're also too much of an asset to kill. So that's your option. Come back with us willingly, or we drag you back. Neither of you is in a position to argue."

I shared a glance with Morgan and her lips thinned as she gave me a sharp nod. She holstered her weapon, and I did mine.

"Good choice," he said, motioning to the rest of his group. They moved forward and fanned out around us. Two of them picked up Adrian and the others kept their guns trained on me and Morgan as they escorted us back to camp.

Their comfortable accommodations ended up being Lyle's living quarters. He wouldn't need them. The entire group was moving out, preparing for their assault on the summit.

"Don't worry now, you just sit tight. As soon as our work is done, I'll come back and we can talk terms," he'd explained right before he sealed us up in the hill. "Wouldn't want you to die in this hole without giving you a chance to see that we're doing the right thing here." His cruel grin was the last thing I saw before the door closed.

The weight of the enchantments sunk around this place was impressive. Every magi on the team must've contributed something to it.

It wouldn't have done any good to explain that the summit was actually meant to discuss a peaceful resolution to this war. Nor would it matter if I told him they knew he was coming. That would probably make it worse because instead of storming in and taking hostages, he'd attack with everything he had and obliterate everyone there, noble or not.

I paced back and forth, going out of my mind.

"You've already checked for weaknesses five times over every inch of this place," said Morgan. "You're making me tired just watching you."

"I can't just sit," I said. "I told Tristan I wouldn't let this happen. I failed. Again!"

Morgan stood and put her hands on my shoulders. "You didn't fail. Tristan upped security, he's taken precautions. You know he has. This doesn't all fall on you. And Lyle may be unhinged, but he's not a mass murderer. There's still hope."

"But I'm stuck in here!" I said, slamming my fist against the wall. The paneling dented but that was the worst of the damage I could do. "He could be dying—"

I broke off, choking on a sob and shooting a guilty glance at Adrian.

Morgan guided me over to the lumpy sofa, rubbing my back.

"Every turn," I said, raging. "Every fucking turn, something goes wrong! I just want to protect the people I love!"

My gaze lingered on Adrian this time and the tears that had been threatening to escape finally made a break for it.

"He suffered so much," I said. "Because of me. If I hadn't—"

"Hadn't what? Reforged the bond? Made yourselves stronger? Looked for comfort and support when you thought Tristan had truly left you? You were trying to move forward with your life. There's nothing wrong about that." The vehemence in her voice surprised me.

"He doesn't deserve to get his heart broken again," I said.

"Maybe not," said Morgan, gently. "But you can't lie to him either."

"He's going to hate me," I said, biting my lip, still staring at his unconscious form.

"Are you sure?" she asked.

I finally looked at her. "Why wouldn't he?"

There was pity in her gaze. "I know you think you're good at hiding emotion, and you usually are. But not when it comes to Tristan. Just a mention of his name and you looked haunted, and so sad. It's obvious to everyone that you still love him." She nodded toward Adrian. "And I'm positive it was to him, too."

She gripped my hand. "You were both trying to convince yourselves you could go back to the way things were. You love each other, I don't doubt it, but..." She shrugged.

We lapsed into silence. My mind was still spinning and the only things I had to focus on to keep the crushing anxiety at bay was waiting for Adrian to wake up and trying to figure out how Lyle found us.

I kept staring at the bed where Adrian was laying. "Where did you go?" I asked.

"What?"

"When you said you had to check on something. Where did you go?"

"My spirits were the ones that brought him back. I needed to check that the portal they used was closed."

I blinked. "How?"

She shook her head. "I'm not entirely sure. Nothing about what we did that day makes a whole lot of sense to me. The best story I can cobble together—their minds got a bit scrambled in the process—is that the spirits that helped you escape the lamia stayed with Adrian wherever he wound up. They made sure he got back here. It was the one goal they had that kept their minds from dissolving completely. Once they got back here, they lost whatever grip they had left. That's what first drew my attention. I could hear them screaming."

"What happened to them?"

She shook her head sadly. "They crossed over. Permanently. I guess we have an answer though. They weren't destroyed by feeding themselves to that portal, but they did lose a good chunk of themselves. There wasn't enough left to save."

"So in the end they were destroyed anyway?" I asked.

"Yes," she said, sighing heavily. "But at least their energy wasn't trapped in some kind of hellscape, so we can be grateful for that." She blinked, realization dawning, and looked at me. "Did you think that I went to find Lyle?"

I ducked my head. "You disappeared and he showed up a little while later. I didn't know what to think."

A flicker of anger crossed her face. "Adrian was also screaming before you put that bubble around us. Anyone in a ten-mile radius probably heard it."

"I know. And that's what I was hoping it was. But—" There really wasn't a good way to end that sentence, so I let it drop. "I'm sorry for suspecting you."

Her hard look softened a bit. "I guess you're not really a stranger to betrayal." She grinned. "I'll forgive you this once. Don't let it happen again."

Adrian stirred and we both rushed over to his side. His eyes opened, and this time they didn't have that vacant nothingness in them. He looked around, every movement stiff. "Where am I?" he asked. His voice was gruff and unused.

"We're being held prisoner at the moment. But I'm working on a way out."

Morgan shot me a look, knowing full well that was a lie.

He nodded, his gaze finally settling on me again. "Who are you?"

"I'm Morgan," she answered. "We've never formally met."

Adrian turned and looked at her with a quick nod of his head before turning back to me. "And you are?"

I gave him a disbelieving stare. "Adrian, that's not funny."

"Well, then it's a good thing I'm not joking," he said, pulling a face.

"Evyn. I'm Evyn. I'm your familiar." I put my hands on his face, peering into his eyes. "You really don't remember me?" I pushed against the bond, hoping he would feel it and remember.

He moved my hands away. "No, why should I? I don't have a familiar." He looked back and forth between me and Morgan. "I don't know either of you." He looked down at himself. "And why the hell am I naked?"

"You were kidnapped, half dead when you found your way here. We healed you." I expected that to knock his memories loose for some reason, but I knew that was a foolish thing to hope for.

"Then I owe you thanks for that," he said with a frigid detachedness. "Are there any spare clothes around here?"

I could only nod, numb and with an ever-growing feeling of dread. Morgan gripped my arm, sensing I was about to lose it.

"Well? Where are they?" he asked, narrowing his eyes and giving me nothing but a mistrustful glare.

I pointed toward a chair with a folded pile of clothing on it. He shuffled over, his movement pained.

Morgan attempted to intervene. "Why don't we just sit down and talk. A lot has happened. I'm sure there are a few things we can figure out."

Adrian struggled into the pair of pants, and wrenched the shirt over his head. "Thank you for your help with whatever it was that happened, but I'm leaving."

"We literally can't leave. We are trapped here. That wasn't an exaggeration," I said. "And where would you go?"

"To the Strangefells. Where I live." He brushed past us and made a circuit of the room. "Where's the damn door?"

"Are you not understanding words? I said we are trapped," I said, clapping my hands for emphasis.

How was this happening? Had I made a mistake somewhere? Was this another side effect of the æther that I hadn't anticipated?

Adrian gave up on his search for a door and sat heavily in the chair that the spare set of clothes had been sitting on. He crossed his arms and looked away from us. I looked at Morgan, desperate and hoping she had answers, but she looked just as confused as I was.

The two of us were speaking quietly, trading ideas and trying to figure out what went wrong, when a rumbling noise caught our attention. There's no way they could've pulled off their attack that fast, but the door appeared. My heart hammered. Had they left anyone alive?

"Finally," Adrian groused, hurrying over and wrenching open the door. He stumbled back when a giant bearded face met him on the other side.

"Knock, knock," said Moshe.

I blew out a relieved breath. "I knew you couldn't leave us here. I've never been so happy to see your ugly mug in my life," I said.

"You have a really bad habit of bringing out the best in people," he said. "Good to see you back, Adrian."

"Great, another stranger who thinks they know me," said Adrian. "Can you move?"

Moshe looked taken aback, but made the tight turnaround and headed to the exit. As soon as we were clear, Adrian huffed off and I felt him tap a portal as soon as he was outside the perimeter.

"What happened?" Moshe asked.

Morgan supplied the answer. "He doesn't remember anything or anyone. We're still trying to figure out why."

"Damn," said Moshe, looking at me with something akin to pity in his eyes. "Some people have all the bad luck."

I snorted. "Then let's go change that."

CHAPTER TWENTY-TWO

When the three of us arrived at the manor, everything was quiet. "Did anyone tell you the specifics of the plan?" I asked Moshe.

He scratched the back of his head. "Sorry, no."

"They have to be inside by now, right?" asked Morgan. "I'm not sensing any of them out here. Unless you think they're not even here?"

I shook my head. "Tristan said the summit was happening here. He laid out all the security they had. It should've been solid. At the very least, we should be seeing bodies lying at the walls right now if they tried to infiltrate. Some kind of sign that they were here."

We'd been making our way slowly across the field, not bothering to hide ourselves. Tristan said he would let the head of security know about all of it, including not to fire on me if they saw me.

"Any chance they just walked in?" asked Moshe.

"You think they had somebody on the inside?" I asked.

As soon as the gate came into view, I caught a brief glimpse of men standing in front of it in a mixture of Resistance uniforms and security uniforms. Moshe shoved Morgan and I behind him, moving us around the corner, just as bullets whipped toward us, ricocheting off the stone and whickering into the darkness.

"Guess that answers that question," I said, drawing my pistols. "Did you get a count?"

The giant shook his head. "A bunch."

"Thanks for narrowing that down," I grumbled.

"This complicates things a bit," said Morgan. "What's option two?"

The sound of gears grinding as the heavy iron gate was lifted creaked across the vineyard. Shouting voices and a heavy truck engine fired up.

Moshe glanced up. "Climb the walls." He chuckled. "I'll give you a boost."

"While you wait out here so we can do all the heavy lifting. Nice try." I grinned at him. "I was going to suggest we go through the walls."

"I'm not the Kool-Aid man," said Moshe, frowning.

"I learned a few tricks since we worked together last." I motioned for them to follow me farther away down the wall. Depending on how thick it was, it might take me a minute. This method was becoming a favorite real quick. With my palm placed flat against the wall, I sped up the vibration of the stone until a wide section of it vanished.

Moshe hummed appreciatively. "That's neat."

I made sure to keep contact with the wall at all times as we moved through it, and once I removed my hand, the stone reappeared back in place. I heard the truck roar by on the other side of the wall.

There was no movement in the courtyard. We'd come out to the side of the manor, near the driveway. It was packed with cars, so the summit was clearly underway; Lyle had plenty of political prisoners to choose from.

"Dammit, I wish we had backup. I was hoping we could at least rely on security."

Morgan pointed toward the front door. "We probably could've counted on those guys." I traced the direction she was pointing and saw several bodies, all dressed in security uniforms, piled against the door like cordwood.

"Fuck," I spat. If they've already killed this many people, they'd gone in guns blazing. How many other casualties were we going to find?

"Side door, back door?" asked Morgan.

"Neither," I said. "Not for us." I jutted my chin upward, toward the balcony. "Moshe will give us a lift up, and then when I give the signal, he'll come crashing in the front door."

"He will, will he?" said Moshe. "You're going to make me move all those bodies?"

I shrugged. "They certainly won't be expecting you to come in that way."

"What's the signal?" he asked.

"Two gunshots and a scream," I said.

"Seriously?" he asked.

"No," I scoffed, pulling a face. "You'll know it when you see it. Or hear it." I waved my hands. "You'll figure it out."

Moshe shook his head, lifting Morgan and I both until we could grab the balcony railing. We hauled ourselves up and disappeared inside as Moshe made himself scarce.

We switched to hand signals only, not knowing where anybody was. Immediately, I heard a dog barking and throwing himself at a door. I rushed over and tried the knob, but it was locked magickally. It would take a minute to break it, and Jake needed to stay put anyway. I knelt. "Jake," I whispered.

He stopped and whined, pawing at the door. "You need to stay here." He barked. "I mean it. Are you safe in there?" His reluctant harumph said he was. "I'll be back for you, soon, baby boy."

I took point as we cleared the hallways, making our way downward. We checked every door, but the majority of them were locked. If there was no sign of life inside, we moved on. I came to a hall closet and heard panicked breathing inside. I held up my hand in a fist before pointing at the closet. Morgan moved into a defensive position where she could cover me as I pulled the door open.

The man inside made a surprised squeak of fear. Of all the people to find here first. "Urquhart?" wheezed Thatch.

I slapped a hand over his mouth. "Stay here. Do not move. And stay quiet," I whispered.

He nodded and I closed the door. Nobody else was on this floor. Big surprise that Thatch had run and hid at the first sign of trouble.

As we neared the grand staircase, I could hear fervent whispering below. The two of us eased out of the shelter of the hallway, just enough to peek over the edge. There were several prisoners, bound and gagged on the floor, surrounded by Lyle's team and their own traitorous security.

We needed to find the back staircase.

Confident that we were alone, I moved much faster this time as we searched for the servant's stairs. Every good medieval fortress-turned-manor has at least one set.

"Hey!"

I had a knife in hand and was throwing it before the full exclamation was out of the man's mouth. It struck the security guy right between the eyes and he dropped like a rock. Morgan hurried back and dragged the man out of the hallway, shoving him in the closet with Thatch. The warlock shot us both a glare before she shut the door in his face.

We exchanged a quick fist bump before we moved on. The door for the stairs was well hidden, carved to match the paneling around it. Cobwebs hung thick as we crept inside. Did anyone even know this stairway was here?

"We're going to have to separate. Do you feel confident enough to do that?" I asked her.

She nodded. "I think so. Are we creating distractions to draw them away in smaller groups?"

"Exactly that," I said. She was already more proficient than most of the other young guns I'd worked with. I guess with an entire team of spirits to guide you along the way, you could become good at pretty much anything in a very short amount of time.

Nobody was in sight as I eased the door open on the main floor. We were in the kitchen. Perfect.

"Give me three minutes. Then make a bunch of noise. Either duck back into the servant's stairs, or take them on, but I have no idea how many are going to come at you at once. And I don't know if I'll be able to help you if you get overwhelmed."

"Got it. I'll take it as it comes."

"Stay safe," I said.

She gave me a confident smile. "Worry about yourself."

I grinned and headed for the dining room. There were too many blind corners here, so I threw up a concealment cloak and reminded myself not to be surprised if there was a counter curse hiding somewhere in the defenses of this place that would peel it off me.

The dining room was massive and featured a gigantic wooden table in the center of the room. Everyone had clearly been in here when Lyle struck. Chairs were tipped over, a few more security lay dead, smears of blood were on the walls. The table itself was scattered with papers, official-looking documents, and plenty of booze. Not sure all those things went together, but maybe they were done for the day.

I hurried through to a sitting room and then into the main hall. Picking my way through this section was much more difficult. Nobody noticed me, so my concealment was still working, but hostages were packed so tightly on the floor that I almost tripped a couple of times. Luckily, they just assumed their neighbor had nudged them.

After a quick run through of the entire lower floor, I didn't find anyone else. There was a small nook to the side of the grand staircase, and I squeezed into it as I waited for Morgan to do her thing. A quick check of all of the people present revealed that the majority were human. There were a few council members sprinkled between them, but this clearly wasn't where they were keeping the most prized prisoners.

Just a few seconds later, there was a horrible cacophony as what sounded like an entire rack of metal pans went falling to the floor.

All the guards spun to face it, and I was horrified to find this was clearly the B team as they *all* went rushing toward the kitchen.

"Shit!"

Just as I was about to sprint after them, Moshe came crashing through the front door. "Help Morgan and meet me in the basement!" I shouted, dropping the concealment cloak and pointing. He didn't even hesitate, just took off, faster than anyone his size should be able to move. There was a wall-shaking roar and the battle was on.

I needed to find the rest of the prisoners fast. Lyle assuredly heard Moshe's roar and might decide to forgo his demands in favor of skipping straight to execution.

Everyone tied up on the floor made frantic noises as I passed by them, but I ignored them, searching out the basement. I'm sure there was also a dungeon down there, because what good fortress would be caught dead without a dungeon?

Luckily—for me, not for them—several security came bursting out the basement door and barreled right into me. Four of them dropped within seconds, their throats cut. I exchanged a series of fast and furious combat with the remaining two before they were all down.

The stairs were carpeted, so it was easy to stay quiet and move quickly. I'm not sure if Tristan was thinking about the logistics at the time that he made that decision, but it was a good one.

"Somebody report!" Lyle was shouting. "Dammit! What's going on up there?!"

"Maybe we should—"

"Gina, if you suggest one more time that we call this off..." Lyle warned.

A peek around the corner showed only a handful of guards left, and every single other Council member and noble. They were all bound and gagged like the others, but alive. That electric blue glow was emanating around the Council. Lyle must've gotten his hands on one of the magick nullifiers the mortals had developed.

Upstairs, things had gone quiet. Faint scuffling sounds reached my ears, which I imagined to be all the upstairs prisoners being freed and running away. Sure enough, a moment later, Morgan appeared behind me. She was a little bloody, but no worse for wear.

"Where's Moshe," I mouthed.

"Couldn't fit through the door," she mouthed back.

Duh. The drawbacks of working with giants.

I held up the number of fingers corresponding to the number of guards in the room, followed by an instruction for her to take the left side, while I handled Lyle, Gina, Veronica, and the other two I didn't know the names of.

A quick countdown and we struck. Morgan was a blur of deadly speed as she rushed toward her targets and then I lost track of her as I went after mine.

Lyle went down first, a bullet between the eyes. Veronica ran. Moshe would deal with her.

Gina... turned on the other two and killed them before they could react. She grinned at me and put her hands in the air. "Thanks for showing up, finally."

I stopped, stunned. "No way were you working against him the whole time," I said.

"Not the whole time. But the minute I saw that this was a peace talk I wanted out."

Morgan, who had dispatched of all her opponents, looked around at us, a new spatter of blood on her face.

"Seriously?" she asked. "Do I have to do all the hard work around here?"

I just laughed and shook my head, going to work disabling the nullifier while Gina and Morgan untied the nobles. Once I got the device turned off, the Council was far less enthused to be free and far more embarrassed.

The Matron was the first to stand and confront me. "Evyn."

Not saying a word, I waited for her to pass whatever judgment she would.

"Thank you," she said, and several other Council members nodded their thanks, to Morgan as well.

I nodded, relieved. "Least we could do."

George stepped up. "No, it was definitely the most. We had no right to expect this of you." He clapped me on the shoulder. "Consider the excommunication withdrawn." Something told me he wasn't the one to issue it in the first place. The wolf looked over my shoulder with a sly grin. "Although I suspect you weren't really doing it for us."

Tristan was standing ahead of the group of nobles who were watching the conversation warily. He truly looked *princely*, with his finely tailored suit and a new air of confidence I hadn't seen before. A man coming back into his own. He turned to the others and there was a brief exchange before they filed out of the room. Sophia caught my eye and to my surprise, she gave me a nod and the tiniest of smiles before following the others.

"If everyone is amenable to continuing these talks in the morning, I think we've earned a little rest," said Tristan.

"Agreed," said George. A hard glint lit his eyes. "I also need to make a few calls."

Code for, there would be a lot more bodies dropped by morning. Malcolm would be busy.

Tristan gripped my elbow. "I need to see that everything is taken care of. Meet me later?"

"The garden?" I asked.

He nodded and I went to see what other trouble I could get up to in the meantime.

First stop was to get Jake out of the room he'd been stuck in and—after I'd taken advantage of the waterfall shower to wash forest grime, Adrian's blood, and everything else I'd gotten into since, off me—we'd headed outside immediately after. Tristan found us lounging on the grass and eased himself sorely down until he was lying next to me, one hand propped behind his head. Jake was snoring, his feet kicking away as he chased his dream quarry. We'd listened as the manor gradually quieted, and Jake finally gave up the battle against sleep.

"You're going to get grass stains on that amazing suit," I warned.

He chuckled. "So be it."

I turned my head, studying his face in the dim light as he stared at the sky. A profile I knew so well, but was also different. "Is everyone settled in?"

"Mm-hmm. Finally." He turned to look at me. "You could've warned the housekeeper about the warlock and the dead body in the linen closet."

I snorted and Tristan's laughter joined mine.

"Please give her my apologies," I said, still giggling and picturing it in my head. Thatch had probably screamed louder than the housekeeper did.

A huge yawn made my jaw crack. "Wow." I massaged my jaw. "I'm really tired."

"Then let's go to bed."

"I—" It sunk in, what he'd said. His eyes burned into me, and I took his hand. "Let's."

Curling up next to Tristan that night, I fell right to sleep.

My dreams were dark, filled with the cackling of the twin sisters I hated most. As the vision came into focus, I was all too familiar with the surroundings. I was back in the lamia's lair.

Then the twins appeared. Without further preamble, I launched myself at them, running across the room at top speed and crashing into Malea, throwing her to the floor and pinning her down. She only laughed.

"Now, Evyn, what is the problem?" she asked.

I wrapped my hands around her throat. "What did you do?" I screamed, tightening my grip. Her laughter strangled but she made no move to stop me, nor did her sister.

"I did nothing that Adrian didn't do to himself," she hissed.

"Lies!"

Amara spoke. "He was asking for it. We could see it in his mind. He wanted to forget. You, your friends, your life together. Everything that was bringing him pain and the reason he was going through his ordeal. It was your fault, Urquhart." She smiled and moved over to me, peeling my hands away from her sister's neck. I couldn't believe what I was hearing.

"You lie," I snapped. "He wouldn't do that."

"Oh yes, he would. He begged us, pleaded with us to stop. He called for you. Over and over again in his torment. But you didn't answer. He felt betrayed."

"That wasn't my doing! You hid him from me!"

"He didn't know that," said Malea, rubbing her neck and finger-combing her hair into place.

I slapped her so hard, her head snapped to the side, a red handprint left behind. "Did you bring me here just to taunt me? To laugh in my face and brag about the pain you've caused?" I said low in my throat, the words dripping with hatred.

"Something like that," said Malea who had snuck up behind me while I was watching Amara. She spoke into my ear with her vile, reeking breath. "We enjoyed the taste of your familiar. A demon bound to a mage has an interesting flavor."

"His lips were my favorite," said Amara, with a sly smile. I must have made a disgusted noise because she shrieked with laughter.

"Is that objectionable to you? I gnawed them off myself," she said. "Bite... by... bite." Her eyes rolled into the back of her head and down again. The grin on her face was terrible.

"I'll kill you!" I screeched, lunging at her. She easily evaded me, and I ended up facedown in a pool of fresh blood.

I stood and angrily wiped at my face. "This isn't over by any means. I will find you, I will fight you, and I will destroy you." I spat. "That's a promise."

"Sister, is she threatening us again?" asked Amara, cocking her head to the side.

"She is not in her right mind," said Malea.

"I've never been more sure of myself," I said.

"So hot-headed and so naïve. I'm surprised you've lived this long," said Amara, narrowing her eyes.

Malea glided over to me and put her fingers on my face. They burned where they made contact with my skin. She wiped away some blood and licked it off her fingers. "Well, pet," she said, hitting the *t* with bitterness. "I guess we'll have to find you first."

"Be seeing you," they said in unison, turning wicked smiles on me.

"No!" I exclaimed, sitting up and staring around, wild-eyed.

"What's wrong?" asked Tristan. Jake growled at a far corner of the room.

I sucked in air around lungs constricted with fear. The whisper of a noise caught my attention, and I slipped out of bed, grabbing my pistol from the side table.

The pajama pants I'd borrowed were too long and I almost tripped as my foot got caught in the leg. Tristan reached for a weapon of his own. Thin moonlight filtered through the window as we crept toward the corner.

There was nothing there.

I lowered my gun. "Must've dreamed it."

Tristan shook his head, just as perplexed as I was. I turned, intending only to climb back into bed and go to sleep, when arms wrapped around me from behind, clawed hands digging into my skin.

"Hello, pet," Amara hissed.

"Evyn!"

I broke away and we both fired at the lamia, only to find a blank patch of wall now riddled with bullet holes.

Thundering feet came down the hall and a heavy fist pounded on the door. "What's going on!" It was George's voice.

Tristan swallowed, Adam's apple bobbing nervously. He crossed to the door and threw it open. Ishani strode in first, her nose wrinkling at the fresh gunpowder in the air. She was still fully dressed with a hint of blood on her breath. George, following right behind, was in his pajamas and barefoot, as were the Matron, Sophia, Morgan and a couple of nobles I didn't know the names of.

Ishani was staring at the wall. "What happened?"

The Matron answered. "A lamia was here."

"It was Amara," I said, nodding.

The sister's cackling filled the room then, and we all flinched back, those of us with weapons drawing them to the ready. The laughter echoed down the halls until it surrounded us from every angle. Then it vanished.

"Do you still sense them?" George asked the Matron.

She was still for a moment, before shaking her head warily. "No. Nothing."

I reluctantly lowered my weapon. "This isn't over."

Chapter Twenty-Three

Tristan's lips on my forehead woke me up, and I blinked in the bright sunshine.

"Good morning," I said, drawing his face to mine for another, longer kiss.

He ran his hand across my stomach and under my shirt, the light skimming of his fingertips on my skin sending gooseflesh over my body.

"Morning," he said, breaking the kiss and leaning back on his elbow with a smile.

Gods, I missed this.

"I have to go make sure everyone is set to continue the talks in light of last night." He frowned. "I'm hoping they're satisfied with the new security the Council and I are bringing in. I even let the human governments call in their own."

My eyebrows rose. "That was generous. You trust them?"

He shook his head. "Not in the slightest, but concessions had to be made. Our teams were clearly compromised."

He shuffled out of bed and I instantly missed his warmth. "You should join us for breakfast. A few of the nobles have taken to meeting in the mornings, keep the conversation casual over pancakes before we get into the nitty-gritty."

"Pancakes? I'm there," I said.

He smiled. "Great."

To my great surprise, everyone from the night before was still on board for continuing the talks. The only people who left were some of the family members that came with the officials. People were dedicated to making peace happen.

They weren't as cool about seeing me there, however. While it didn't become openly hostile, in the minds of humans, I was still at the top of the *Public Enemies* list.

I overheard a few political leaders from multiple countries saying how they wouldn't be surprised if I was behind the attack myself, and swooped in to "save the day" to get back in the good graces of the Council.

But there were pancakes, so it didn't bother me.

It was the sitting down at a table of nobles, who I've only ever heard about in legends and histories, that turned out to be the most intimidating part of my morning.

"Just a few nobles, huh?" I asked Tristan in a whisper. There were at least twenty people here.

He flashed me a grin and kissed my cheek before pulling out a chair for me. "Forgive me."

Jake sauntered in and sat next to me, his head easily able to rest on the table as he sniffed at the food.

I noted the sour faces of some of the nobles as they saw him and crossed them off my list of people to get to know.

Tristan sat next to me, taking the seat at the head of the table. He looked so at ease, so much like a high lord at court... a *king*. I'd noticed it last night, but with him at the head of all these nobles, it really sank it. Was I getting into something that was way over my head?

He must've sensed my unease, because he reached under the table and took my hand.

"I'd like to introduce my partner, Evyn Urquhart," said Tristan, as soon as everyone's plates were filled and we were tucking into a delicious breakfast. I might've grabbed pancakes *and* French toast, but dammit, I'd earned it.

I gave a shy wave to the table.

There were some nods and some scowls, the usual mix of reactions my presence elicits. Even though we'd come to some small understanding, I was glad to see Sophia sitting toward the middle, several seats away.

"Is the introduction necessary?" asked a woman wearing a white fur stole while eating a Monte Cristo dipped in copious amounts of ruby red strawberry jam. "Is there anyone here who doesn't know who the brat is?"

Well, then.

Tristan's voice was still light but there was a warning edge to it that sent shivers down my spine in all the best ways. "It seems you've forgotten how manners work, Tabitha, but I have not."

She sniffed and went back to her sandwich, and I hoped she spilled jam all over her furs.

The talk quickly moved on and I was gratefully left alone to my pancakes until I felt a hand rest on my shoulder.

I turned and instinctively my hand flipped the fork around into a "stabbing-ready" position as I spied the man standing at the entrance to the room, half-hidden behind the doorframe. "Malcolm," I growled.

George took a step sideways to block Malcolm from my view and smiled apologetically. "Can we speak for a moment?"

"Everything okay?" Tristan asked, getting to his feet. I stood and spoke low into his ear. His noble buddies didn't need to know my business.

"It's fine. I'm sure George is about to attempt to broker another peace."

George tipped his head in acknowledgment. "Might as well rip the bandage off, right?"

There was still a lot that I hadn't had time or mental fortitude to fill Tristan in on yet. "Malcolm was at the head of the hit squad the Council sent after me." I smiled a vicious, predatory smile at Malcolm, who blanched and ducked completely out of view.

Tristan stiffened beside me and George held up his hands. "There is no threat." He grinned and amended himself. "Other than the one Evyn poses to Malcolm."

"I'll catch up with you later, okay?" I said to Tristan.

He slid his arm around my lower back, resting his hand on my opposite hip. "Later," he agreed. I tilted my head up to kiss him and followed George out of the room.

"It was nothing personal," said Malcolm, the instant I came into view. "I was following orders, you know—"

"Yeah, I know," I said, cutting my hand in a sharp motion. He stopped babbling and settled for a pout.

"This way," said George, leading us to a smaller room with a writing desk, luxurious rug, and not much else.

He closed the door behind us. "Malcolm is still the head of our teams. He's going to be with us for the duration of this summit."

"How many people did you bring with you?" I asked Malcolm. I'd left at least ten of his group dead when they attacked me.

"A bunch," he said, noncommittal. "Some of them were my friends, you know."

Darkness crowded the edge of my vision. I shook my head to clear it. "Did you expect me to just give up and go quietly?"

"No, we would never expect you to do the honorable thing," Malcolm sneered.

"Malcolm," George warned, moving in between us.

I stared the merc down. "Don't put that on me, Malcolm! You forced my hand."

He just scoffed and folded his arms, confident his boss would protect him. The black shadows crept closer and I couldn't push them back. My anger was boiling over.

"Evyn?" George's voice sounded fuzzy in my head.

"What the fuck do you know about honor?" I asked, trying to push past George. He wouldn't move.

"More than a washed-up, has-been, traitor," he spat.

Streaks of red shot through the black.

"Say that again," I warned.

Malcolm smirked. "You're just a murderer, plain and simple."

The world narrowed down to a pinprick and my only thought was killing Malcolm, and George if he got in my way. The wolf put a hand on my shoulder and I flinched back at the contact, reaching for a knife. "Evyn!" he barked, claws extending and gouging into my skin.

The pain cut through the haze enough for me to realize George was my friend. I didn't want to kill him. I loosened my stance and backed up a couple paces just as the door banged open behind me and the Matron appeared, Morgan in tow.

I threw myself into a corner, reaching again for my knife as the darkness closed back around me.

The Matron shouted, skirt billowing as she conjured power. She hit me with a hex that froze me to the spot and it felt like my entire body was on fire. I couldn't make a sound.

Her lips moved but I couldn't understand the words.

Pressure built in my head and popped as suddenly as a cork out of a champagne bottle. The power surrounding me faded, and I sank to my knees.

Morgan rushed forward to catch me, easing me to the ground. I blinked and looked around at them.

"The fuck just happened?" I asked, words slurred.

The Matron's face was covered in a sheen of sweat. "The lamia," she said. "I felt their power appear again and followed it here. To you."

I gritted my teeth. "Possession."

She frowned. "Yes."

"Are they—"

The Matron shook her head quickly. "They're gone. I was able to seal them out of your mind." She gave a shaky laugh. "I suppose it's a good thing it happened now. They hid their link to you so well, I couldn't even tell it was there."

"Me either," said Morgan. "Are you okay?"

I nodded. "I think so." She helped me to my feet and I looked at George. "Sorry about that."

He waved me off. "No hard feelings." He shared a glance with the Matron. "This would seem to prove your innocence with the Riverwalk murders. You weren't acting of your own volition."

A pang of guilt at the memory of Ivan's bloody face hit me. "Ivan's still dead because of me."

George clapped me on the shoulder. "We will stop these monsters. You'll get your revenge. For Adrian, too."

My eyes widened in surprise. "Who told you?"

Morgan spoke up. "I couldn't sleep last night, so I ended up talking to Ishani about all of it."

"All of it?" I asked, careful, the unspoken question revolving around the highly illegal ritual we performed to find Adrian in the first place.

"Most," she said.

George took note of the interaction but said nothing. "Ishani gave me a rundown earlier this morning when we were going over casualty reports from the extra cleanup we needed to do."

And by *cleanup*, he meant hunting down the other traitors that aided Lyle.

"Is there any sign that they're still here?" asked George.

The Matron shook her head. "None."

"The session will be starting soon," he said, looking back and forth between Malcolm and I. "Can I expect that you'll be able to work together?"

"Hell no," I said immediately.

George looked surprised. The Matron did not.

"Evyn, I—" George tried again.

"The answer is no," I said. "Moshe and I will be hanging out, watching over things, but I'm not working with the Council teams." I looked at Morgan. "Have you been reinstated as Frige's second?"

She nodded and I smiled, relieved. "Good. Then that's that. Are we done here?"

George looked at the Matron, who gave a subtle shake of her head. He sighed. "Yes."

"Great." I hurried out of the room.

Jake and I stalked around angrily until we found Moshe sitting under a tree in the back courtyard, reading. The instant he saw my face, he asked, "What's wrong?"

I plopped down on the ground beside him while Jake demanded pets from the giant.

"Hey, pal," said Moshe. "We haven't formally met. I'm Moshe."

Jake barked and flopped down beside him.

"Smart dog," he said, chuckling.

"Jake's a guardian," I said.

Moshe's eyebrows rose. "Huh. Makes sense."

"Why's that?"

He shrugged. "Lots of people are invested in keeping you out of trouble."

I rolled my eyes. "If that were true, they've been doing a shit job."

Jake harrumphed and looked over at me.

"Not you," I said. It wasn't his fault Tristan took him with him. And if he'd stayed, the lamia would've killed him, no question

Jake accepted my answer and went back to soaking up Moshe's attention.

"George expects me to keep working with the Council," I said. "And the lamia tried to possess me again during our conversation."

Moshe grumbled and then looked at me, alarmed. "Run that last bit by me again?"

"The sisters were still clinging on to me. They tried to posses me like they must've done before. I almost attacked George. I wouldn't have felt bad about Malcolm, though."

"Are you okay?" he asked.

"I'm fine," I said. "Honestly, I'm so tired of those bitches I don't even want to think about it right now."

Moshe nodded. "So you declared yourself an independent contractor?"

"Not officially," I said. "I might stop being angry at them at some point."

"They excommunicated you. Mostly for political reasons. And they were going to use you as a pawn to negotiate for peace after lying to you and saying they wouldn't pursue you." He paused. "Am I getting the story straight?"

"Yes." I ran a tired hand over my face. "I said 'might.' Chances are low."

"What do you need from me?" he asked.

I smiled at him. "I told them we'd be working security on our own."

He closed his book and gave Jake a few more pets. "Sounds good."

We steered clear of Malcolm and the other teams as we took up a position on the second floor landing. It gave us a nice view of the hall and all the comings and goings, we were near enough to the action that we could reach the session room in seconds if something happened, and we had plenty of cover.

The magi had combined their magick to put a ludicrously strong shield over the building and grounds, and I couldn't help but wonder if that would harm more than it helped. Nobody could get in, but unless you were magi, you couldn't get out either. But it was the Matron's call.

Human reinforcements had arrived about an hour previous, and they were stationed at every doorway on the main floor with dozens more surrounding the building.

News crews had also shown up. All the activity drew them in, any secrecy completely blown. They couldn't get anywhere near the property, but long-range cameras were pretty great quality these days.

Now we just had to hope nothing happened, because with this many armed guards things would get messy fast, and innocent people would get caught in the crossfire.

I yawned, the drone of voices from the summit lulling me into sleep. Maybe we should've chosen a spot outside.

"I've had more fun filing paperwork," said Moshe, scratching his beard. He paced a little, shaking out his arms and legs.

"Hey."

Moshe and I started, reaching for weapons as we searched for the source of the voice.

"Gina?" I asked. Jake barked and growled. She was standing in the middle of the hallway. "How the hell did you sneak up on us?"

She shrugged. "I was just walking."

She came over to join us, leaning against the banister, not giving the giant dog that clearly didn't like her the time of day. I watched her closely, something not sitting right.

"Shouldn't you have been out of here the instant they decided not to detain you?" I asked.

"I was going to, but I want to see this through. Lyle still has friends. I figured I'd be able to help spot them."

Moshe was looking at her with the same suspicion. "Did you stay the night here? I don't remember seeing you in the servant's quarters with the rest of us peons," he said, shooting me a grin.

"Sorry," I said.

Gina shook her head. "I headed back to the States, but turned around last minute."

"What time did you get here?" I asked.

She cocked her head to the side. "Why all the questions?"

I shrugged. "Just curious. Humor me."

Moshe moved in closer.

Gina looked back and forth between us, frustrated. "About an hour ago. I thought it was pretty obvious I was on your side." She pushed away from the railing. "If you don't want my help, I'll go find another spot."

"That shield has been up for hours. Unless you came in with the human military—"

Gina took off running, leaping down the stairs in a single jump. "Gina!" I yelled, taking off after her, Moshe booming behind, floors shaking with the force of his speed. Jake made it there first.

The guards at the doors all had their weapons pointed at us as Jake tackled Gina, taking her to the floor. Her palms hit the marble and made an awful squeaking noise as they skidded to a halt. I jumped in and Jake rolled away, letting me pin Gina. He stood guard, ready to step in.

I could hear chairs pushing back and raised voices heading our way from the summit chamber.

As I wrestled with Gina, she started laughing.

"Evyn?" Ishani asked. "What's she doing?" The other guild leaders were pressing in around and beside her while their human counterparts stayed well away.

I shook my head. "Something isn't right. Get people clear."

Gina shrieked. "Nowhere is safe!" Her laughter reached a fever pitch.

"Go!" I shouted at Ishani.

She nodded and turned to the others, shouting orders. Screams and running feet dashed off to a safer location as a single gunshot rang out.

A hole the size of my fist appeared in the side of Gina's head, a small entry wound on the other side leaking a small trickle of blood as her body went limp.

One of the uniformed soldiers was staring, wide-eyed, at his rifle. "I didn't mean to—"

"Shit," I said, jumping off Gina's body and scrambling away.

"This has to be the lamia!" I shouted. "Everybody get back!"

We all drew away to a safe distance. I could see soldiers running outside the windows, ready to move in. "Keep everyone back!" I shouted again, pointing at the front door they were about to storm through. A young man on my left nodded, speaking quickly into his radio.

Running feet came back toward us, and I saw Malcolm in the lead. "What have we got?"

"Not sure yet," I said. "The lamia are up to something." I nodded my head toward the soldier that shot her. "They made him kill her."

The soldier took in my words. "That wasn't me?" he asked, hopeful.

"No."

He breathed deeply and nodded.

"So she's dead. End of story," said Malcolm, staring at Gina's still corpse, blood seeping in an ever-widening pool around her. It was too much blood.

"No," I said. "It's not."

"How do you—" he began, but a rumbling boom cut him off, a sound like thunder.

"How are you second best?" I asked, shaking my head in disgust.

Additional running feet came in our direction.

"Evyn!" Tristan shouted.

I whirled. "Get out of here!"

He kept coming at a jog, not stopping until he was standing with me. Morgan, Ishani, Atum, the Matron, Percy, and a few others were with him.

"I'm not leaving you again," he said.

"You have to. People need you to stay safe." I put my hand on his cheek. "It's bigger than just us, now."

The floor around Gina cracked, the blood boiling before it seeped through.

"Please, go," I said. I looked at Jake. "You, too."

He barked and shook his head. "Please," I said again.

Tristan grabbed me to him for a kiss. By the time we broke apart, we were breathless. "You *will* make it back to me," he whispered.

"Always," I said.

With one last look and a hug from Jake, they jogged off.

"Where will they go?" I asked Ishani.

"There's a Council team and magi ready to move them to the other side of the barrier." She grimaced. "Pity we'll lose more than half our forces to protect them though."

"No George?" I asked.

She grinned. "I told him much the same thing as you told Tristan. Without the passionate embrace."

I was about to tell her where she could shove that comment, but Morgan gasped. "It's a bridge," she said, staring at the scene before us.

She looked at the Matron, who frowned. "The minute that woman's blood hit the ground, the magick was set."

"A bridge to where?" Percy asked.

"The realm they made for themselves a long time ago," said Atum. "If that bridge solidifies it'll leave us vulnerable to attack from all sorts of creatures."

"Great. Earth will have an open door policy," I said. "Just for the record, I'd like the next villain not to use portals and ancient blood magick."

"How else do you expect giant beasts to move around?" Morgan asked.

"They can get small. They don't have to be so dramatic."

"We agree." Twin voices spoke in unison as ghostly figures appeared.

Chapter Twenty-Four

The soldiers immediately opened fire, the bullets passing through the twins' semitransparent forms as they walked out of the bridge they'd created between worlds.

"Hold fire!" Percy shouted.

It fell silent. Malea and Amara stepped forward.

"Do we have a plan here?" asked Percy.

"Don't die," said Baqi. He was the leader of the djinn on the Council. I'd not spoken with him much, but it was a formidable prospect just sharing space with the man. Having him as an enemy would be a nightmare.

Amara's face was twisted in anger. "That little stunt that you pulled, calling your geist's spirits and getting us lost between realms caused us a headache. You weren't supposed to escape. And you made us go to great lengths to come to you."

Malea slunk forward, hips swaying, becoming more solid with each step. "We will take the æther by force, and then we will consume this entire household. The world will be plunged into further turmoil because so many of their leaders will be gone. Because of you." She sneered. "Because you can't accept when you are beaten."

"You're right on the latter, but you can't put global turmoil on me," I said, taking a step forward. "All of this is on you." Another step. "Two monsters that lost their minds and wanted to exact vengeance on gods that forgot them a long time ago."

"Best not to mention that part," said Ishani, glancing at Atum.

"They'll remember soon enough," said Amara, a whisper above the ever-present crackle of the flames.

"You aren't so powerful as you'd like us to believe," said Atum. "I can see your weakness. You expended much of your power to return here."

The sisters glared at the god. "It's simple enough to restore," said Amara.

"You'll be a great appetizer for the feast," said Malea.

I felt it then, just a spark of magick coalescing around the sister's feet. Baqi was weaving something, lines of power so fine I could only detect them with Sight. As it warbled and activated, it formed a seal, a complex rune of some kind.

Its purpose wasn't clear to me, but it didn't have to be. I just needed to keep them talking, so he had time to work.

"How did you two manipulate the DIWR attack and Tafford's bullshit? Possession?"

"Tafford is an idiot," said Malea. "His hatred made him amenable to many ideas. We weaponized him with very little effort, and for the most part, he took care of it on his own. The attack wasn't us, but I'm sure he was involved." She gave a flippant wave of her hand.

"And the train? Those secret weapons the military pulled out of their asses that were so effective against us? Was that your doing too?"

Amara tapped her chin. "The plague demons were my idea." She frowned. "I might've overlooked a few things, but it moved your downward spiral along nicely."

"Glad you can be so casual about it," I said.

Baqi's binding looked almost complete.

"All the way down to the Nyx," said Malea, ignoring my comment. "You should thank us."

"How's that?"

"That ring is a focus for the power." Amara sounded bored. "You're supposed to use it to bend the æther to your will. It is sentient. But without that immersion in the Nyx, your connection was tenuous." She rolled her head toward me and stared at me, eyes raised. "The æther would've overwhelmed you eventually."

Amara lashed out with her hand as Baqi was about to snap the binding shut. The force they threw at him should have knocked him off his feet, but he stayed upright, only a grunt of pain rushing out of him.

The twins rushed forward, and in a heartbeat, Percy had transformed into her massive wolf. Ishani took a raking swipe with her metal hand, the diamond-tipped nails catching Amara across the face. The lamia spun to the side and struck back, launching Ishani across the chamber. Gunfire erupted and I had my .45 to hand the second they started their rush. I fired off three shots, all but one of them missing Amara's face. That one was just a glancing blow across her temple.

Atum manifested his full strength, while keeping his glowing, lightning-infused godform under fifteen feet tall.

Baqi was frozen to the spot, a vacant expression on his face. I traced the lines of magick from the binding back to him with my Sight. Somehow, they had reversed the effect and turned it back on him.

Malea was heading right for him, and I sprinted, tackling Baqi to the ground and severing his ties to the binding. He took a startled breath and was back in action in the same heartbeat.

The twins exploded out of their skin, giant, writhing snakes the size of fully grown Burmese pythons landing with a heavy *thwack* on the ground. The snakes twisted and lashed, growing larger. One second they were manageable, but in the blink of an eye they were towering over us, bursting through walls and the second floor before the ceiling crumbled.

Percy and Ishani launched into a coordinated attack on Malea, their teeth and claws unable to get purchase on the thick scales. She struck, her massive head darting down blindingly fast, missing Ishani by a hair's breadth. Percy went for the eyes, digging her claws into the bottom of the socket. Malea roared and reared back up, taking Percy with her. She shook her head, and the wolf went flying, landing heavily on the stone floor instead.

Baqi's binding was still good. If I could find some way to activate it, we could at least hold one of them while we concentrated on the other.

My attention was so focused on solving that problem, I almost missed Amara's tail coming straight at me.

"Evyn, down!" Ishani yelled. Automatically, I dropped to the floor, Amara's whipping tail coming within inches of me with a rush of wind so forceful that it made my head spin. If that had gotten a piece of me…

Ishani rushed past me, leaping at Amara's face and landing between the beast's eyes, stabbing, swiping, and clawing. One of her hits landed dead-on, and Amara screeched as her eye burst, oozing viscous fluid.

Malea, going head to head with Atum and the Matron, the god now growing to his full size, heeded her sister's cry, disengaging from the battle. Her bulk slithered unnervingly fast, and Ishani jumped away just before Malea's tail swiped with pinpoint precision in a strike that missed her sister's face, but would've caused devastating damage should the vampire have been there.

Atum lunged, grabbing Malea's tail mid-swing and using the leverage to wrench her around and fling her across the rubble of the fortress, right over my head. She crashed through the one remaining solid wall and everything still standing tumbled around us. I heard screams of pain that quickly faded to nothing. Our numbers were dwindling fast.

Our fight was out in the open now, in plain view of the world that was sure to be watching. I only hoped the others had gotten away safely and that the barrier would hold.

Amara struck as soon as Atum was turned to the side, sinking her fangs into his back and shoulder. The god's fury was instantaneous, the lightning crackling across his body, concentrating at the bite. It lit up blindingly brilliant, and Amara convulsed like she was being electrocuted. The Matron added a storm of curses, hitting the lamia from all angles.

She retracted her fangs and reared away, but Atum wasn't letting her go that easily. He gripped Amara in a wrestler's hold, throwing his weight down on her and pinning her as she writhed to get free. Her massive tail thrashed against the ground.

But I could see he was weakening, his power being drawn back into the earth. An Ætherim couldn't hold their form in this realm for long.

He pried her jaws apart and Malea slithered toward them, screaming.

Baqi saw the same thing that I did. She would have to cross right over his binding to get to her sister. As soon as she came into contact with it, he activated it. She slowed, but didn't stop, and I conjured heavy rods of pure energy, sinking them into the ground and lacing them together, like I was tying a corset overtop her.

The Matron appeared at my side along with Morgan, who had a nasty cut on her collarbone. They joined me in binding Malea and in seconds we had her pinned.

Atum plunged his hand inside Amara's mouth. There was a flash, a boom, and the back of her head disintegrated. Malea's scream was ear piercing as her sister slumped to the ground, thrashing like an eel on dry land in her dying spasms. We almost lost our grip on the bindings holding her in place, my feet sliding backward from the invisible force of her agony and fury pressing against the barrier.

Baqi cursed as the bindings shattered. Malea's eyes blazed and she thrashed her tail, so quickly it was all we could do just to stay out of the way.

"You will pay!" she screeched. She only had eyes for Atum.

He readied himself just as she launched at him, taking them both to the ground and wrapping herself around him, constricting her coils and sinking her fangs in deep. Lightning flashed against her, but was absorbed.

All of us were throwing everything we had at her but it was all deflecting. His blazing power grew dimmer, Malea consuming it until his movements became feeble. She was killing a god?

"Can't you use the æther?" asked Ishani, staring in helpless horror.

"No," I said. "The minute I bring it out, she'll take control of it."

Percy threw herself at the lamia, attacking her face and every soft spot our spells and curses opened up, but every injury healed in an instant.

Malea reared back, opening her jaws wide and biting Atum's head clear off. His light blinked out and he dissolved into ash. She swatted the others aside, brimming with stolen power. I was too slow to avoid her tail as it wrapped around me and lifted me into the air, bringing me face to face with her.

"No more games," she hissed.

Her tail tightened as she stared at Amara's felled body. "I will finish this, for her." She reared back and struck, her right fang sinking into my body. Her poison pumped through me, and I screamed. It was deadening my resistance to her.

The æther woke, boiling up at the attack that threatened my life. It wasn't going to let me die, but in doing so, it was making itself available to her. She'd take her prize and that would be the end.

Baqi and the Matron hurled spells while Ishani ripped scales from the lamia to make way for teeth, claws, swords and spells, but Malea didn't even feel it.

She'd drained Atum's power. How could *I* hope to resist her?

The æther strained near the surface, fighting the venom and working its way toward the fang embedded in my body. She was getting something from me, there was no way out of it now. But what if—

I didn't have time to come to grips with what this idea would ultimately cost me before I redirected the æther's attention, Solomon's ring glowing warm as I joined the two halves of the puzzle together, issuing my command. There was resistance, cold chills blistering through me as I fought for dominance, but

I bent it to my will. The æther flowed through me and sought out every anchor that bound my magick to me.

And severed the ties.

One by one, those anchors fell away until my mage power was a kite on the wind, one thin string keeping it from flying away into the brilliant blue sky above us.

A whirlwind encompassed my body and that last remaining cord was cut. Blinding pain seared through me, and I watched the power draining from me. I screamed, unable to form coherent thoughts, only able to watch with darkening vision as the glistening fang drank up my essence. My magick, everything that made me who I was, leeched out of me as Malea absorbed it into herself. Every nerve ending burned and frayed, only to be cut open and doused with acid.

A pressure around my heart boiled up as the æther swirled within me. I thought I was about to lose control of it, but the pressure burst and the turmoil inside my body and mind stilled. I was filled with a gentle warmth and there was a presence with me, like an old childhood friend.

The pain ceased and the whirlwind subsided. A shudder ran through me as my body convulsed in shock. My power was gone. The last thing I remembered was a bright flash of light and a lamia's wail, before... nothing....

"Evyn."

Pain. The lingering agony imprinted on my bones, my nerves. Nothing felt the same. My body was alien to me as I floated on a hazy sea, flashes of the battle playing through my mind. We'd won, hadn't we?

"Evyn."

A woman's voice, reaching toward me from so far away. It was familiar. Where did I know it from?

"I know you can hear me." The voice was slightly chastising.

"Wake up!" said another woman. A voice I knew well.

"Fuck off, Percy," I mumbled, tongue thick.

She snickered, and I heard someone pour a glass of water.

"Can you sit up?" This from the first voice.

My eyelids felt scratchy, and the light was too bright. My muscles were stiff and weak at the same time. When I could focus again, I found myself surrounded.

"There she is." Hands pressed a cool glass of water at me, and I followed them to the owner.

I grinned. "Frankie. It's been a while."

She dipped her head. "This isn't how I would've liked to meet again, but here we are." Her cherubic face beamed at me. "How are you feeling?"

"Been better." I looked around at everyone, feeling like Dorothy fresh out of Oz. Derfael, Percy, Ishani, and Morgan were there. Motion at the door caught my attention, and I glanced over to find Tristan walking in. We locked eyes, his ringed with heavy circles and painfully bloodshot, but he still had enough energy to fix me with one of his brilliant smiles.

"You're awake," he said, crossing the room and sitting on the bed beside me.

Frankie tutted. "I've been telling this man to get some sleep for three days, but he refuses. Maybe you'll have better luck."

"You've been defying Frankie?" I asked, threading my fingers through his. "I'm surprised she didn't knock you out."

Tristan chuckled. "Pretty sure she tried, but I have a hard head."

Frankie grumbled, "Gods know that's the truth."

The ultimate vibe in the room wasn't cheerful by any means. "Is there some news you need to share? Kind of feels like a funeral home in here."

"How much do you remember?" asked Derfael. His face was drawn and sad.

"I already know my magick is gone, if that's what you're trying to tell me."

There was a collective burst of breath. "You knew?" Percy asked. "Gods, we've been debating drawing straws to figure out who had to give you the bad news."

"It was a choice I had to make. It was hand over the æther, or sub it out for something else."

"It was a sacrifice?" Ishani asked. "Knowing what will happen now?"

"What's going to happen?" asked Morgan.

Ishani gave her a look that was not appreciative of her naïveté. "What do you think? She is a person with many enemies. And now she has no magick to defend herself. How long do you think it will take until they find that out? They will come after her without hesitation."

"But we can protect her, right?" Morgan looked around.

I looked at her sadly. "They can't be with me all the time. But I still have good old-fashioned weapons."

Tristan made a noise. "Not to mention my entire security team."

Oh, yeah. Now that he's back on the nobility train, he'll have his own team at all times. "That's going to take some getting used to."

"We'll have plenty of time," he said.

We must've been staring at each other for too long, because Percy cleared her throat. "You realize we're still here, right?"

I rolled my eyes but smiled congenially. "What happened. At the end?" That section was still a big blank.

Percy and Ishani exchanged looks.

"Where does your last memory leave off?" Percy asked.

"Malea's fang was sticking into my torso, and I decided to let my magick go."

Percy nodded. "There was this crazy flash of light and Malea just... froze. A petrification started with the fang sticking into you and then it traveled down her entire body. It turned her into a statue. Baqi had to break the fang off and break her tail to get you loose." Percy ran a hand through her hair and looked down at the floor, wiping her eyes furiously. "We all thought you were dead again. You need to stop doing that to us."

Tristan shuddered. "I had to watch the whole thing from the other side of that damn bubble..." He moved closer to me and wrapped his arm around my shoulders, like he needed to remind himself that I was here and alive.

"We're not sure how it happened, to be honest," said Ishani. "Ordinary, everyday magick shouldn't have affected either of them like that."

A niggling feeling crept up the base of my spine. There was that moment, right when I had to make that decision to relinquish my magick, and again before I blacked out, where it felt like something *else* came through. Or pushed forward. A presence that was familiar from a long time ago.

"What about the peace talks?" I asked.

Tristan kissed the top of my head. "We continue tomorrow. The general cease-fire is in place, and after the entire world got a look at that battle, it'll be interesting to see how that pressure lands on the humans." He hesitated. "You're trending on social media."

"The woman that almost destroyed the world by letting in giant snakes?" I asked.

"Um, no. You seem to be becoming a folk hero, of sorts," said Derfael.

"What?"

"It kind of looks like you and Atum were the ones that saved us all," said Percy, folding her arms. "The cameras were too far away to see everything and after Malea captured you there was just a bunch of flashing light and the bitch turned to stone." She tapped her foot and rolled her eyes to the side. "It actually looks really impressive."

"Oh, and uh," Derfael scrubbed his beard, a grin on his face. "Tafford will no longer be an issue."

My eyes widened. "Why is that?"

"Seems he was discovered plotting the DIWR attack, on camera, with a great microphone, with his pal, Senator Yards. Those bombs had been placed weeks prior. They were just waiting for you to show up. Turns out they learned their lesson from the last time you went invisible on them. Upgraded their tech."

"This all seems too good to be true." I couldn't quite let myself believe it, because to be proven wrong would be too heartbreaking after all of this.

"Sometimes good things do happen, Talulla."

"We're not out of the woods yet though, just keep that in mind," said Percy.

Ishani punched Percy in the arm, not with her metal hand. "Why are you always so negative?"

"It's called realism," said Percy, a defiant grin on her face.

"Whatever," Ishani said, throwing her hands in the air before blasting me with a bright smile. "Anyway, I'm going to take Ms. Realism and get out of your hair." Her smiled faltered a bit. "We'll figure something out, to keep you safe. It will look pretty bad if the Council turns its back on the woman who keeps showing up to save their asses, despite everything they've done to get rid of her."

"And she's the world's sweetheart, now," said Percy with a simpering smile.

I swatted at them, laughing, and the two of them left.

"I need to get going too," said Morgan.

Derfael gave me and Tristan a knowing look. "I'll walk you down. I know when I'm not wanted." He chuckled. "I'll see you tomorrow."

Frankie sighed when they were gone. "Ten minutes, Mr. Iraklidis. Then you have to leave. I'm putting my foot down with that one."

She gave me a squeeze on the shoulder and bustled out of the room, Tristan immediately snuggling closer. "They told me what happened with Adrian."

"Nobody's heard from him, I take it?"

His thumb stroked my arm. "No. But George has been keeping tabs on him, just in case."

That surprised me.

"Things are complicated right now," he continued. "It's okay if you want to take more time apart. Figure things out."

"Shit's always complicated with me and him. I feel horrible about all of it. Malea and Amara targeted him because of me. They waited until we reforged the bond before they abducted him because they knew it would hurt both of us more." I paused. "I do love him."

I looked up at Tristan, whose expression had grown cautious. "But I'm not *in love* with him." His face softened, and he leaned in for a kiss, but I put my hand against his lips. "Woah. That's a bit presumptuous. I didn't say I was in love with you, either," I teased.

He pulled my hand away, laughing, and snuck a quick kiss. "I won't say we should start over, because there were more good times than bad. And this was a helluva storm to weather, and we both came out the other side. But I don't want to pick back up right where we left off, either."

I nodded. "Agreed."

Tristan reached into his pocket and pulled out a simple silver band.

My eyes widened, and my gaze darted to his. He gave me a nervous smile.

"This is a promise." At my dumbfounded expression, he rambled, "No pressure, and you don't have to say anything if you don't want."

"I—" My heart raced and heat flooded my cheeks. "Are you sure?" There was no way I could be interpreting this correctly.

He laughed, his entire face lighting up. "Is it so hard to believe I'd want to marry you?"

"Kind of." I looked between him and the ring. "You know how I can get." Uncertainty crept in. "I'm bad at... love," I finished lamely.

"No, you're not. I promise you that."

The collection of befuddled sounds that left my mouth said everything my words could not.

"Look at everything that happened over the past few months," he said. "We still found our way back to each other. I love every part of you, Evyn. Even the spiky bits." He laughed. "And there won't be any more mind-controlling lamia running around."

I slapped a hand over his mouth. "Way to jinx it."

Tristan's shoulders shook with laughter as he pulled my hand away. "There's no hurry. I just wanted to make sure you knew without a doubt that I want to spend the rest of my life with you." He held out the ring.

My hand trembled as I offered it and when Tristan slipped the band onto my finger, I could only stare. A happy, relieved smile spread across his face as he twined his fingers through mine and leaned in close. "When you're ready for the real one, just say the word. I love you, Evyn."

I tilted my face up for a kiss. "I love you, too, Tris."

Frankie bustled back in, two adepts flanking her. The amount of effort it took for her to appear stern was considerable. A severe frown etched into her face, she said, "I've given you *fifteen* minutes. Don't make me escort you out."

Then she spied the ring, and the ruse was up. She broke into a giddy grin. "Congratulations!"

EPILOGUE

I was just getting back from a walk around the grounds when there was a knock at my open door. When I turned, Keanu Reeves was standing in my doorway, looking at me with an amiable smile. Even though he'd appeared to me in this form before, it took me a minute to process who I was actually looking at.

"Uh-oh," I said, easing my tired body onto my bed. I'd been taking longer walks every day, but building up my stamina was slow going. Not having my magick meant relearning how to function.

It sucked.

"Come to fetch the remnants of my former life?"

"That's defeatist of you," said Death.

"Is it? Because from where I'm standing, my whole life is about to look very different."

"Indeed," he said, eyeing the ring on my finger.

I smiled shyly and tucked my hair behind my ear. "Not all of it's bad," I admitted.

"Since I was in the neighborhood—" I snorted and he raised his eyebrows. "Don't believe me?"

"Death never does anything casual." I leaned in conspiratorially. "Have any tricks up your sleeve to keep me alive?"

He sighed. "My dear, you are not powerless."

I blinked at him. "That's exactly what I am. Have you not heard the word? I'm not a mage anymore."

"You still have the æther," he said, sitting on the edge of my hospital bed.

"I can't use it without my magick to help keep it in check. Solomon's ring doesn't respond to mundanes, I've tried. I can't even get it to answer, let alone summon it. It's just sitting there, out of reach. Taking up space, but refusing to pay rent."

"You know that's not true." There was a spark of something in his gaze. Mischief. "You've felt it."

"Felt what?" I asked.

Death narrowed his eyes but said nothing, and I fidgeted uncomfortably.

"It was nothing. I was half out of my mind."

"It's always been with you, Evyn. Ever since you were a child. When you summoned it for the first time."

I picked at my nails and took way too long to reposition the pillow behind my back. "Even if it is dark matter, it's too dangerous. I can't access it. If I lose control—"

"You're acting like these things function the same way your magick did. Being able to manipulate energy in certain ways and harnessing primordial forces that are living things in themselves is far different. And it's already taken a shining to you. That's why you survived the first time you touched it. It stayed with you because it knew what you would become."

"Not to be disrespectful, but it feels like you're really shining me on here. That 'chosen one' bullshit." I bit my tongue to resist making a Matrix reference.

He shrugged. "Maybe not *chosen*, but you are elite. There are exceptional people in the world."

"You need to stop with the compliments," I said, narrowing my eyes to slits. "It makes me not want to trust you."

Death smiled. "How Midwestern of you."

I sniffed. "My people have been weaponizing compliments as long as we've been slinging pasties and hot dish."

He threw his head back and barked a laugh. "Do you know I haven't personally come to collect a soul in the Midwest ever since a train accident with a dozen victims? One woman began our interaction with 'Ope! How the heck are ya?' and proceeded to invite me to dinner and gave me her mother's recipe for cherry pie. And then it took ages for me to get the souls to leave because they kept insisting on being the one that got to hold the door open for everyone else to pass through."

"That checks out," I said, chuckling. It still hurt to laugh and I held a hand to my stomach.

Tristan knocked on the door. "Hey." He looked at Death. "Am I interrupting?" He did a double take. "Johnny Cash?"

"Um," I said, hesitating. "Tristan, meet Death. Death, Tristan."

Tristan froze, mouth agape, and I rose to join him. It was a lot to take in, especially when meeting an egregore for the first time.

"Charmed, I'm sure," said Death, flicking a piece of lint off his coat. "I came by to offer your fiancée a few words of advice. Congratulations, by the way."

"Th-thank you," said Tristan.

"Anyway, think about what we talked about," he continued. "Have a good rest of your day." Keanu/Cash made for the door, but paused.

"Oh. While I'm here, there is one more thing. I'm putting together a team..."

DEAR READER

Thank you so much for reading! It means the world to me that you shared your time with the Strangefells universe. Have a moment? I'd love it if you could leave a review. It's immensely helpful for indie creators like me. Have questions or comments? I'd love to hear from you! Reach out at author@gwydionroyce.com and let me know what you think! Or keep up to date on all the things, get fun extras and stay in the loop on everything I've got coming up at gwydionroyce.com

THE CATALOG

The Death's Left Hand Series:
(Dark Paranormal Urban Fantasy)
Book 1: Iron-Forge Crossroads: Metanoia
Book 2: Iron-Forge Crossroads: Remeant
Book 3: Coiled Phantoms: Exuvia
Book 4: Coiled Phantoms: Kairos

The Primordial Embers Series:
(Reverse Harem Dark Fantasy Romance)
Book 1: Trickster's Ashes
Book 2: Illusion Razed
Book 3: Stone Captive
Book 4 : Enemies Remade
Book 5: Primordial Fall